MW00930177

The Treasure of Adonis

Enjoy the adventure!

By C.S. Kjar

C. S. Kjar

ISBN-13: 978-1508516620
ISBN-10: 1508516626

Dedicated to my teachers and professors who taught me to read and write. And to my family who have always encouraged me to try new things.

Chapter 1

The dappled morning sunlight warmed the sidewalk in front of the library where Charlea Ludlow hurried up the steps of the refurbished old building and toward its oversized wooden doors. The librarian for the small east Texas town, she was beautiful in an aging-gracefully way, slender enough to be a model, with her long brown hair immaculately styled in a French roll. She was always punctual as a good librarian should be. Except for today. Today she was late. And she was not happy about that.

In her mind, being late for work was inexcusable. She had made the five-block walk to work as fast as her pencil skirt allowed, chiding herself with every step. Mr. Woodson was coming in to see her this morning. If he knew she was late, he would accuse her of being incompetent at next week's City Council meeting. She had barely fended off his accusations of embezzlement at last year's budget meeting with the city. She dared not give him any more ammunition. Nothing would prevent him from bringing up those accusations again. Had she known that her coffee pot and toaster would both go out on the same morning, she would have gotten up earlier. Why they would both pick today to break, she could not fathom.

Pausing for a moment with her last thought, she wondered if her reasoning skills were also broken. Appliances don't conspire together. Her brain wasn't working without her morning cup of coffee. That, or her arteries were hardening now that she was middle-aged. She shook her head to erase the thoughts and start all over.

She picked up the newspaper lying by the front door and tucked it under her arm. Grabbing the brass handle of the large door, she gave a mighty pull. The door did not move, but her hand did. She stumbled backward on her high heels and teetered on the edge of the top step for a few seconds. Catching her balance, she leaned forward and stumbled toward the door. She grabbed the door handle to steady herself. Clutching her chest to still her wildly beating heart, she looked around to see if anyone had seen her mishap. Mr.

Woodson's spies were everywhere. Relieved to see no one, Charlea turned to face the door and took a deep breath. She leaned against the door to allow composure to return to her body. She tried the door again. Locked.

Where was Bonnie? The library assistant was supposed to always be the first one there in the morning. That was their agreement. Bonnie opened in the mornings and Charlea closed at night. So where was the girl? The door should have been unlocked at least twenty minutes ago.

Charlea put her hands on her hips. Her schedule might be out of kilter, but there was no reason why everyone else's should be too. A part of her was relieved that Bonnie wouldn't know that she had been late but she was still perturbed with herself and her out-of-sync day.

Digging through her purse, she found the keys and worked to get the door unlocked. The key was hard to turn, so she tried jiggling it and turning the knob. Her efforts made her drop the newspaper. As she made a grab for the paper, her purse fell off her arm, spilling the contents across the front step. She looked up with a why-me prayer, looking for divine intervention, before kneeling down to pick up her purse's contents and the paper.

Rising, Charlea looked around again to see if anyone was watching. No one. *Good,* she thought, *at least I'm not embarrassing myself in front of witnesses.* No staring or laughing eyes. Now to open the door. She jiggled the knob, turned the key, and prayed until the lock granted her request.

Stepping inside, she flipped on the light switch. The fluorescent lights blinked awake to shine on a well-ordered world called Library. Here was her haven from troubles. Her shelter from storms. A sense of calm came over her. The day held more promise now.

Her footsteps on the tile floor echoed off the rich wood paneling as she walked by the canyons of bookshelves to the center of the room. Here was the hub, the circulation desk, where library transactions and community interactions took place. Charlea laid the paper and her purse on the desk. She straightened her fitted jacket and pencil skirt and made sure her belt was still centered on her small waist.

Charlea picked up her purse and started for her office in the back of the library behind the massive staircase that had a Gone-With-the-Wind look. The staircase had a large landing halfway up and smaller stairways leading to opposite sides of the second floor. A hand-me-down velvet rope from the local theater stretched across the staircase to discourage library patrons from going to the second floor. The museum would be located up there someday, when time and funding allowed. For now, the second floor was a storehouse of boxed items gathering dust.

Charlea entered her office and slipped the silk scarf off her head. Once a broom closet, it was just large enough to hold a pair of file cabinets, an old wooden desk, and an extra chair for visitors. A few newly acquired books and magazines lay on her desk, awaiting her approval to become part of the library. She didn't mind being cramped as much as she wished she had windows for light and checking the weather. She checked her hair in a wall mirror behind the door and smoothed a stray brown tress back into the perfect Jackie-Kennedy hair style.

Where is Bonnie? Charlea wondered again. *She's usually punctual.* Her absence was a little worrisome. Bonnie's car often broke down. Could she be stranded somewhere? Or was one of her kids sick? Or was her husband sick? Or...there were so many reasons to worry. Charlea forced her mind back to the tasks at hand.

Returning to the circulation desk, Charlea spread the newspaper out on the countertop and scanned the headlines. As usual, the paper was full of news about the upcoming presidential campaign between President Johnson and whoever the Republicans would nominate, along with news of the escalating war in Vietnam. Reading the newspaper left her depressed. Her Air Force fighter-pilot husband, Mark, had never come home from the last conflict in Korea, so it was difficult to read about other women losing their husbands and sons in another war. Rubbing the finger where her wedding ring used to be, she flipped the pages to the local section to see if she knew anyone listed in the obituaries. Not today, thank goodness again.

Starting the morning chores, she picked up a small stack of returned books and went into the rows of books.

"Hello!" Bonnie McGregor yelled from the backdoor, breathless with hurry. "Sorry I'm late!" A loud bang from the slamming backdoor interrupted the quiet.

"You had me worried," Charlea called out, relieved that Bonnie was finally there.

"Tim couldn't find one of his shoes. Typical six year old boy!" Bonnie called back, her voice echoing down the bookcase canyons. "We all had to dig through his messy room until we finally found them. By then, the bus had come and gone, so I had to take him to school, but halfway there, he couldn't find his lunch box and we realized it was still at home. So we had go back to get it and that took twice as long. That boy! He'd lose his head if it weren't screwed on.

Bonnie came around the corner and saw Charlea sliding a book onto the shelf. Her cheap canvas shoes padded on the tiles and her out-of-style dress stretched around her large figure. Even though she was younger than Charlea, the years of caring for her crippled husband and their three children on one small paycheck had aged her more. Charlea was one of the few people who had ever heard Bonnie complain about her situation, and even then, it was rare. Financially, the McGregors were hurting, but Bonnie was thankful for what she had. Most people saw her cheerful demeanor and assumed all was well. Her slightly graying hair was the only indication of how much her troubles weighed on her.

"How're you today?" Bonnie asked in a please-don't-dock-my-pay voice while twisting the edge of her blouse.

"You had me worried," Charlea said in her don't-worry-about-it voice. "I'm glad you're here now. The weather is forecasted to be sunny and warm. Maybe people will go to the park instead of coming to the library.

"I hope so. I might have time to process the new magazines and get them out on our display.

Charlea slid a book onto the bookshelf. "Do you mind working out front alone? I need to work on our budget. The city council is asking for preliminary numbers at their meeting next week, and I'd like to get it done while it's not busy."

Bonnie took the last few books out of Charlea's hands. "That sounds like a good idea. We don't want a repeat of last year's budget meeting."

The year-old memory twisted Charlea's insides so much it made her head hurt. The confusion over the missing $1,000. The implications on her reputation. The accusations of embezzling. The damage to her library's good standing. The sleepless nights.

Charlea's hand moved to her temple to hold back the pounding. "I still don't know what happened. How could I've gotten so far overdrawn in our accounts? I keep very meticulous records."

"Maybe you need help with it," Bonnie offered. "You know, Mr. Woodson has offered—"

"Stop right there." Charlea's harsh tone left no doubt about her distaste of that name. "I don't want that man anywhere near here. I don't like him. I don't trust him. I don't want him around."

"But he's a city councilman—"

"I don't care if he's king of the world. He's a foul man, and I don't want him messing in our business. I'll take care of it."

"Sorry I brought it up," Bonnie murmured. She hurried around the end of the bookcase to get out of firing range. Over her shoulder, she called out, "While you're working on it, could you see if you can get them to throw in a raise for us. It's getting harder to feed the family. And the kids need new coats and my car needs new tires…" Her voice trailed off as she went to unlock the front door.

"I'll see what I can do," Charlea called after her. "Surely they can find a few spare pennies. Come get me if you need me."

As Charlea reached the security of her office, the front door creaked, announcing the arrival of the first customers of the day. Charlea closed the door to avoid disruptions from people asking questions or dropping in to visit. The budget needed her full attention and concentration.

She brushed a few eraser crumbs off her desk. Unlocking one of the file cabinets, she pulled out a large ledger from one of the drawers and laid it on her desk. Organizing a budget was her least favorite part of administering the library, but it could not be avoided. Turning to the last page with figures on it, she pulled out her pencil and eraser and began working.

A single knock at the door broke Charlea's concentration. No one came in, but she understood the signal. Mr. Woodson was here. Here to see her. Here to touch her. Here to make her sick to her stomach. Her blouse was instantly damp with fear, knowing that she would have to defend herself from his trespassing hands.

6

Chapter 2

Panic swept through her. Her office had no escape route. She had to get out. She rushed to the door, opened it, and rushed out…straight into Mr. Woodson. Face-to-face with him, all she could see where his large saliva-dampened teeth exposed by a malicious smile.

"Can't wait to see me, Charlea? What a pleasant surprise!" He swept his arms around her and tried to pull her closer. Charlea pushed him away before he got a firm grip on her.

"No, I was going to the circulation desk. Want to join me there?"

"What I have to say needs to be said in private, so let's step inside your office. Much cozier in there." He nudged her back inside her office without waiting for an answer. He sat on the extra chair and patted his knee, inviting her to sit. He was dressed in a tailored suit, with a stylish narrow tie. With a different personality, he might have been considered an attractive man, but his lecherous behavior made him gag-impulse ugly in her eyes.

Charlea went behind her desk and sat. Her usual seat offered the only place out of his reach.

Mr. Woodson pouted slightly. "I want to know if you'll have budget figures ready for next week's meeting." The leering in his eyes reflected his ugly heart's desires.

"I'm working on it now. The numbers will be ready by meeting time." Charlea replied.

"I need to see what you have now. The mayor asked me to brief him on budget requests so there are no surprises." Rising, he came around her desk and scanned her work spread out on her desk. Picking up several papers, he began to read through them.

Incensed with his rude behavior, Charlea quickly grabbed the papers out of his hands and closed the ledger to keep them from his view. If he had politely asked for information, she might have considered sharing it, but his prying made her defensive. "I've told you before, keep your hands off of my desk and off of me." She shook her finger at him. His arrogant assumption that he could do as he pleased made her as angry as a mother bear protecting her cub.

Mr. Woodson chuckled spitefully and held his hands up as if to surrender. He didn't fool Charlea. She knew he'd do it again when the opportunity arose.

"I didn't mean to rile you, Charlea. I just want to see your budget."

"It's not yet complete," she said with undisguised animosity, "so any numbers I give you now would be premature and useless for a proper briefing. Tell the mayor I'll call him as soon as I have things organized." She watched his eyes narrow, a sign he was not pleased with her lack of compliance.

He sneered as he walked back around her desk. "Charlea, it would be advantageous for you to cooperate with me. I hate to see you go through a repeat of last year's budget meeting. You couldn't explain missing funds or unbalanced books. We can avoid that scene again if you let me help you with it."

"Or you'll accuse me of embezzling funds again? You know I would never do that."

"It looked like you did. Come on, Charlea, I know you're no embezzler. I want to help you make sure all is in order."

"I appreciate your offer to help," Charlea lied, "but I am capable of doing it myself."

Charlea sat back in her chair so he would know that she was through listening to him. She tapped her fingertips together, the only power gesture she could think of at the moment. To further close the door on him, she added, "Now if you'll excuse me, I have a lot of work to do."

A flicker of anger sparked in his eyes before he looked away. He backed away a step, and then gave her the same forced smile he gave everyone when displeased.

"Of course you're capable. Just because you looked like an embezzler last year, doesn't mean you will this year. Let me know when you have the numbers. The mayor asked me for this information and I don't intend to disappoint him." After a final look of distain, he turned and walked out the door, leaving Charlea to stew.

Charlea understood his message. If she wouldn't open her books for him now, he would work against her on the City Council. He had the influence and power to deny her budget requests or trim them back so far that it would, in effect, harm the library. Charlea banged her clenched fist on her desk, but the action did little to assuage her anger. He could make her job miserable. He could imply she was an embezzler again. He could get her fired by claiming she embezzled. He could ruin her and her library. No matter how he did it, he would look like the hero in the story, saving the town from a crook. Saving the town from her.

Charlea fumed. Mr. Woodson was firing warning shots and threatening a battle. If that's what he wanted, then she would storm City Hall like the hungry peasants on the Bastille. This library was her professional success and she would fight for it before she let him take it over. She stood in the middle of her office, her fists clinched, ready for a fight.

A light tap sounded. "Charlea?" Bonnie asked through the door. "Are you all right?"

Charlea opened the door for Bonnie, but said nothing as Bonnie came in.

"How did it go?" Bonnie asked, scrutinizing Charlea's face. "Don't tell me. I already know. I knew it was bad when he left without saying a word. What went on? He obviously upset you."

"Don't worry about it, Bonnie. He wanted to see the library's budget, and I told him no. Something in me says he's up to no good, that he's digging for…I don't know what, but nothing good!" Charlea paced in a small circle, all the room she had to release her anger. "Why do I let that man upset me? He's only one vote on a council of five. I work well with the rest of them, so that should be good enough, right?" She looked at Bonnie for support or a word of encouragement.

Bonnie avoided her gaze and shifted her feet. "Is there something in the budget you don't want him to see? You're not hiding anything are you?"

Charlea stopped pacing, surprised by the lack of support offered by her friend. "Why would you ask such a thing? I'm not hiding anything! The budget is not ready, simple as that." Charlea sat and straightened her desk. "I'm upset because of the way he asked for it. He didn't ask. He came in and demanded things. He made me mad and I reacted badly. I'll get the budget in order and take it to the mayor so we can go over it together. Cut out the middleman."

"Mr. Woodson will be really mad to be skipped over. I mean, if the mayor asked him to do this, then maybe you should let Mr. Woodson do it."

Charlea grew more uncomfortable with Bonnie's continued defense of Mr. Woodson. "Yeah, he'll probably get mad, but he'll get over it."

"I don't think you should make him any madder than he already is."

"I don't care how mad he gets. When I'm done with the budget," Charlea's voice rose in volume, "I'll give it to them. Whose side are you on anyway?"

"Yours, of course." Bonnie fumbled with her watch, avoiding eye contact. "I should get back to the circulation desk and let you get back to work. I just wanted to make sure you were all right." She hurried out of the room and pulled the door shut behind her.

Charlea was puzzled about why Bonnie was defending Mr. Woodson. In the past, Bonnie was the one person Charlea could complain to about him because Bonnie felt the same way about him. Something had changed.

Charlea spread her papers out again in front of her and opened the ledger. She'd talk to Bonnie about Mr. Woodson on another day. For now, it became imperative that she get the budget figures done as soon as possible. If she took her data to the mayor before Mr. Woodson came back, it would save her from dealing with him again. She bent over her desk and began her work with renewed vigor. Mr. Woodson might come back to check on her progress. She didn't want that.

Chapter 3

"I hate to interrupt you, but can you come help me for a little while? Mr. Wilkerson is here."

Charlea looked up at Bonnie, relieved to be interrupted for a good reason this time. She had made little progress in the budget and, rather than waste more time drowning in numbers, it would do her good to get away from it. She straightened the papers on her desk and closed the ledger. Her now-dulled pencil rolled across the desk.

Brushing the eraser crumbs from her skirt, she said, "I'm happy for the break! By the way, whose turn is it?"

"I think it's mine. You can watch the circulation desk while I show him some of the new books." Bonnie stepped inside the tiny office. "How's the budget coming?"

Charlea shrugged as she stood and stretched a little. "It's coming together, slowly but surely. I hate accounting and budgets. Maybe I should let you do it. You're better at math than I am. And you seem to like Mr. Woodson." Charlea spoke tongue-in-cheek and expected some sort of resistance from Bonnie.

"I would be happy to," she said.

Not the response Charlea had expected. Puzzled, she said, "I think the Council expects the head librarian to complete the budget. But thanks for offering."

Charlea said no more as they left the small office to attend Mr. Wilkerson, the lonely widower who visited the library almost daily to socialize with Charlea and Bonnie and whoever else happened to be there. In spite of his advanced age, he was still spry and youthful in his behavior, flirting with women of every age. While Charlea and Bonnie liked the man, his long-winded stories often kept them from their duties for extended periods. Neither of them had the heart to cut him short, so they took turns listening to him and recommending new books, which he would check out and bring back two days later. He was always pleased with the individual attention.

Charlea went out to the circulation desk where Mr. Wilkerson was already deep into a story with a woman, whispering so loudly and so continuously that it seemed he hardly took a breath. He handed his book to Charlea without stopping his story. When he finally paused to take a breath, his captive audience quickly excused herself and hurried away.

"Hello, Charlea," he said grinning. "My, you look beautiful today. Will you marry me? I'm in love with you, you know." He reached out and took Charlea's hand.

"Not today, Mr. Wilkerson," she responded, pulling her hand back. "Maybe some other time, but I appreciate your offer."

"You've broken my heart again, but I'll keep asking." He feigned sadness. "You need a man and I'm a good one. I'll take good care of you."

"Yes, you're a good one, but I'm doing fine on my own. And speaking of today, Bonnie can help you find whatever you need. We may still have a few books that you haven't read yet."

Mr. Wilkerson chuckled like the cheerful man he was. "Some books are worth reading twice. I love coming to see you. Since my precious Mabel left me, I get lonely sometimes and your beautiful faces cheer me up. I don't want you to be as lonely as I am. That's why I want to marry you."

Bonnie stepped in. "She'll marry again someday. One day, Mr. Right will come walking through that door and sweep her off her feet."

"That's why I come here as often as I can," he said. "Someday, you might see *me* as your Prince Charming. But hurry up! I'm not getting any younger, you know." Their unmuffled laughter was shushed by one of the other patrons as Bonnie took his arm to lead him away.

Mr. Wilkerson began another story as he and Bonnie turned into an aisle of books, looking for the next one to check out. His voice reverberated throughout the library as he relayed his continuing story about growing up on a farm. Bonnie repeatedly asked him not to speak so loudly, but he ignored her. His impression of cows mooing and his laughter lofted over the bookshelves and filled the library. Several library patrons looked up at Charlea, frowning at the noise breaking their concentration. Others who knew Mr. Wilkerson snickered to themselves.

Bonnie's vain attempts to quiet Mr. Wilkinson left Charlea feeling relieved that it was not her day to be with him. She was not in the mood to deal with all his questions, incessant talking, and good-natured flirtation. The dark cloud that had formed after Mr.

Woodson's visit still hung over her head and she didn't want to hurt Mr. Wilkerson's feelings by being curt with him. She quietly busied herself with checking books in and out as patrons wandered to the circulation desk, glad for the quiet respite from her troubles.

The bright sunshine warmed the room as it poured through the front windows. Their prediction of a slow day turned out to be correct. Only a few people read at the nearby tables and a mother and son looked at the children's books.

As soon as Mr. Wilkerson went on his way, Bonnie could easily handle everyone by herself, and Charlea could get back to the budget. With the budget woes roiling in her mind, she was anxious to get back to it, but at the same time, she dreaded it. Maybe Bonnie was right. Maybe she should ask for Mr. Woodson's help with it. He might save her time and aggravation. After all, he was a businessman with experience in these matters. Yet it would give him an excuse to touch her and threaten her if she didn't comply with his will. An involuntary shudder ran through her at the thought of working with him.

Charlea picked up a stack of books to return to their places when the front door opened and she, out of habit and curiosity, glanced in that direction to see who was coming in. She did a double take as she watched a stranger strolling through the door. Her mouth fell open slightly, and the books slid out of her hands back onto the counter as she stared.

The man walked in with such confidence. He had the appearance of a Greek statue or maybe Michelangelo's David come to life. Chiseled, beautiful, perfectly formed. No doubt, he was used to being viewed by all, admired by all, loved by all. By women, that is. Embarrassed to be caught staring, one by one, each woman in the library quickly turned away when he looked in her direction, only to sneak a peek at him after he passed.

Turning, his dark eyes scanned in Charlea's direction and stopped when he saw her. Their gazes met and she quickly looked down, suddenly self-conscious for staring. Desperate to look busy, she opened the book on top of the counter, *Greek Mythology*. The book answered her question about who he was: *Adonis*! The Greek god of beauty and desire had come down from Mount Olympus to her library. To check out a book?

Charlea restacked the dropped books on the counter and then peeked at him to see if he was still watching her. He looked at a magazine display for a minute and then pulled a book from a shelf and thumbed through it before putting it back. He quickly scanned through several other books and put them back, obviously not finding what he sought. She debated whether she should take the lead and offer her assistance. As head librarian, the duty fell to her.

She drew a deep breath and started toward him, but when he moved away from her around the corner of a bookshelf, her courage dissipated like a snowflake on a hot sidewalk. She made a fast U-turn and hurried back behind the circulation desk and fumbled with whatever her hands could find to do. She heard people whispering to each other and wondered if they were talking about *Adonis* or her overt display of cowardice.

Charlea tried to turn her attention back to her work, but she couldn't keep her mind focused. The image of *Adonis* overwhelmed her thoughts and her imagination ran wild, carrying her away to long-forgotten places. Butterflies stirred her stomach with the vision of talking to him, being in his arms, being kissed.

Suddenly and uninvited, her voice of reason roared in her head, trying to talk sense into her. *You naughty girl! How dare you think such things! He is out of your league and you are too old for him to be interested in you. He's obviously the kind of man that only likes the younger ones. Not 42-year-olds like you.*

You're right, but I like to dream, she told her inner voice, *Lord, forgive me.*

The stranger walked out from behind the bookshelf and over to a small display to look at the local history books Charlea and Bonnie had set out to encourage support for the county museum that was soon to be organized upstairs. Every female head in the library followed him along his path. Either unaware of the women's stares or choosing to ignore them, he seemed focused on an unknown purpose. He searched for a specific reference in each book's index. Not finding what he wanted, he glanced around until he spotted Charlea standing behind the desk and started in her direction.

The closer he came, the harder her heart pounded, making her nervous and giddy. Without her permission, her hand smoothed the side of her hair to make sure her hair was still neat. She looked down and tried to concentrate on writing until she could get control of her emotions. Failure. She couldn't think of anything to write. Her hand began to tremble, and she fumbled with the pencil until it went flying over the front of the counter.

Not only was she a coward, she was a klutz. Her face burned as *Adonis* stepped forward, picked up the pencil, and handed it back to her. She found herself hypnotized by his stare, while he, staring back at her, seemed satisfied to let a few moments pass before saying anything.

She tried her best to look professional, so he would not know of the effect he was having on her. "May—" her voice squeaked, betraying her feelings. She cleared her throat before restarting. "May I help you find something?"

"Good morning. Yes, I hope you can," he said in a deep voice.

He looked at her so steadily that it felt like he was delving into her soul.

Can he see what I'm thinking? she wondered. *I want to jump over this desk and wrap him in my arms.* Her heart fluttered with embarrassment and desire. Transfixed by his eyes, she was unable to break the spell he had cast over her.

A twinkle flashed in his eyes as he held out his hand for her to shake. "You have the most beautiful eyes I've ever seen," he said.

Charlea blushed as she fumbled for his hand, still unable to break the gaze they shared. Just a few minutes before, she had felt melancholy and now this *Adonis* had lifted her spirits higher than they had soared in a long time. The simple comment made her feel young and happy. His charming manner enveloped her and swept her off her feet. Charlea made her hand release his and held it against her stomach with her other hand, as if cradling a precious thing. When she noticed what she was doing, she quickly dropped her hands and hoped he hadn't seen her.

Then, against her will, alarms went off in the back of her mind and a cloud overshadowed her excitement. Practicality, or perhaps reality, reared its ugly head and told her that this was too good to be true. Men didn't talk like this around her, especially men like this stranger. If he didn't mean what he said, then he must want something from her.

Torn between the conflicting emotions of strong attraction and even stronger suspicion, she composed herself. "Thank you, that's very kind of you to say. What can I do for you?"

He seemed somewhat surprised at her reply. "Kindness has nothing to do with it. I think you have lovely eyes. Don't people tell you that? You look nothing like the stereotypical librarian."

Charlea weakened a moment, but the voice in her head brought her back to the improbability that he spoke truthfully. Only in her dreams would a man like this desire her. The spell was broken. He definitely wanted something and her suspicions carried her forward.

Finding part of her confidence again, she replied, "No, they don't. Is there something you want? I don't recall you ever coming in before."

"That's because I've never been in before. I have a friend who needs help."

"Did your friend lose one of our books? Or does he have an overdue fine?"

"No!" he interrupted, "No one lost a book! I mean—what?" He seemed genuinely confused, making her feel very guilty for suggesting he was trying to con her. He laughed softly which made her feel even worse. "I'm in town on vacation. I came to look for information on local history, old homesteads, and addresses. For my friend, like I said. Can you help me?"

Charlea studied his face closely, but could find no deception in it. "Um-oh," she stammered, embarrassed by her cynical presumptions. "I'm sorry. I just thought…it seemed to me…most people want something from me when they say what you said." She wished she could rewind time and try this exchange again. "I'm sorry for thinking that—"

"There's no need to apologize. Forgive me for not introducing myself. I'm Roland Parker."

I like "Adonis" better, she thought. "Nice to meet you, Mr. Parker. I am Mrs. Ludlow. Charlea Ludlow, the head librarian."

"So glad to meet you. May I call you Charlea?"

That seemed very presumptuous to her. Properly raised people who had just met did not address each other by first name, but she knew social manners were changing. Charlea nodded.

"Please call me Roland."

"All right, Roland." *But you'll always be Adonis to me*, she thought. "How may I help you?"

He reached inside his coat pocket and pulled out a yellowed envelope. "I'm trying to find out more about this letter. It—um—I got it from my aunt who died recently. I thought it would be interesting to find out more about the people who sent the letter. I mean, I need to know where their house is. Sentimental stuff, you know." He held out the old envelope for her to examine.

"Let's see what you have here." Charlea took the envelope from him. The date stamp was faded and illegible. The letter was addressed to Theodore Williams, from someone named Robert Williams. The moment she saw the handwriting, she knew who had written it, and several unexplained mysteries became clear to her. She couldn't help but laugh silently. Fine. She'd play along for now and see what happened. Who knows? It might be fun. "Interesting. The letter wasn't addressed to your aunt. How did it come to her?"

"I'm not sure how she got it, but I'd like to find out who this is and where he lived." Roland pointed at the return address. "Have you ever heard of the person it's addressed to?"

Charlea handed the envelope back to him. "I don't know anyone named Robert Williams. Have you checked the phone book?"

"Yes, but there is no Robert Williams listed. Someone told me to go to the library. He said there might be old city records here that would hold a clue to his whereabouts."

"He said? Who is 'he'?"

"I'd rather not say, but he said to start here." Roland smiled at her and she could not resist. She had an idea where this might be going and wanted to play along.

"There's no date on the envelope. Any ideas on when it was written?" she asked.

"Probably 1945 or so. Just after the war."

"That old? I have several old town plats in our museum section, but they aren't organized yet. We can look for the name there, but it might take a while to do a search. Have you checked at the county courthouse? Their files are more organized and the information may be easier to find."

"And who might this gentleman be?" Mr. Wilkerson interrupted as he came to the circulation desk with Bonnie. "I can see my marriage proposal might be in jeopardy."

"Mr. Wilkerson! Really!" Charlea chided the elderly man who appeared unashamed of himself. "Bonnie. Mr. Wilkerson. This is Mr. Roland Parker. Roland, Bonnie McGregor and Asa Wilkerson."

"Mind if I call you Mr. Right?" Mr. Wilkerson laughed as he said it and winked at Charlea.

"I'd rather you didn't." Roland laughed along with the elderly man, apparently unembarrassed by the banter. "I've been mistaken for him before and things didn't turn out very well."

Charlea touched her forehead with her fingers and closed her eyes, seeking one drop of dignity and a way to end this uncomfortable conversation. Opening her eyes again, refreshed after her millisecond timeout, she tried to save face. "I see you found another book, Mr. Wilkerson. Bonnie can get you checked out and on your way home for your nap." Mr. Wilkerson harrumphed his disapproval of being sent home, but went quietly.

Roland turned to Charlea. "Shall we get started?"

Chapter 4

Charlea led Roland into a large room on the second floor. A table and a few chairs sat close to the door, a little dusty but otherwise ready for use. Beyond them, boxes and file cabinets lined the walls. Dirty windows filtered sunlight through the windows along one side. The air had a musty smell that made Charlea wrinkle her nose. She made a mental note to have the janitor open the windows more often in the coming summer to air it out.

Although the room seemed to be a chaotic mess, Charlea knew the location of most everything, or at least the general area where it would be found. As her library duties allowed, she looked through the old files in the cabinets and the many boxes stored on the second floor—maps, books, business ledgers, antiquated medical tools, endless files, trunks filled with old clothes. All of these and more made up the inventory of the museum thus far. Time, soap, and elbow grease would eventually organize it into some semblance of order.

Charlea walked to the back corner of the room and searched through a box of large, rolled-up maps. "Here it is!"

Roland wiped off a corner of a table with his handkerchief and helped her spread out a large plat. The dark ink on the yellowing paper illustrated the town around 1940, with the gridded lots and their owners' names neatly drawn out and labeled. Roland ran his fingers across each lot and name, searching for the name Williams among the many entries.

As they stood together, his arm occasionally brushed hers, sending an intoxicating shot of adrenaline through her each time. The butterflies tickling her insides made it hard for her to focus. She stared at him as he studied the plat and hoped he didn't notice.

"A-ha!"

Roland's exclamation startled Charlea and she took a step back.

Roland seemed excited by the quick progress of his search. "Here's a lot that belonged to an Arthur Williams. Do you know anything about him?"

Charlea stepped closer to see where Roland was pointing. "Arthur Williams was a doctor and an administrator of the hospital for many years. I thought you were looking for Robert Williams?"

"I am, but he's still a Williams. Maybe Arthur is related."

"That's quite a leap in logic. Williams is a common name, so it might be someone unrelated."

"It's the only Williams on the map. Robert had to live there too."

"Maybe. The official maps of the town are at City Hall. If Robert lived in town after 1940, you should be able to find it there."

Roland shook his head. "Robert was not here after 1946. He was probably Arthur's son. Is Arthur's house still there on this lot?"

Charlea studied the plat, following the street names with her fingers. She could smell Roland's aftershave as he bent close by her. "I don't think so. The house that is there now was built only a few years ago. The old one must have been demolished."

Charlea heard Roland whisper a curse.

Charlea frowned. She allowed him to call her by her first name, but no gentleman would use such language in front of a lady.

Roland noticed her displeasure at his vocabulary. "I'm sorry. I shouldn't have said that, but I really wanted the house to be there."

"Is it that important? Is there something in the letter about the house?"

Roland suddenly seemed a little nervous. "No, no. I just wanted to see the house. And maybe see if the family still lived there."

"So you want to see the family or the house?"

Roland ignored her question. "Would anyone from Arthur's family still be around?"

"There are several Williams families in town, but I don't know if any are related to Arthur Williams or Robert Williams or whoever it is you want to find. I'm reluctant to have you poking around in our citizens' backgrounds. I don't know what your intentions are, other than looking for a house. Perhaps if I read the letter, then I could help you better."

"Since the house is gone, it doesn't make any difference. It was a crazy idea anyway." He put the letter back into his jacket pocket.

"Which is most important? The house or the family?" Charlea wondered why he seemed so reluctant to share information and the letter with her.

Roland shuffled and backed away from the table. "It doesn't really matter now. Both are gone." He held his hand out to shake Charlea's. "Thanks for your help this morning."

Panicked at the thought of him leaving so soon, she quickly searched for excuses, anything to keep him around a little longer. "We have old newspapers. We could look for a news article about the house or what happened to Dr. Williams' family, if you want. We might find some insight that you could use."

Roland fumbled with the edge of the plat while he mulled over the suggestion. He was either hesitant or reluctant. Charlea could not read his face well enough to tell.

At last he answered. "It really doesn't matter all that much. I was just curious about my mother's letter and how she might have known the family."

"I thought you said your aunt left it to you?"

"I meant my aunt. My mother's sister." He rolled the plat, but the roll kept going askew. He unrolled and tried it again. After several attempts with no luck, he let the plat lie flat and started to leave.

Charlea knew that *Adonis*—or Roland or liar or whoever he was—was hiding his true mission. She knew he wanted quick easy answers to his questions. Obviously, he was not a patient man, especially when he wanted something for himself. Yet, she didn't want *Adonis* to leave. She wanted to know the truth about why he was here. She wanted him to stay a little longer. She wanted to know why she cared. Mark's memory was enough for her, wasn't it? But *Adonis* had stirred something long buried in her and she wanted to feel it more. He made her feel like more than a woman. He made her feel like a young woman.

Roland stopped at the door and waited for her to follow him. His attention was directed to the large disarray of boxes, cabinets, furniture, and other stuff around the room. "So what is this? A storeroom?"

"No," Charlea came to the door to stand beside him, surveying the town's history captured in the artifacts in the room.

"It's the beginning of a museum that we hope to have ready in the next year or two. Shall we look at our newspapers?"

Roland seemed hesitant.

Charlea prodded him a little to get her way. "Arthur Williams was such a prominent man in the town's history that there are probably articles about him and his family. Papers back then had very trivial information and might have some mention of Robert Williams. It wouldn't take very long to look and we might find what you're looking for."

Roland glanced at his watch. "I guess I have time. Can you help me with it? You could make things go a little faster." He took her hand and looked at her with pleading eyes. "Please?"

Charlea smiled slightly, flattered by his pleading while at the same time knowing that he was using her to get something he wanted. "That's why I'm here, to help. Where should we start? We have almost 80 years of papers here."

"Let's start in 1945 when he sent the letter. I know that the house was there then. Whatever happened to it happened after that."

She took him to a large map cabinet that held old newspapers. After she delicately handed a stack to him, Roland took them to the table. They quickly scanned the headlines on the front of each newspaper and went through ten years of papers quickly.

"Nothing," Roland said.

From his tone of voice, Charlea knew he was discouraged even though they had only just begun their search. She normally had no patience for short attention spans, but she made an exception this time. His deceptive story had piqued her interest and she wanted to find out what he was really after.

"Let's go through them again," Charlea said, "but this time, look through the whole paper. Maybe the hospital administrator didn't always merit being front page news. That is, if you can stay." She held her breath, hoping for the answer she wanted.

"Time spent with a beautiful woman is always well spent. Let's keep looking."

Her heart skipped a beat with excitement and spread a broad smile on her face. But then, against her will, her voice of reason reminded her that she was being foolish. He wanted something from her and his charm would hypnotize her into submission to get it. *But,* she told her voice, *I like being charmed and called beautiful. Let me enjoy it for a little while.* Pushing the warning away from her mind, she separated the papers.

"I'll take 1947 and you take 1946. We should be able to look through them fairly quickly for any hint of Dr. Williams."

He nodded and took the papers she gave him to the table. Pulling the top one to him, he began to scan through it.

Charlea sat across from him with her stack and followed suit. As they perused the papers, they talked. She surreptitiously surveyed his left hand for a gold band and, finding none, felt relieved. She would hate to be so twitterpated over a married man.

Although she didn't ask the questions, Roland easily shared details of his life, growing up on a farm, his current job working as a waiter at an exclusive, top-notch restaurant in Dallas, his last divorce with his ex-wife had taking everything, and moving in with a brother until he could get back on his feet financially.

His last divorce? Charlea thought. "How many times have you been married?" Charlea asked before she could stop the words from spilling into the air. When Roland didn't answer right away, she was afraid that he was angry at her for asking. "I'm sorry. I should not have asked such a personal question."

"I've been married twice," he replied casually. "Once right out of high school. Her parents had it annulled—something about how they didn't like me. Then I married Grace. A lovely girl with a lovely name and a lovely—um, well—you know what I mean. She decided I couldn't give her everything she wanted so she chose money over me. She left me for a rich old codger and then had the audacity to sue me for everything I owned."

"I'm sorry."

Roland chuckled, apparently finding some sort of humor in his misfortune. "I'm better off without her, but enough about her. Are you married? I noticed you aren't wearing a ring." He turned the page of the newspaper, acting nonchalant about it.

"Yes." Charlea fidgeted with the corner of the newspaper. "No." She felt embarrassed at her indecision about a yes-or-no question. "I don't know. He was shot down over Korea and never came home. The Air Force has presumed he's dead, and I guess they know what they're talking about. He was the one great love of my life and now he's gone."

"I didn't realize that we only got one per lifetime. Who set that limit?" Roland flashed a mischievous grin. When she didn't return his smile, he grew serious. "I'm sorry. It must have been very hard."

Thinking of Mark pushed *Adonis* out of her head. Where was he? Was he still trying to get home? *No one will ever take Mark's place in my heart*, she thought. *I made a vow and will honor it until death parts us.* She knew *Adonis* wouldn't understand, so she didn't say it out loud. The long silence echoed through the room, ending any further conversation.

"I think I've found it!" Roland exclaimed as he leaned over a newspaper, interrupting Charlea's thoughts. "Look, here on page three."

Rushing to his side, Charlea leaned over him to read the article he had pointed out. *He smells so good*, Charlea thought as she closed her eyes. She quietly breathed in deeply, letting his sweet cologne warm her blood. Opening her eyes slightly, she could see Roland's flawless skin, his strong shoulders, and feel his irresistibility. She fought the urge to put her arm around his shoulders. An image of Mark floated through her mind. She took a step back.

Roland read aloud to her.

HOUSE BURNS DOWN

The home of Dr. Arthur Williams, City Hospital Administrator, and that of his family burned to the ground yesterday. The police have not determined a cause for the fire, although it appears to have started in the kitchen. Mrs. Williams and a maid were the only people in the home at the time of the fire and were able to get out without injury. The home and its contents were a total loss. Dr. Williams, his wife, and son will move to a living area at the hospital until their new house can be built.

"What's the date on the paper?" Charlea asked.

Roland looked at the front page. "July 15, 1946. There isn't much here. Seems strange though. Wouldn't the hospital administrator be a big man around a town this small? I wonder why they didn't have a bigger article about it."

Charlea stood back and walked to the other side of the table. "I don't know. Maybe the doctor didn't want the attention drawn to his family. At least we know the house burned down and they built another one. Does it say where they built the new house?"

"No, it doesn't. It says they lived at the hospital for a time. Is that building still around? We saw a hospital as we came into town, but it didn't look very old."

"We? Did someone come with you?"

"Did I say we?" Roland nervously chuckled as he closed the newspaper. "Where is the old hospital? It wasn't torn down, was it?"

"No, it wasn't. You're standing in it." Charlea spread her arms wide.

Roland looked around. "This is it? No kidding! Where was the family living quarters? Is there any way to find out?" He moved around the room, looking around the crates and boxes stacked against the walls.

"There's not an apartment or anything like that in this building so I'm not sure where they stayed. I think we have an old plan of the hospital somewhere. Maybe it's one there. Give me a minute to look in another room." Excusing herself, she went down the hallway. She felt a little uncomfortable leaving Roland alone in the other room with the historical items. Though not rare, they were still valuable. He was hiding something. Something that had to do with a house. Or something that had to do with the Williams family. Which was it? She would have to pry deeper to find out exactly what he wanted. Excitement ran through her like an electric shock as she realized that meant spending more time with him, but then she shook her head. *Get a hold of yourself! He's just a customer. Calm yourself down before you make a fool of yourself.*

Charlea went down the hall to the room that held the most valuable items of the museum collections, including old hospital records, rare books, and fragile artifacts. She would not allow just anyone in this room, a rule stemming from an incident with an angry woman who destroyed an old Bible from her ex-husband's family.

Charlea walked along a row of dusty shelves, rubbing her fingers on the binder labels until she came across one marked "Hospital." Inside, she found several neatly folded blueprints and thumbed through them until she found the one she wanted. A quick glance around before leaving told her that the janitor had used his broom and feather duster in here recently. She was pleased at his efforts.

She stopped in front of a glass case to see her reflection. She smoothed her hair and bit her lips to give them color. Calming herself, she went back down the hallway. Before entering the room, she peeked around the corner and saw Roland looking at labels on the cabinets. Opening a few of the drawers, he quickly rifled through the contents, but didn't take anything. He ran his hands along the wall and tapped quietly, looking for something. Studs? A secret passage? A hidden vault? Backing up a few steps, she coughed before entering the room, giving him time to pretend to be innocent.

Roland was sitting at the table when she entered.

"This may show you what you need to know." She spread a blueprint out on the table in front of him. "The first floor of the building has been extensively remodeled so this layout may not be of any use." Charlea leaned over Roland again, drinking in his scent that made her slightly dizzy. "The second floor is basically the same as it was when Dr. Williams was here, a series of large rooms with smaller rooms off of them. We are here in this room—um, the quarantined patient room." They looked at each other and wrinkled their noses. Reading his mind, she assured him that the room was safe now.

Charlea continued. "I don't see any mention of a small apartment."

Roland let out a soft moan of disappointment and pointed to a room on the blueprint. "It shows the administrator office on the second floor. Do you think they lived in there?"

"I don't know. I thought you wanted to find their house?" Charlea asked again, hoping to pry another bit of information out of him.

Roland opened his mouth as if to answer, but closed it without saying anything. He heaved a great sigh and rubbed his forehead, as if conjuring an answer.

"Still not going to tell me the whole truth?" Charlea asked, prodding for more. "Why are you being so mysterious about it?"

Studying his face as he searched for an answer to her questions, she found nothing. But one thing was for certain: he didn't want to share the whole truth with her. When he did not answer her inquiry, she added, "Keep your secrets then."

"Can I look around the building anyway? I promise I won't steal anything."

"I guess I believe you since I didn't see you take anything when you were looking around here while I was gone."

Roland looked surprised, but then laughed. "Sorry about that. I thought you might not approve of me searching on my own. I wouldn't take anything without your permission."

"I should hope not," Charlea replied, half-jokingly and half not. "This is a public building, so you are free to look around, but please do not bother any of our library customers. And leave things as and where you found them."

"Yes, ma'am. Where should I start?"

"At the beginning, I guess."

Chapter 5

Charlea went to the circulation desk where Bonnie and Mr. Wilkerson were standing. Roland went off on his own, studying the map as he went.

"I thought you went home." Charlea stared at Mr. Wilkerson who returned a broad smile.

"I'm not leaving my sweetheart around a guy like that!" he told her. "I have to make sure he's the better man."

The trio stood there, watching Roland as he explored the library. Roland carried the blueprint with him and stepped off approximate distances. He disappeared down the bookshelf canyons and reappeared at the far ends. Occasionally, he rubbed his hands along the walls or knocked on them. Once, he knelt and rapped on the floor. He walked around the exterior walls where he could, moving his hands up and down the paneling with an occasional tapping.

Bonnie and Mr. Wilkerson looked at Charlea for an answer to their unspoken question, but Charlea only shrugged. She had no explanation for his strange behavior. While they watched him as he moved around the library, other library patrons joined in the observation, occasionally looking at Charlea who gave no hint of what was going on.

Walking back to her, Roland said, "I'm surprised to see that your office was a closet under the stairs. You're the director of the library. Surely you deserve better."

"It's not glamorous, but it serves the purpose in a low-budget organization. Have you found what you're looking for?"

"No, but I think I'm getting closer. Would you mind if I looked in your office?"

"As long as you don't bother anything, I suppose not."

"Thanks!" Roland walked toward her office.

Bonnie sidled up behind Charlea and whispered, "What's he trying to find? Why is he feeling the walls?"

"I'm not sure yet. He says he's researching a letter his mother or his aunt gave him. Somewhere in our discussion, he decided that he's interested in Dr. Williams and the hospital. I have no idea what the walls have to do with the letter or the doctor. He's lying about something for some reason."

"Lying? Or maybe he's got a fetish with walls." Bonnie giggled quietly.

"Or he's a nut!" Mr. Wilkerson exclaimed. All three of them laughed. Roland poked his head out of Charlea's office.

"Shh!" Bonnie managed to say. "He's acting very strange for such a good-looking man."

"*Adonis*," Charlea said, "that's what I call him...but not to his face. He's being too vague about what he's looking for."

"Do you think he's up to no good?" Bonnie asked.

"I'm not sure. Time will tell. It will take more...um...research, if you know what I mean." The two ladies giggled like teenagers.

"Sounds like fun," Bonnie sighed. "I almost wish I was single again. I'd help him with research any time. Weird or not, he seems quite the charmer, although I'd want to know what his deal with the walls is."

"Bonnie, I can't believe you said that! You're a married woman."

"You should flirt with him, Charlea," Mr. Wilkerson inserted, much to Charlea's shock. "Get him to ask you out."

"You can't be serious!" Charlea whispered loud enough for Mr. Wilkerson to hear. "He's a total stranger!"

"You're a fool if that's the extent of it," he whispered back to her.

"Or blind," Bonnie added. "Charlea, wake up. Someone wonderful and mysterious has dropped in on you. Grab him!"

The trio turned to watch Roland feeling along the staircase with his hands.

"I'd better get back to him before he rubs the paint off." Charlea left Bonnie and Mr. Wilkerson shaking their heads.

"Looking for termites?" Charlea asked when she walked up behind Roland. He spun around and laughed uneasily.

"Can we go to the second floor to look in Dr. Williams' office?" Roland asked. "Or if you point it out, I can look by myself if you have work to do."

"I suppose I can spare the time. I can help you look if you tell me what you're looking for." She watched his face closely, but saw no clue to his purpose. "Or do you want to feel the walls there too?" She smiled at him so he would know that she was joking with him.

"No, I'm only curious," Roland said. "And we could spend more time together." He winked at her. Charlea was on to him and hesitantly let his charm roll away without affecting her. She nodded and led the way.

Chapter 6

Returning to the second floor, Charlea and Roland entered a large room with several doors on one side leading to smaller rooms. Roland mindlessly reached out and wiped the dust away from the face of one of the doors. His stroke revealed very faint letters on the door. He excitedly took his handkerchief out and wiped the door more thoroughly. The word "Administrator" could be seen faintly against the faded paint. As he pushed it open, the door creaked in protest.

Just like the other rooms, this one was also in need of a good cleaning. Cobwebs hung from the ceiling and a thick layer of dust lay on the furniture. Sunlight peeked through two windows that would make the room bright and cheerful with cleaning. On the left, there was a large roll top desk, an old wooden office chair, and a large file cabinet. On the other side of the room, boxes and books were stacked against an enormous halltree. Charlea sneezed as the dust went up her nose.

While Roland examined the walls of the room, Charlea opened the closest box and found file folders filled with crumbling yellowed papers. Using what little light came through the large, dirty window, she saw that they were patient records. The next box she opened was full of more patient records, pages from a hand-written journal, childish drawings wishing "Father" a pleasant day, and notes on patients. She would ask hospital personnel what to do with the records.

"This room needs a lot of work to get it cleaned up," Charlea said. "I've avoided these small rooms because there's so much to do elsewhere." She ran her finger through the dust on top of the old desk.

Roland was running his hands along the walls again. "Do you think this might have been their temporary home?" he asked. "It's not big enough for a residence." He went to the back wall to look in a sink below a window. Brushing the dirt from his hands, he surmised, "Even without the furniture, it's too small for three people. And no one would want to live just off the patient room."

Charlea peered over his shoulder. Dead flies littered the bottom of the sink that had once been white, but now was brown with dirt. The sight made her flinch and she backed away. "They only lived here long enough to get another house built. This room has such poor access for a family to come and go. They probably lived on the first floor. And since that floor was remodeled, there's no way to tell for sure."

Adonis looked around the room and shook his head. "Is there a basement to this building? Maybe they lived there."

"No one would live down there in the dark and damp. The place gives me the creeps." Charlea shuddered as visions of ghosts fluttered through her mind.

"Is it haunted? This is an old building where people died. I bet there are ghosts around here, aren't there? Do you mind if I go look at the basement? I'm not afraid of ghosts."

Charlea put her hands on her hips, growing impatient at being led on. "Can you clear something up for me first? Why this is so important to you? I thought you wanted to find out who the letter was written to and where the writer lived. Then you needed to find the house. Now you seem obsessed with this building, which is neither the address on the letter nor is it connected with someone named Robert Williams. I'd really like to know what's in that letter that makes you want to crawl around in a dirty basement." Getting no answer from him, she asked him pointedly, "What's going on?"

A long pause followed her question while Roland nervously shuffled in place. "My brother tells me I get carried away with things, but I prefer to think that I'm a determined person. Or maybe I'm thorough. If you don't have time to help me, I can do it on my own." He pouted a little as if he intended to make her feel guilty.

Inwardly, Charlea laughed at his feeble attempt at a guilt trip. Her mother had used the guilt strategy so much with her that Charlea was immune to its effects. She was determined not to fall under the spell of his charm again. She dropped her arms and shook her head.

"I can't help you if I don't know what you're looking for. What's important here? Is it the person, the house, or the hospital? May I read the letter?"

Roland was noticeably nervous. "I don't want to share it. It's very personal." He ran his hand through his hair. "I'll...I'll go to the courthouse like you suggested. That's a very good idea. Thank you for your time. It has been a pleasure." He bowed slightly to her and walked past her out of the room.

Surprised by his sudden departure, Charlea quickly followed him. She didn't intend for her prying questions to run him off. In spite of his deception, she didn't want him to go away angry. She called to him as she hurried down the stairs behind him.

"Roland, please wait. If you want to see the basement, I can make arrangements with the maintenance man to escort you tomorrow. He knows this building inside and out, so he could answer many of your questions. How long did you say you were staying in town?"

Roland stopped and turned to face her. "I didn't say. I wanted to get my business done today so I could relax during the rest of my vacation. I'd really like to see it today."

"It's not a good time for me, but Milt, our maintenance man, knows the building inside and out. He might know where to find whatever it is you're looking for. He's not here today, but I could set an appointment with him first thing tomorrow. You could enjoy your vacation this afternoon."

"It won't take me long to look down there. Are you sure we need to wait for him? I'll protect you from any ghosts we find." He smiled at her. "Really, I will."

"I'm sure you would," she replied as she reached the bottom stair. "But yes, I'm sure you need to wait for Milt. He only works part-time and won't be in until tomorrow. He worked here when the building was a hospital and knew Dr. Williams, so he can answer all of your questions. It'll be worth the wait, trust me." Charlea smiled at Roland, attempting to charm him. She doubted it worked because she hadn't practiced that skill as often as he obviously had.

Roland was unhappy, but Charlea gave him no choice. "I guess I can wait that long." He took her hand in his and caressed it softly. Leaning closer, he said, "You've been very patient and helpful this morning. Can I take you to lunch, Charlea? To repay your kindness. And we could get to know one another better. Go over some of the town's history as well as more of your own."

Charlea was stunned by the offer. Was this another ploy to get information out of her or have free access to the library? Too many unanswered questions left her unable to trust this guy. Prudence and her voice of reason felt it was best to steer clear of him until she knew him better. But her heart told her this was a one-time offer and she would be crazy not to take it.

Her voice of reason won the argument.

"Thanks, but no. I, um, have other plans," she lied. That said, her voice of reason vanished, and she immediately regretted her answer. But the words were spoken, and she couldn't summon the courage to change her answer.

Roland seemed genuinely disappointed as he released her hand and stepped away. "Well, maybe tomorrow. Will I see you before the tour of the basement?"

Charlea was relieved to hear that he would come back tomorrow. She hoped for a second chance at lunch. If he asked, she would tell her voice of reason to shut up and accept his invitation.

"Of course. I'll call Milt this afternoon. I'm sure he'd love to show you around. He'll be able to fill in the blanks for you better than I can. After I get a hold of him, is there someplace where I can call you with the time?"

"I'm staying at the Stop and Sleep Inn. You can call me there or leave a message. I think I'll have a closer look around town to see what's here. Can you show me how to get to where the old house was? I'd like to drive by and look, even if it's not the Williams house anymore."

Charlea drew a map for Roland and then escorted him to the circulation desk where Bonnie stared at him.

Bonnie suddenly blurted out, "Did you look what you're finding for?" When she realized what she had said, her face turned red.

Bonnie's outburst elicited a smile from Charlea. Even Bonnie wasn't exempt from *Adonis'* charm. Attempting to rescue her from this uncomfortable situation, Charlea said, "*Adon*…I mean Roland is doing some historical research on our town. He'll be back tomorrow to look through more records and study our building's architecture. Hey, you've lived here all your life. Do you know anything about Dr. Williams?"

"I heard his name when I was younger, but I didn't know him. Maybe some of the older people did. We can ask Mr. Wilkerson. If anyone remembers him, it'll be Mr. Wilkerson."

Charlea looked around. "Where is he?"

"He left a little bit ago," Bonnie replied. "Said he was tired of waiting on you to finish up. He will likely remember Dr. Williams, Mr. Parker. And he'll tell you every detail he can remember as well, which will take him hours to tell it all." Charlea and Bonnie laughed as they told Roland about Mr. Wilkerson's long stories.

Roland stepped away from the counter. "Charlea, thank you for all your help today. You have work to do and I have a house to find. Until tomorrow, ladies."

Roland left the two women looking after him as he left, each lost in their thoughts about him. Every female eye in the building watched him as he walked out the door. When the door shut, a collective feminine sigh resounded, indicating *Adonis* had left the library.

Chapter 7

Only a couple of people were in the library, so Charlea slipped into her office for a few moments of solitude, mentally exhausted by the morning's events. The emotional rollercoaster with Roland had drained her, and she was relieved to be away from him for a while. She needed time to clear her head. She dropped into her chair and laid her head on the desk, but she jerked upright again when she heard footsteps hurrying toward the door.

Bonnie slipped inside and excitedly asked question after question, not waiting for Charlea to answer. "Did you find out what his fascination was with the walls? What does he want? Is he married? Did you kiss him?"

Charlea waited for Bonnie to draw breath before answering, "No, I don't know why he likes our walls so well. No, he's not married. He's divorced. And no, I didn't kiss him. What a thing to ask!"

"But you wanted to, right?"

"I admit the thought crossed my mind. I'm confused about him. Something in me says not to trust him, at least not completely. I even turned down a luncheon date with him."

Bonnie's mouth dropped open. "He asked you out to lunch? And you said no? Are you out of your mind?" she exclaimed, waving her arms in the air. "Who cares if you can trust him or not? Go to lunch in a public place. What can he do with other people around?" Bonnie sat down in a chair across the desk from Charlea, staring at her in disbelief. "What were you thinking? It's a meal, for heaven's sake, that's all. What could happen?"

Charlea shook her head and put her hands over her face. "I know, I know. How could I be so dumb! I regretted saying no the second I said it. But I didn't know how to tell him I changed my mind."

"How about, 'On second thought, yes, I'll go.' Women are known for changing their minds. That's our prerogative. Men expect us to change our minds."

"I try not to be that fickle. I can't figure out why he would ask me. I mean, you know he has women falling all over him. What does he want with me? I'm too old for him."

"You're not too old. You're an interesting, attractive woman. You might fall in love, get married, and leave here..." Bonnie's voice trailed off.

Charlea leaned forward in her seat. "Think about it. He's "*Adonis*," the kind of man who can have any pretty, young woman in visual range. I can't compete with that. I'm past my prime and I accept that."

"Not all men want young women."

"Oh please, Bonnie. Men who are my age are either happily married or are looking for someone young to cheat with so they can feel young. They can't feel young with an old woman. I don't have a chance because I can't do that. Or at least they think I can't."

"If he's divorced, then he's not in either of those categories."

"Women don't divorce men like him unless he's a cad. Maybe he cheated on his wife. I wouldn't put it past him. Look at the reaction of the women here? Given the slightest push, they all would have thrown themselves at him. For a woman to leave *Adonis*, there has to be something really annoying about him."

"I don't think that's it at all. I think you're a coward. Don't look at me that way. Yes, you're a coward. Some man shows the slightest interest in you and you look for any excuse to dismiss him."

"It's not cowardice. I don't need a man in my life."

"If you didn't need a man, you wouldn't still be talking to Mark's picture. Don't look so surprised. I know you do that."

"I still miss him, even after all these years. I keep hoping he'll walk in that door someday."

"I know you do," Bonnie said softly. "Maybe *Adonis* can help you with that."

"Maybe, but it's unlikely."

"You can hope he can."

"Hope is a very fragile thing. But to end this debate and to make you happy, I'll keep him in mind. Maybe tomorrow he'll ask me to lunch again. If by some miracle he does, I'll say yes."

"And what if he doesn't ask?"

"I will be disappointed for missing the opportunity." Charlea avoided Bonnie's gaze so she couldn't see her face. If he didn't ask again, Charlea would be bitterly disappointed. She would have to be charming enough to make sure that he did ask. And she'd spend more time getting ready for work, take more time fixing her hair, and wear her blue dress that brought out the color of her eyes. Maybe she would have one of her "pretty" days tomorrow.

Bonnie interrupted her thoughts. "Will you take some advice from a friend? Say yes if someone asks. Maybe it's nothing more than a free meal. But maybe it will be more. You never know!"

"I'll make you a deal. I'll accept the next date offer I get, if that will make you happy. I won't say no unless the guy's a jerk," Charlea told Bonnie. "Do we have a deal?" Charlea held out her hand.

Bonnie eyed her suspiciously. "How do you define a jerk? Roland is not a jerk and you told him no."

"No, Roland is not a jerk. You know what I mean; a jerk is a man who is a drunk or doesn't have a job or someone like that. Deal?"

Bonnie nodded in agreement, and shook Charlea's hand. "We have a deal. Next time you accept the date. I'd better get back to work."

Bonnie got up to leave. "Mr. Wilkerson and I think you should. We think you need a love life."

"You two were discussing my love life?"

"No, we were discussing your lack of one."

"Please. Don't discuss my private life with him." Charlea waved Bonnie out the door. "Why don't you go to lunch while I watch things? You've had a busy morning."

"No more than you have," Bonnie said, winking at Charlea. "But I need to run home and check on things. The baby was fussy this morning and I'd like to see if she's better. I won't be long."

Chapter 8

Back in her office after lunch, Charlea worked on the budget again. Being away for a time had done her good, and she started the chore with renewed vigor. She stopped long enough to call Milt and set up an appointment to show Roland around the building. Milt's excitement came through over the phone as he enthusiastically agreed.

The next order of business was to leave a message for Roland. She rehearsed several ways to accept his invitation to lunch, just in case the topic came up. Prepared with answers to fit all the situations she could imagine, she dialed the Stop and Sleep Inn. The butterflies returned to her stomach as she listened to the phone ring in his room, but they turned into lead when there was no answer. She had to leave a message with the front desk and hoped he'd get it. Perhaps later she'd call again just to make sure he did and to give him another chance to ask her to lunch.

With tomorrow's appointment set up, she turned back to the budget, but the zeal for it was gone. *I give up,* she thought to herself. *I'll try again later and hope it works. I have too much on my mind right now to concentrate.*

Charlea went out to the circulation desk and checked the clock. Almost closing time. While she was chatting with Bonnie, another man that neither of them knew came in the door. If Roland was *Adonis*, this new man was one of the lesser gods. A fine looking man, tall, well built, with an air of self-assurance, but as handsome as he was, he came in a distant second to *Adonis*. Just like *Adonis*, he appeared to be searching for information, looking through the books on the front bookshelves.

Bonnie nudged Charlea in the ribs and whispered, "Go help him. Maybe he'll ask you out too. Remember your promise!"

"Don't be ridiculous!" Charlea whispered so loudly that one woman looked up from her reading to see what was going on. Charlea heeded the warning and whispered more softly, "I meant that I would accept a date from *Adonis*. Not just anyone! Besides, how do I know he's not married? Men like that are always married."

"You said you'd accept a date from anyone who is not a jerk, remember?"

The truth of the statement elicited a groan from Charlea. "You're right. I said that, but I didn't really mean it. You can't seriously hold me to it."

"Of course I can. He doesn't look like a jerk. In fact, he looks pretty good, and I don't see a ring on his hand. He looks older than *Adonis* so that negates your whining about age. He meets all the criteria. Time to keep your word. Go help him," Bonnie whispered loudly.

The man, hearing the loud whisper, turned to look at the two women standing at the counter. They both smiled and nodded to him. As he turned back to perusing the books, Bonnie winked at Charlea and pushed her toward the man. Angry for being shoved, Charlea turned back to Bonnie with a frown that would have melted butter.

"What about *Adonis*?" Charlea whispered. Bonnie shook her head and pointed to the man. When Charlea turned to go, Bonnie gave her another nudge in his direction. Charlea was tired of fighting the battle and surrendered to the prodding.

"Can I help you find something?" Charlea asked as she approached him. As he turned to face her, she was immediately drawn in by his brown eyes that were honest and direct. He was better looking up close, with thick brown hair well groomed, as she liked it.

"I'm visiting the area and would like some history about this town," he said. "Do you have a book that's not too lengthy?" His smile immediately put Charlea at ease, so different from the reaction she'd had with *Adonis*. No butterflies. No jitters. No voice of reason screaming in her head—all qualities that endeared this man to her, much to her surprise.

"That's really odd," she said. "You're the second person today to ask for local history."

"It must be tourist season." He smiled, which gave his face a warm and welcoming expression and her heart melted slightly.

"Must be. So you want just the history high points? I think we can help you out. Let's look through these books over here." She directed him to the display near the front of the library. As she showed him several books, they talked about what might be of local interest and locations to visit.

The man thumbed through each of the books and set one aside. He seemed very appreciative of her efforts to accommodate him, asking appropriate questions, and listening closely to her answers. Finding a book with a town map in it, he asked her if he could check it out.

"This book is available at our local bookstore," Charlea told him, looking at him out of the corners of her eyes in an attempt to flirt.

"I only need this book for one day. I'd rather check it out."

Disappointed in his lack of response to her attempted flirtation, Charlea took the book from him. He had chosen an inexpensive book that was still in print, easy to replace. It was against library policy to loan books to anyone outside of the county, but as head librarian, she had the power to make exceptions. He would have to come back to return it. The book would be her assurance that she would see him again. The thought excited her.

"How long will you be in town?" she asked regarding the book, but also to pry into his plans.

"Just a couple of days. I can leave a deposit, if that would make things easier."

His easy smile put her more at ease, just like Mark's smile used to do to her. Mark. His memory flashed across her mind, but she shoved it aside for later.

"I normally don't allow anyone from outside the county to check books out," she said quietly, not wanting the other patrons to know she was granting an exception to her own rule. "But since you don't want your own copy, I will make an exception for you. No deposit will be necessary, as long as you give us your address so we can send the police after you if you don't return it." For an instant, he looked concerned by that, so Charlea flashed him a smile.

He mirrored her bright smile. "I'd rather check it out. That way I get to come back for another visit."

Charlea's heart skipped a beat when she understood that he might want to see her again. Flattery made her face and heart warm. The pair joined Bonnie at the circulation desk where Charlea gave him a form for a library card. From that, she got his name—David Collins—where he lived—Dallas—where he worked—a utility company. She especially liked this—only two years younger than her.

While Bonnie typed up his card, Charlea asked him, "What brings you to our town?"

"I needed a vacation. I'm a tourist."

"We don't get many tourists around these parts. Why here? Our little town must seem dull compared to Dallas."

"I was hoping to meet interesting people. And I have."

Charlea felt the heat turn her face red. "That's nice."

"Now that you know all about me, what's your name?"

She was embarrassed that she had neglected to introduce herself. "My name is Charlea Ludlow. I am the head librarian."

"So nice to make your acquaintance, Miss Ludlow." Turning to Bonnie, he asked, "And you are…?"

"Bonnie. Bonnie McGregor. Charlea, here's his card." She passed a freshly typed library card to Charlea with a secret wink. "I have work to do, so if you will excuse me." She picked up a book and disappeared behind a bookcase.

"Charlea," David said, "That's a very unusual name. Is there a story that goes with it?"

"My parents wanted to name me after their mothers, Charlotte and Leah. But they couldn't agree on which one, so they combined their names. Charlea. My mother told me it means 'peace in the family.' It doesn't really, but it makes a good story."

David smiled widely. "Family peace is always a good thing. It's a lovely name that fits you, Miss Ludlow."

As Charlea checked the book out to David, Bonnie quietly told the few remaining customers it was closing time. Charlea reluctantly left her conversation with David to check out books for other patrons leaving. She was delighted to see that David seemed to be hanging around, waiting for everyone else to leave. As the last one left, Bonnie ambled to the front door and stood, waiting for David to leave as well.

"Well, I guess I should go too," said David, having delayed his departure as long as possible. He fumbled with the book as he started toward the door, then turned around to look at Charlea. "I noticed a dinner club on the edge of town, and well, since I don't know anyone in town, would you go to supper with me? I hate to eat alone and I've enjoyed talking with you."

From the doorway behind David, Bonnie mouthed the word 'yes' to Charlea and nodded in an exaggerated way. Charlea expressed her annoyance of the action with a scowl. David followed Charlea's gaze and turned to see what had her attention. Bonnie smiled innocently at him, having stopped her motioning before he turned around. Bonnie played with the door's lock, trying to appear as unobtrusive as possible. David turned back to Charlea and waited for an answer.

Charlea rubbed her forehead, trying to iron out the aggravation in her brow. "I know which place you're talking about," she replied more sweetly than she actually felt. "It's a nice place and the food is good."

The request presented quite a conundrum. As much as she liked him, she wasn't sure about going out with him. Her voice of reason urged her to be prudent and decline. Mark's memory wafted across her mind. Glancing at David again while her emotions roiled in her, she could see the sincerity in his eyes. She was sorely tempted to accept, but she couldn't summon the courage.

Charlea looked at her feet, still struggling with her emotions. "Thanks, but I can't. I don't go out with men I don't know. I'm not good at blind dates."

"Oh, brother!" Bonnie groaned from the doorway. She shook her finger at Charlea and frowned to remind Charlea of her promise.

"I beg your pardon?" David asked Bonnie after turning to look at her.

Charlea glared at Bonnie. "Bonnie—um—is anxious to get home. Aren't you, Bonnie?"

"I'm mad because you're going back on your word!" Bonnie said angrily, putting her hands on her hips.

Charlea glared at her friend who was exposing her vulnerability. "Bonnie! This is not the time to discuss it!" Turning back to David, she said softly, "Don't pay any attention to her, Mr. Collins. She gets grumpy at the end of the day. I'm sorry."

David shuffled his feet and looked disappointed. "I'm sorry too, because I'll have to eat alone tonight."

"Can I say something so I can go home?" Bonnie called from the doorway to remind them she was still there. "If I may be so bold to ask, are you a respectable gentleman?"

David seemed taken aback by the question. "What?" He looked from one woman to the other before seeming to comprehend the point of the question. "Yes, of course, I am. I neglected to bring a list of references, but I assure you that I have nothing but honorable intentions."

"Are you currently married?"

"No, I have never been married."

"Then Charlea accepts your offer. I happen to know that she has no plans for tonight, so she'll be happy to have dinner with you. Won't you, Charlea?" Bonnie narrowed her eyes, daring a contradiction from the other woman. "Charlea, I'll take you home so you can freshen up." Transitioning into her sweet voice, she asked David, "Can you give her an hour to get ready?"

David nodded. "Of course!" He turned back to Charlea to get her concurrence.

"Bonnie! Mr. Collins," Charlea exclaimed. "I—"

Bonnie didn't give Charlea a chance to finish, "Sorry, Charlea, but a promise is a promise. He meets the criteria." Turning back to David, she continued, "Miss Ludlow lives at 440 Pine Street, five blocks east of here in a white apartment house with blue trim."

"I think I should have a say in this!" Charlea cried out, angry at being left out of the decision-making process.

"No, you don't. You're going to keep your promise." Bonnie moved closer to David and poked his chest with her finger for emphasis, "And if you're not a perfect gentleman, a lot of people in this town will come after you, including me. Get my drift?" She gave him a look that wiped any doubt in David's mind what she was talking about.

"Bonnie," Charlea stammered, "Please—Mr. Collins, I'm sorry—I can't—"

He held his hand up, "Please, Miss Ludlow, since it seems we have a date, call me David." He turned to Bonnie and said, "I understand, and I'll remember your words of warning. Trust me. I'll treat Miss Ludlow with the utmost respect. Pine Street, did you say?"

"Wait, you two! I haven't—"

Bonnie held her hand up to Charlea. "Yes, five blocks that direction. You can't miss it. The apartment house is the biggest building on the block."

Charlea opened her mouth to argue with both of them again, but it was no use. Bonnie and David were ignoring her protests, so no matter how much it frightened her, she knew she would be going out to dinner with Mr. Collins tonight. Deep down, she could feel the growing excitement inside, but she wasn't ready to admit it to herself, much less them.

David told her with the excitement of a schoolboy, "I'm really looking forward to this. I'll see you in an hour." With that, he walked out the door and Bonnie shut it behind him.

Charlea turned to glare at Bonnie. "How dare you accept a date on my behalf! You have no right to do that!"

"You made a promise, and I'm holding you to it." Bonnie flipped the lock with a determined flair.

"I don't even know this man! I can't go out with him. It's not—not—"

"Proper? Quit being so proper! Your no-blind-dates policy has kept you alone far too long! He seemed like a gentleman to me. You'll have a good time tonight. If you give him a chance, I bet you'll be glad you did."

"But—"

"Face it, Charlea, you're going on a date tonight and there's nothing you can do about it."

Charlea rubbed her temples. "I can't believe this is happening."

"Quit being so melodramatic. Look, you got two invitations today. The first one you turned down and regretted it—regretted it so much that you sat in your office fantasizing about ways to accept if he asked you again."

Charlea felt embarrassed. "You heard me?"

"Overheard you. I was walking by your door and couldn't help but hear. But I understand why you'd do that. You're out of practice and you need to work on it. You should have used one of those lines with this guy. You had some good ones."

"I had *Adonis* in mind while I was trying them out."

"He's no *Adonis*, but he seems really nice. You two seemed to get along well, and you look good together. Grab the opportunity and go with it. Live a little!" Bonnie walked behind the counter. "What kind of friend would I be if I let you regret not taking this one either?"

Charlea wrung her hands, trying to release the anxiety. "This doesn't seem right. I know nothing about him. What if he's a criminal or something like that?"

"Stop letting your imagination run away with you. Trust me, you'll thank me tomorrow. I have a good feeling about this."

Charlea knew there was no use in arguing with her. Bonnie turned the lights off, took Charlea by the arm, and led her to her office.

"I hope you're right," Charlea said as she got her purse and tied the scarf over her hair.

Bonnie collected her other things and headed toward the back door to leave. "Just think, you can go out with this guy tonight and go out with *Adonis* tomorrow. That'll be a new record for you, Charlea, two dates in two days. Mr. Wilkerson won't believe it. Let's go. There's not much time for you to turn yourself into a dream girl."

"I'm not a girl anymore, and that makes me even more nervous. Makes me wonder what he sees in me. Look at me! I'm an old woman. Why would he want to go out with me?"

"It doesn't matter. All that matters is that he does."

"That dinner club's a pretty fancy place. What am I going to wear? What will we talk about? What if I make a fool out of myself?" Charlea shut the door to her office. As they made their way through the back entrance, Charlea turned out all the lights, locked the door, and tested it to make sure it was secure.

Bonnie got into her car. "Wear that cute dark blue dress you had on at the Chamber of Commerce dinner last fall. It looks good on you. We need to hurry. You've got less than an hour before he comes."

Bonnie's rusty old car sputtered as it started and smoked as it went down the street. On the way to the apartment, Bonnie gave her advice on what to do and not to do. What to say and not to say. How to act and what to wear.

At some point, Charlea began to lose track of what Bonnie was saying because her own thoughts were crowding her mind. Charlea's stomach was churning at the thought of going out with a stranger. *Am I crazy for doing this? How did I get into this mess?* she asked herself. *I don't even know him! What if he's a murderer or something like that? If I turn up dead tomorrow, I'll come back and haunt Bonnie. I should have never promised her anything. I know how she is about those kinds of things. If he's like all other men, he should be looking for someone younger. Is he looking for an easy mark? Why would he pick me? Something must be wrong with him. Otherwise, he would be married. Didn't he say he had never been married?*

"Are you listening to me?" Bonnie asked when she pulled up in front of Charlea's apartment house. The car shuddered and coughed, but kept running while it was parked next to the curb.

"Of course, I am," Charlea lied. "Be on my guard, be charming, and remember every detail so you can hear about it tomorrow. I need a man in my life, according to you and Mr. Wilkerson. And last but not least, I'm not getting any younger, so I should grab every opportunity that presents itself, whether it's a good idea or not."

Bonnie looked at her with a why-do-I-even-try stare. "At least try to have a good time. And keep a good attitude. See you tomorrow."

"Thanks for the ride home. Tell Allen and the kids hello for me." Charlea got out of the car and headed up the walk to her apartment. Behind her, she heard Bonnie's car sputter, then roar to life as it pulled away. *I need to get her a raise*, she thought as she walked toward her apartment.

Charlea opened the door to her apartment, feeling triumphant that she hadn't run into her landlady, Mrs. Butterfield. She didn't want to explain things to the older lady who was old-school and as protective of Charlea as a mother wolf. She would not approve of Charlea going out on a blind date and wouldn't mince words in saying so.

Charlea walked straight to Mark's picture on the wall. "Well, honey, I guess I'm going out on a date tonight, but I still love you. I'm so nervous! Give me strength." She blew a kiss at the picture and went to her bedroom. She got out the dress that Bonnie told her to wear. One less decision to make. She looked in the mirror and wondered if there was any way that she could hide the little wrinkles on her face for one night. Probably not, she decided, and let out a sigh of resignation.

She let her hair down. Ordinarily, she liked to have her hair pulled back, but with it down around her shoulders, it hid her graying temples. She fluffed it up by adding a little water and drying it and then refreshed her makeup. Looking at her image in the mirror, she shook her head and wished time didn't show so much on her body.

Charlea pulled her dress on. The dress fitted her figure quite well, fitted at the bodice and full in the skirt below the waistband. The dress made her look very slim and classy and would swirl nicely if they danced. Looking in the mirror again, she was pleasantly surprised at how pretty she looked. The excitement of the looming date brought new color to her face and a sparkle to her eyes. Maybe Bonnie was right after all and this would do her a lot of good.

Opening the top drawer of her bureau, Charlea pulled out the Baby Browning revolver her father had given her on her wedding day. An odd gift for such an occasion, but he had told her that if she was to be an Air Force wife, she would spend a lot of time alone and would need some way to protect herself. She and her father had spent many hours at the shooting range so she knew how to handle a gun.

She debated with herself. *Should I take it or not?* Her father's voice spoke to her from a memory, always be prepared. She didn't really know David very well. Following her father's advice, she strapped on the stocking holster and then packed a purse.

Just as she finished, there was a knock at the door. "Charlea," called out Mrs. Butterfield from the other side of the door, "there's a man here saying he's looking for you. I haven't seen him before. Do you know anything about him? I can call the police if you need me to."

The thing Charlea had dreaded most had happened: Mrs. Butterfield had found out about this. Charlea flung the door open. "No, that won't be necessary. We're going out on a date."

Mrs. Butterfield stood there, a baseball bat held limply at her side. She always kept it close at hand in case something frightened her. In spite of her short stature, she was a husky and imposing woman who liked to be in control of every situation. A no-nonsense kind of person. A person who could give a good tongue lashing. A person who was not afraid to use her trusty baseball bat,

"My stars, Charlea. Tonight?" Mrs. Butterfield asked. "It's not even the weekend! How long have you known this man? He's not from around here is he? What do you know about him? Back in my day..."

The elderly woman's meddling annoyed Charlea. "Times have changed, Mrs. Butterfield. I'm a grown woman, and I can go out if I want to, even on a weeknight. I met him at the library this afternoon and he seems to be a very nice person. Bonnie approves of him."

"How well does Bonnie know him? Is he a friend of hers?"

"No, she just met him today too."

"This is not a good idea. Let me call the police and check up on him. What's his name and where is he from?"

"No, that's not necessary. I'll be fine. I'll tell you all about him tomorrow. But I really appreciate your concern." Charlea motioned for Mrs. Butterfield to leave so she could follow her out the door. "I shouldn't be too late." Charlea closed the door and locked it behind her. She could feel Mrs. Butterfield's disapproving stare following her as she went down the hallway.

David stood in the front foyer in a suit and tie. He looked even more handsome now than when he was in the library, which made Charlea smile as she came down the hallway. *Yes, this was a good idea, and it's going to be a good night*, she thought, as she saw a look of admiration in his eyes as she approached.

"Good evening," he said in his strong deep voice. "You look wonderful."

"So do you. You met Mrs. Butterfield?" The older woman came up behind Charlea, no doubt glaring at David over Charlea's shoulder. She tapped her bat with more than a hint of menace.

David cleared his throat. "Yes, we met." Clearly, words had passed between them.

Mrs. Butterfield's finesse with her bat made it perfectly clear that she did not approve of him taking Charlea out. "You didn't tell me where you're taking Mrs. Ludlow," she softly growled like a wolf and took a step toward David.

Wanting to change the subject, Charlea asked, "Did you have trouble finding the place?"

David took a step backward. "Not at all. Bonnie's directions were perfect. Shall we go?" His eyes were not on Charlea, but on Mrs. Butterfield and her bat.

"Don't wait up, Mrs. Butterfield!" Charlea said over her shoulder as she walked through the door. "See you tomorrow." She heard a grunt as the door shut behind her.

Chapter 9

Arriving at the club, they found a space toward the end of the parking lot as the sun blinked and went below the horizon to sleep for the night. The stars twinkled awake in the sky, around the sliver of the moon. The neon lights of the club became brighter, lighting the parking lot with a rainbow of colors.

As they walked toward the door, David took Charlea's hand in his and a little shiver ran through her that she hoped he didn't noticed. She knew it was a silly schoolgirl reaction, but her excitement was growing. She didn't have to pretend to be someone different when she was around him. His relaxed, unpretentious ways put her totally at ease. Mark used to make her feel that way. *He reminds me of Mark and that's why I feel attracted to him*, she reasoned. Relieved to discover the reason for her heart's rapid beating, she held his hand tighter and walked closer beside him.

The club was a relatively new business in town, but was very popular with local residents. Its Caribbean resort motif with soft lights, candles on each table, warm atmosphere, and live music set a tranquil mood. The exotic food was a change of pace from the usual meat-and-potatoes fare found around town. The bar was teeming with people talking and laughing while they waited for the small band to provide music for dancing.

As Charlea and David were led to one of the last empty tables, a momentary pause in the din of conversation swept through the restaurant. All eyes were on them. Whispered comments behind hands and staring eyes made Charlea uncomfortable as people made little effort to hide who they were talking about. Their rude behavior irritated her more than usual because she feared that David would be uncomfortable which would ruin her evening.

Charlea spotted Mr. Dunwoody, who owned the furniture store, and his wife, who minded everyone's business but her own. Her beehive of red hair was like a beacon announcing her presence. Mrs. Howell from the church was there, quickly hiding her shot glass behind the flowers in the table center. The banker Mr. Burnett and his too-young second wife were in a corner table, oblivious to what was going on.

David ordered glasses of wine for them and looked around. "Everyone seems to be looking at us. Are they watching to see if I'm being a gentleman? Do I have something to fear?"

"It's one of the disadvantages of living in a small town. Everyone knows everyone else. As long as you behave yourself, you'll be free to leave town peacefully."

"That's a relief!" David chuckled, leaving Charlea glad he had a sense of humor about the situation.

She leaned across the table and whispered, "The reason they're so interested in you is that you dared to take out the old spinster librarian. Seeing us together is shocking, maybe even scandalous. That makes you an item of intense curiosity. And by the number of eyebrows raised, some may disapprove."

"Shall we shock them a little more?" David reached across the table, took her hand, and kissed it. A soft, collective gasp echoed through the room. The sound amused the pair so much that they couldn't help but laugh.

"Bonnie told me I'm supposed to get to know you better," Charlea said after a sip of wine. "Tell me about yourself."

David sat back in his chair and told his story of growing up in a large family on a farm, going to college, and getting a job with a utility company. After their dinner of shrimp and fish was served, he told of how he worked his way up through the company into management.

"You never married?" Charlea was surprised that the words had slipped out. She hadn't intended to ask.

"No, I never married. You seem surprised by that."

"I am. Most men your age—not that you're old or anything. I mean men are usually married in their twenties and it seems unusual that you are not." Charlea blushed. "It's really none of my business."

"I never found the right woman. I thought I did a couple of times, but it didn't work out."

"Didn't worked out?"

David took sip of wine. "I was engaged twice. First, to my high school sweetheart. I was drafted into the Army right after high school, and we were going to get married after my tour of duty. Or so I thought. She ran off with someone else. I found out about it in a letter from my mother."

"How cruel!"

David waved off her sympathy. "She's now working in a factory, supporting her sot of a husband and their six kids." David gave a she-got-what-she-deserved laugh. "She should have waited for me."

"She probably wishes she had." Charlea ran her finger along the top of the wine glass, making it sing a melody while she summoned the nerve to ask the obvious question. "You said you were engaged twice?"

David took a deep breath and played with this food, seemingly lost in a memory for a few seconds. "After I got out of college, I met this woman at church, and for me, it was love at first sight. She was beautiful and talented and I loved her deeply. We dated for several years, and I was absolutely sure that she was the right one. Then on the day of our wedding, she ran off with my best man. She literally left me standing at the altar. It took a long time to get over it."

"I'm sorry for your pain. Are they still together? She and your best man?"

"No, they never married." David saluted Charlea with his wine before taking another sip. "Now tell me about you. What about your family?"

"My family and I were very close while I was growing up, but that ended when I married someone they did not approve of and they cut me off. Mark, my husband, was an Air Force fighter pilot. He loved flying and was almost more comfortable in the sky than he was down on earth. While he was on his deployments, I went to college—which probably kept me from worrying every minute. Then it all came to an end." Charlea paused long enough to swallow the lump that had found its place in her throat. "His plane was shot down in Korea during the war. The Air Force said he was missing in action and presumed dead."

David reached out and took her hand. "I'm sorry."

Charlea shrugged, refusing to expose her inner torment. "It's the cost of war. He was proud of his service and we often talked about the risks he faced. He said he would gladly give his life for his country and made me promise not to grieve for him if it happened. I broke that promise when I found out he had been shot down. What made it worse was that they never found him. He never came home.

Even now, I keep wondering if he's out there somewhere, trying to come back. And maybe someday, he'll come walking in my door."

"Is that why you were so reluctant to come with me tonight? Because you still feel like a wife instead of a widow?"

"Maybe. Maybe not. Saying no is easy. It's a habit."

"Are you glad Bonnie forced you to come?"

A smile escaped Charlea's control before she knew it. "Yes! I'm having a great time."

As they finished their dinners, Charlea told him of her family. How they reconciled after Mark was lost. How her parents were killed in a car accident. How her brother kept in close touch with her. How she set up the library and her plans for the museum on the second floor. David's soft eyes and timely questions made her feel special and lovely. She found her heart tugging at her, pointing to David. But Mark was still there, too.

With dinner finished, they danced and talked, lifting more eyebrows around the room and stimulating more gossip behind hands. Charlea knew the rumors would be flying tomorrow as word spread across town. Mrs. Butterfield would find out and march down to tell her how a lady acted in the old days. But tonight, she was having fun.

As David led Charlea back to their table, she thought she spotted Roland at the bar, but the person was soon surrounded by several women who blocked her view. She wouldn't be surprised if he was here. Roland would be attracted to the hot spot in town, and women would be attracted to him like ants to a picnic. With the memory of his handsome face still fresh in her mind, she was probably imagining things. Turning her attention back to David, she felt guilty for letting Roland invade her thoughts.

"You are a wonderful dancer," Charlea told David.

"My mother insisted that all of her rough-and-tumble boys learn to dance," he replied. "Although most people thought of us as country bumpkins, my mother insisted that we be well educated and could conduct ourselves like the 'up-town' folks. She said she couldn't give us much of an inheritance, but she could give us culture."

"Your mother sounds wonderful and wise."

"Yes, she was. I miss her a lot." David half-smiled at Charlea, revealing that he still mourned her passing. "She passed on many years ago, but sometimes I feel like she's still—"

"Excuse me," a voice cut in. "Miss Ludlow, do you have the library budget in order yet?"

Charlea was startled by the unexpected interruption and turned to look up. Her anger flared like a spark on a dry kindling when she saw Mr. Woodson standing next to their table, wearing the same suit from earlier in the day, still accessorized with a snarky look on his face.

"I was surprised to see you on the dance floor," he continued, remaining arrogant and condescending, as if she owed him an explanation. "I didn't think you came to places like this?"

Her spark of anger grew into a raging fire. "Why shouldn't I? The food is great and I like to dance. I don't need your permission to be here."

"I trust your work on the library budget will be done on time? Maybe you need to work overtime to get it ready, instead of gadding about."

David threw his napkin on the table and started to rise.

Charlea grabbed his arm and held it tight. "David, please don't."

Slowly David sat down again and gripped the edges of the table with white knuckles. His narrowed eyes never left Mr. Woodson's face.

Charlea turned her body to face Mr. Woodson, but didn't rise. Her hands were already curled into fists and she would have punched him in the mouth if she had stood. Through gritted teeth and with a tone that rose with each word, she said, "The budget will be ready in time for next week's meeting. Now leave me alone. I am here with this gentleman and three's a crowd."

"You heard her, mister," David said in a low growl that reflected Charlea's anger.

Mr. Woodson's shot them a look that left no doubt his anger equaled theirs. He excused himself and left.

Charlea turned back to David, taking great effort to gain control of her wildfire of anger. "I'm sorry about that. I usually don't act that way, but I couldn't help myself. I hate that man."

David shook his head. "I think you handled that well. He was way out of line. Who is that jerk? Your boss?"

"Mr. Woodson is on the city council, so in a way, he is my boss. He has harangued me about the library budget for the last several years. Practically accused me of being an embezzler. I'm not!"

"I know you're not. Anyone who thinks you are is crazy."

"He's a politician. A charmer to other people. But I seem to bring out the worst in him, especially after..." Charlea stopped. She really didn't want to go into it.

"After what?"

Charlea was hesitant to answer his question, but decided it would do no harm. "When he and his wife moved here, he started propositioning me. You know, indecent propositions. He won't give up. He keeps propositioning me and I keep rejecting his advances. He comes on to me whenever he can get me alone. I think that's why he wants to make me look like an embezzler."

"Now I hate the guy too."

Charlea pushed herself away from the table. "Let's not ruin this evening by talking about unpleasant things. I need to calm down. Will you excuse me for a few moments while I visit the ladies room?"

David stood up as Charlea left the table to walk toward the back of the club. She slipped into the ladies room and found an empty stall where she could be alone for a few moments.

For a little while, she stood in the quiet and let the anger drain away from her. To be sure it would not return, she flushed the toilet to symbolize what she wanted to do to Mr. Woodson. The simple action helped ease her mind.

Charlea replayed the day's events in her mind. So much had happened to her during this day. How could it have started out so wrong to end up so right? Two men had come into her library and both had swept her off her feet. She tried to remember how long it had been since she had been out on a date. Two years, at least.

She wondered if David was too good to be true. Her heart pounded as she thought about the feel of David's hand on her arm, on her hand, and on her back as they danced. No one had made her feel that way since Mark. At the thought of Mark, she felt a pang of guilt for being so happy. Still, she loved the way David made her feel. These strong emotions scared her and made her feel guilty, but at the same time, left her feeling alive again.

Enjoy the moment while it is here because soon it will be gone—but I can't do that here in the restroom. She quickly freshened up and went out to find David. As she passed the bar area, someone grabbed her by the arm and pulled her back toward the kitchen door. As Charlea stumbled along, she glanced up. Mr. Woodson.

"I need a word with you," he said sternly as he led her through the kitchen doors. The hubbub in the kitchen continued around them, with the cooks and wait staff preparing food and frowning at them for this invasion of their territory.

Charlea started to protest, but he held his finger over his lips to shush her as he pulled her toward the back door. He looked around to make sure no one was close enough to hear what he had to say.

"I just thought you should know that while you were in the ladies room just now the gentleman you're so taken with was in deep conversation with another man at the bar about what you might have in your purse and something about the library keys."

"You heard them talking?"

"No, but someone else overheard them and told me about it."

"Who?"

"The bartender. But I saw the way they were talking and it was very suspicious. You need to be careful around those two."

"Who was he talking to?"

Mr. Woodson pulled her back to the kitchen door to peek into the bar area. "See that guy in the sports coat and no tie? That's him."

Charlea followed his gaze and spotted Roland in a circle of women on the far side of the bar, but within sight of the table where David was sitting. She watched David turn and look toward Roland who nodded and raised his glass in salute. David quickly turned around and took a big drink of his wine, as if building up courage for some dangerous mission.

Charlea's heart sank into its usual place in the depths of loneliness. So she hadn't imagined seeing Roland earlier. And now Mr. Woodson was saying that he and David were conspiring together about something. It made perfect sense. Both men in her library today. Both looking for similar information. They obviously knew each other. She should have known it was too good to be true. Or maybe it was a setup. She would have to check that possibility out.

Unwilling to show her disappointment to her nemesis who was doing her a favor, she shrugged and said, "Thanks, Mr. Woodson, for your concern. Actually I met the other gentleman today at the library and we have an appointment tomorrow to do some research. Perhaps he noticed me and—"

"But what about the library keys? They sounded like they're planning to break into the library. I think we should call the police. Don't be charmed into submission by some crook who asked you out...."

"I am not blind to what is going on, Mr. Woodson," she said, almost spitting the words at him. "What do we have at the library that they would want to steal? Books? None of them are rare or worth much money. The museum only has local history stuff with no value except to the people around here. I really doubt they're here to steal a...a...an old family Bible or something." Charlea struggled to control her anger. She'd been made a fool. That stung worst of all. And she was furious with David and Roland for using her in their game of whatever-it-was.

No, she told herself. *I will not let Mr. Woodson see how I feel*. She shrugged. "My keys to the library are at home, so even if they stole my purse, they'd be out of luck. There's absolutely no reason to call the police."

"Well, it's a situation worth keeping an eye on." Mr. Woodson again looked through the kitchen door.

Looking past Mr. Woodson, Charlea saw David checking his watch. "I'll be extra careful and keep a tight hold on my purse. I made double sure that the library was locked up tight when we left tonight, and I will continue to do so until they leave town. They are both passing through, so this perceived threat is not a long-term one."

"Do you think it's prudent to keep company with someone who is just passing through? What do you know about him? It seems to me—"

"It seems to me," Charlea interrupted in a tone that left no doubt that she was through with this conversation, "that you're stepping in where you've no business being."

"My primary concern is your welfare."

"Mr. Woodson, this is my business. Not yours. Leave it at that."

"I don't think you know what you're getting into. I think you should be more careful."

"I really must get back to my date." Charlea pushed past him through the kitchen door, glad to get away from him and back to David. But David was now more a stranger than before. Who was he and what were he and Roland after? She felt the disenchantment billow up around her.

While finding her way back to David, she formulated a plan that might help her find the answers to her questions. She would call her brother and talk to him about it. Depending on what she found out, she'd either enjoy the ride or call their bluff.

David stood up as she returned to the table. His smile now seemed somehow fake. Her heart and her mind fought a great civil war. To trust? Or not to trust? This was the question she had no answer to.

"Sorry it took me so long," she said, flashing a fake smile of her own. "I ran into someone who wanted to talk business. I got away as quickly as I could."

"I hope you don't mind, but I got us another glass of wine while you were gone," he said.

That made her feel better and she relaxed slightly. At least he had had business at the bar when he ran into Roland. Maybe it was an inadvertent meeting. But what about the overheard conversation? She wasn't sure about anything any more. For now, she decided, she would put on a happy face and finish out the night as quickly as possible.

They danced again. As much as she distrusted him, she loved the feel of his muscular body next to hers, leading her around the floor. She felt at home, like she had with Mark. David smiled at her and she could feel her heart melting, in spite of her efforts to fight it. Even the harsh looks of Mr. Woodson from his table didn't dampen her heart's delight.

As they made their way back to the table, she decided to make her move. "David, I see someone I need to speak to at the bar. Do you want to come too?" She didn't give him a chance to decline, holding on tightly to his hand as she led him to the end of the bar, past a number of women who were trying to catch Roland's eye. Leon Reynolds, the local whose drinking had driven his family into poverty, cheerfully greeted Charlea as they stopped in front of Roland. Leon was a massive man, having built his muscles by carrying bricks for the masons around the area. She acknowledged the drunken man with a slight nod, but her true focus was on reading Roland's expression when he saw her there with David.

A surprised look flickered across Roland's face as he turned his attention away from two attractive young women next to him, but he quickly regained his composure and became his charming self again. "Charlea, how nice to see you here," he said, taking her hand to shake it. "I saw you dancing, but didn't want to cut in. It looked like you were having too much fun to interrupt."

"That was thoughtful of you," she said, still watching his reactions closely. "May I introduce my date, David Collins?"

"Nice to meet you, Mr. Collins," Roland said, shaking David's hand. "I'm Roland Parker." David had an odd look on his face and muttered a response. *Yes*, Charlea thought, *they know one another and they both seem unwilling for me to know it.* Roland was plainly the better actor of the two.

"Did you get my message about the appointment tomorrow?" she asked Roland, still studying him closely.

"Yes, I did. Thank you for setting that up for me."

"I was happy to do it. Well, if you will excuse us, we'll leave you to—"

"If I may be so bold, Charlea," Roland said, rising from his barstool. "May I have this dance? That is, if Mr. Collins doesn't mind."

Charlea looked at David. He had an unhappy look on his face, but graciously said that he didn't mind.

"Ladies, if you'll excuse me," he said as he took Charlea's hand and led her away.

The soft pouting whimpers from the young women he deserted gave Charlea a selfish satisfaction, and she silently acclaimed this victory for middle-aged women everywhere.

When they reached the dance floor, he pulled her close and her heart started pounding. He put his face against hers and whispered in her ear, "You look lovely tonight, Charlea. I see I should have asked you out for tonight, but when you turned me down for lunch, I thought there was no chance of that. And now here you are with that Collins guy. I'm so hurt!" He pulled his face away from hers so she could see him pout a little.

"I'm guessing you don't get turned down very often." She wondered if he could feel her heart pounding in her chest.

He turned thoughtful and replied, "No, I don't, but at least I get one dance with you." He swung her around and into a dip. "Do you regret coming with him, instead of me?" He pulled her back up to her feet and danced on.

Breathless, she replied, "Mr. Collins is a very nice gentleman. We have a lot in common and it's been a very pleasant evening. No, no regrets." She looked at him coyly, teasing him.

"I don't believe you."

He spun her around and drew her near again, breaking her determination not to smile. She couldn't help it as they glided across the floor. All too soon the song ended and Roland was leading her back to David. Roland bowed slightly to her and thanked her for the dance. The ring of young women quickly began to close around him again.

David asked her for one last dance. A slow song wafted through the restaurant and he held her very close as they swayed to the music. She closed her eyes, trying not to think of Mark. She could always trust Mark, but she was not sure about trusting David. Yet, being with David made her wish she had someone to love her again. Her doubts and misgivings about David were quickly evaporating while he held her close.

After the music ended, they stood there holding on, looking into each other's eyes. From across the room, Charlea heard Mr. Woodson clear his throat, indicating the limits of discretion had been reached. Coming to her senses, she stepped back and thanked David for the dance. He held her hand as he led her back to the table where she picked up her purse and they left the club. Outside, the stars were twinkling around the sliver moon and the air was clean and cool. David put his arm around her shoulders to keep her warm.

As they walked toward David's convertible, Charlea saw movement a few cars over. She knew it was Roland. His silhouette in the dim lights of the parking lot was unmistakable.

"David, how is it that you and Roland know each other?" She nodded toward Roland as they walked. She felt David stiffen next to her when he heard the question.

"How did—er—what makes you think we know each other?" David pressed his lips together and tapped his fingers against his thigh.

Charlea stopped and turned to face David. "Call it body language. Or intuition. But it's obvious that you two know each other and are pretending not to. Why?"

"Well, I—"

"Besides, someone overheard your conversation at the bar about getting the keys out of my purse. Wanting to explore the library on your own?" She paused for a moment, then added in an I-want-some-answers-now tone, "Tell me what's going on. And I want the truth."

"You've always been a lousy liar, David!" Roland replied from the darkness behind her. Charlea spun around to face him.

"Yes, we know each other," he said as he walked closer. "We are trying to get information about the letter. I am a very impatient guy and I didn't want to wait until tomorrow to explore a little."

Charlea saw his charming little smile on his face, as if he thought he could charm himself and David out of this uncomfortable situation. His conniving manipulations didn't work on her this time. "I'm not buying it. I want the truth," she said which took that smile off his face and replaced it with a look of resignation.

"I told you it was a stupid idea," David said to Roland. "You might as well tell her the whole story, Roland. She's got a right to know and she can help us better if she does. She knows this area better than either of us and it would save a lot of time in finding the stones."

"Stones?" Charlea asked. "What kind of stones? Rocks of some sort?"

"But she'll make us split it three ways!" Roland said under his breath to David. He had David by the arm, pulling him away so they could talk out of Charlea's hearing. "I don't even want to split them with you, much less her!" He waited, but got no response. He added quietly, "Do you think she'd consider a deal?" David looked back at Charlea, who stared back at him. He pulled Roland a little further away so not to be heard.

Charlea kept her distance, although she was sorely tempted to walk closer. Occasionally, their whispered volume raised enough for her to catch phrases of their discussion. "No, no, no!" she heard more than once from Roland, as well as "Stick to the plan!" David kept shaking his head to all of Roland's arguments.

Both men walked back towards Charlea who was tapping her foot, waiting impatiently while they had their little huddle.

"So what was the consensus? Am I in on whatever little secret you have going or not?" Charlea asked them, angry at being played for a fool. "If I'm not, then our appointment tomorrow is cancelled, Roland. Either way, I'd like to be taken home as soon as possible, David. On second thought, I'll just call a cab from the club." She turned toward the club.

"Please don't go, Charlea," David called after her. He came up behind her, grabbed her arm, and turned her around to look at him. "I'm sorry. You have every right to be mad at us, but please, give us a chance to explain. We'll tell you everything, won't we, Roland?"

Roland looked at David and then at Charlea. Acquiescing, he nodded and said, "Yes, we'll tell you everything, even though we have to split things three ways." Releasing a loud, disgusted sigh, he drew close to the other two and looked the parking lot over to make sure no one else was around. Drawing Charlea even closer to him, he whispered his story to her.

"You know that letter I have?" Charlea nodded. "It's from a soldier that fought in Europe at the end of World War II, driving Germans out of their strongholds and stuff. In a castle that had been used as a German headquarters, he came across a fortune in gemstones. At least, we think they're gemstones. And we think it's a fortune."

"You don't know for sure?"

"The letter just says 'stones.' They have to be gemstones. Instead of turning them in, he hauled them home and hid them somewhere in town. Why would he be so secretive about it if it were plain rocks? The letter gives some clues to their whereabouts, but not being familiar with the area, it's hard for us to figure out where his hiding place was. And we need your help to find it." He stared at Charlea.

"Where did you get the letter?" Charlea asked.

Roland shuffled his feet like a little boy caught stealing watermelons from the neighbor's patch. "I won it in a poker game."

"What kind of a poker game? Who would allow someone to bet a letter? Got a name?"

"If you must know, I was playing with a customer who needed a fourth. His name was Richard Breyerman. You may have heard of him. He's some rich guy in Dallas."

Hearing the name of the poker player who lost this letter in a game, Charlea wanted to burst out laughing, but kept her poker face on.

Roland pleaded with her. "So will you help us? Please?"

"Please," David said, "or he'll never let either of us rest, if you don't."

Charlea continued to stare at Roland, then she began to laugh. She walked away, leaving Roland and David looking first at her, then each other. They followed her as she walked across the parking lot until she turned back towards them, smiling. She walked up to them, grabbed their arms and steered them toward David's car.

"Come on, boys," she said. "Let's call it a night. We've all got a big day tomorrow. We have a mystery to solve."

David and Roland stopped short.

"You believe us then?" David asked.

Charlea turned around to speak to them and walked backward toward the car. "Let's just say that we should investigate the possibility." Charlea spun back around and continued walking toward the car. As she passed a truck, she turned back to look at them to see if they were following her. As she turned her back, someone grabbed her around the neck and put something cold and sharp under her jaw.

"Stay back!" a man's slurred voice shouted behind Charlea's ear. "Give me the map or I'll kill her!"

Chapter 10

The smell of alcohol permeated the air around Charlea. Who would do this to her? The growling voice next to her ear was deep and husky. Something sharp was pressed against the skin of her throat. Her mind spun at possibilities until she remembered seeing Leon at the bar. Was he holding a knife at her throat? What had she ever done to him? A swirling of fear muddled her mind as she tried to grasp what was happening. She was dizzy. Confused. Desperate to be free. She clawed at the massive arms around her throat.

"Stay back!"

His yell made Charlea's right ear ring. She tried to push his arm away, but it was like pushing on a boulder.

"Give me the map or I'll cut her throat!"

Charlea was certain that it was Leon who held her captive. The knife touched her throat as he flung her from side to side. He seemed unsteady on his feet as he slowly backed away from the two men, dragging her with him. She worried that he might stumble and cut her throat anyway.

She struggled to make a sound, but the drunken man's hold on her throat was choking her, curtailing her air supply. Charlea grasped Leon's hands to loosen their grip, but she didn't have enough strength to pull them away. His excessive consumption of alcohol had not diminished his strength.

David and Roland ran toward Charlea, but stopped cold a few feet away. "What map?" they said in unison to the man behind her, voicing the same question racing through her mind.

"Don't play dumb with me! The map showing where the treasure is! I heard you talking about it in the bar. I want it. I want it now or I knife the broad." Leon was becoming increasingly agitated which made the situation even more threatening. One slip of his hand and Charlea's throat would be sliced.

Charlea grabbed the man's fingers and tried to pull them away from her throat. She succeeded enough to hoarsely say, "Leon, you fool, there is no treasure. No map."

"I ain't no fool!" he screamed in her ear. "I heard them talking about the treasure." He knocked her hand away from his with the butt end of the knife, cracking her knuckles as he did so. He gripped her throat even tighter.

Charlea's hand throbbed where he had hit it. Her comment had pushed Leon closer to the edge of losing control. Her ears were ringing so loudly from his shouting near her ear that she could hardly hear anything else. Her terror and diminished supply of oxygen were causing her to feel like she was going to faint. At this point, she knew there was nothing she could do to free herself from him. Unless she could reach her revolver. She fumbled with her skirt, trying to pull it up so she could reach the holster. At that moment, Leon swung her around and she grabbed his arm trying not to fall. She managed to keep her balance, and his, and hoped that Roland and David could rescue her from this dangerous predicament.

Tears welled in her eyes as Charlea felt the point of the knife at her throat, the sharp tip pressing deep against her skin. She wondered how much pressure her skin would withstand before being cut. Through her watery eyes, everything began to dim, but she could just make out Roland trying to calm Leon, but Leon had no intention of calming down until he got what he wanted. She couldn't see David, but she knew he was still there somewhere. Blackness threatened to swallow her so that she wouldn't feel the ending.

"Stay back or I cut her throat!" Leon threw Charlea to the side where she saw David, then swung her back and forth while he looked from Roland to David and back again. His steps were unsteady as he backed away, pulling Charlea with him.

The motion brought her back to her senses. A renewed fear of stumbling and falling on the knife flashed through Charlea as Leon used her as a shield against the two men creeping closer to her from two directions. She struggled to stay on her feet, trying to match his movements so she didn't trip or fall. When she could, she tried to reach her revolver, but had no luck.

"I swear to you, we don't have a map," Roland said slowly as if talking to a child. "Put the knife down. You really don't want to hurt her. Think of the mess it would make. Blood everywhere, sirens, cops, handcuffs, jail. Nasty stuff. Let her go and we'll talk sensibly about this. Talk to us instead of the cops."

"No talking and no cops! Just give me the map and I'll let her go." Leon was growing increasingly impatient, not slurring his words as much as before. "I will cut her unless you do what I say."

"There…is…no…map!" David yelled, obviously growing impatient with the situation. "You must have heard us talking about the book, *Treasure Island*. You know, pirates, maps, buried treasure. Charlea gave us the book and my friend and I read it. You know Charlea is the librarian, don't you? We were just talking about the book she gave us."

"No, you weren't. I heard you talking about finding treasure here, somewhere in town. You're the pirates on the treasure hunt!" Leon was getting more confused and held Charlea even tighter, pressing the knife more into her skin.

Charlea was convinced that any second now, her skin would give way and the knife would slide easily into her neck. Utterly helpless, she hated feeling out of control. Hated it passionately. Hated it enough to risk everything. She grabbed his hand again and pulled with all her might.

Leon tightened his grip more, fighting back her attempt to loosen his hand. He growled in her ear, "Stop it!" He quickly thwacked her knuckles again with the butt of the knife.

Charlea let out a silent scream of pain.

From the sound of his voice, Roland was creeping closer as he talked. "Hey, John Silver, are you saying that pirates buried a treasure in this town? That seems pretty far-fetched to me since we're a long ways from the sea. But that would be really nice, wouldn't it? We'd all like to find a treasure. We'd all like to be rich. No one would like to find a treasure more than me."

Charlea's mouth involuntarily opened as she tried to gasp for air. She struggled to get his hand away from her throat, but he had a firm grip on her. Panic overtook her as she clawed at his arms in an effort to pull them away to catch her breath. If he didn't cut her throat, he would suffocate her. Either way, she was dead.

Chapter 11

"What's going on here?" Mr. Woodson's loud voice reverberated across the parking lot. "Leon, what are you doing? Put that knife down and let her go before I call the police!"

"No police, Mr. Woodson!" Leon yelled, holding Charlea a little tighter and choking her.

With Mr. Woodson's distraction, David had moved behind Leon and jumped him, pulling the man's knife arm away from Charlea. Leon still had his arm around her throat and so pulled her to the left with him. She stumbled as she felt the heel on her shoe break off.

With David's quick move, Roland lunged from the front and tried to pull Charlea away from him, but Leon's grip was tight. The impact of Roland's lunge sent all four of them down in a pile, thrashing across the parking lot as David, Roland, and Leon struggled for the knife. In fighting to keep his hold on the knife, Leon let go of Charlea's throat.

Charlea gasped for air, coughing and choking with each breath. She attempted to move away from the struggling men, but was partially pinned under them. She was battered by their struggle for the knife, as missed blows and stray elbows hit her. With all the strength she could muster, she pushed the closest body away so she could crawl free. The maneuver failed.

She heard the thuds of Leon's fist as he hit one of the men. The thud was followed by a loud, "Huhgg!" indicating that his fist had hit its mark. Dust and gravel flew all around. The sound of tearing clothes and shoes being scuffed on the ground and unintelligible sounds filled the air as the men struggled.

With another heave, Charlea finally managed to roll out from under the struggling mass of men. She rolled away from the fight, still coughing from the choking and the dust. She reached under her skirt and drew out her revolver strapped in the holster on her thigh. She crawled over to the melee and held the gun next to Leon's face.

"Leon!" Charlea yelled hoarsely, "Stop it! Now!" She started coughing, but kept the gun pointed directly at her attacker.

Hearing her yell, Leon looked over to stare down the gun's barrel. At first, he looked at it in disbelief and kept struggling to be free of the two men holding him down.

"Drop the knife!" she yelled at the drunken man.

Her words finally sunk in and his face distorted in agony as he realized the futility of his struggles. As he went limp, Roland knocked the knife away while David kept the large man pinned against the ground. Roland helped David turn Leon face down and each man held an arm against the aggressor's back. The struggle was over.

Charlea sat up on the parking lot pavement and pushed the safety latch on her pistol. She shook so badly that she wasn't sure she could walk, so she sat there, panting along with Roland, David, and Leon.

Roland was the first to speak. "We got him, Charlea." He stopped long enough to slow his breathing. "It's okay."

Mr. Woodson helped her get to her feet, steadying her as she took a step and stumbled. Opening the door of a nearby car, he guided her into the seat. He reached for the gun, but Charlea pulled it away, giving him an icy stare.

"Let me have the gun," he told her calmly.

"No," Charlea said in a touch-it-and-I'll-use-it-on-you growl.

"There's no need for bloodshed," he said to her, holding his hand out. She still refused to give it to him.

"I know how to handle a gun, Mr. Woodson. I have no intention of shedding blood. I only used it to bring things to a quick and peaceful end." She coughed more as she put the gun back into its holster strapped on her leg. She quickly pulled her skirt down over her leg when she saw him staring at her thigh.

"Are you all right? He didn't cut you, did he?" Mr. Woodson lifted her chin so he could see her neck for himself.

"I'm fine, just shaken up," she said, pushing his hand away. His touch made her skin crawl. Her dress was torn and dirty and she only had one shoe on. The other one was nowhere to be seen, probably under a car somewhere. Her nylons were ripped to shreds and the sleeve of her dress was badly torn, exposing her bruised and bleeding shoulder where she'd been hurt during the struggle on the ground. Her heart was still racing, but the fear she'd felt a short time before was giving way to rage. The drunken Leon had ruined her evening and her favorite dress. And she had worn those shoes only once before.

The commotion had drawn a crowd in the parking lot. "Someone call the sheriff!" Mr. Woodson shouted. A man immediately threaded his way through the crowd and ran back into the club to make the call. Mr. Woodson pulled out his handkerchief and gave it to Charlea, motioning to her to wipe her face a little. She looked up at him and grudgingly felt a twinge of gratitude for the small gesture of kindness. She wiped her face and hands off with it and handed it back to him. He stuck it in his pocket without saying a word as sirens were heard approaching.

Charlea's hand started swelling where Leon had hit it with the knife and her arm throbbed all the way to her shoulder. Rubbing her neck with her good hand, Charlea watched as David kept Leon pinned to the ground. Roland knelt beside him to make sure Leon stayed under control.

Leon was sobbing loudly, "I didn't mean to. Please, no police. I just wanted the map. Please let me go. Mr. Woodson, please, help me! I want to go home."

"Are you all right, Charlea?" David called out to her. "Are you hurt?"

"Just bruised, I think. I see blood on the front of your shirt. Is it yours?"

"I think it's mine," said Roland, looking at his arm through a hole in his jacket sleeve. "I got nicked, but it's not bad. I only need a Band-Aid."

The club owner brought out a first aid kit and bandaged Roland's arm. The knife cut didn't need stitches, but would leave a small scar. Roland called it his battle wound and seemed proud to have taken a knife for the sake of Charlea.

When the police got there, an officer relieved Roland and David of their prisoner. They handcuffed the sobbing man and put him in the back of the squad car while they interviewed Charlea, David, Roland, and Mr. Woodson about the incident.

"No, I won't press charges," Charlea insisted when the officer asked her to come to the station. "The guy is obviously drunk. He misunderstood something he overheard in a bar and did something stupid. Lock him up until he sobers up and tell him to leave me alone. If he bothers me again, I'll file charges."

"You don't have to. We will do it for you." The officer put away his notebook.

"Do you have to?" Charlea asked. "He's normally harmless. He got drunk and wasn't thinking straight. Just warn him to stay away from me. Threaten to arrest him if he doesn't. Hopefully he'll get the message. Right now, I want to forget this whole sordid affair."

The policeman shook his head. "It's the law, ma'am."

"Do what you must then," Charlea said while rubbing her forehead. "Now, gentlemen, if you don't mind, I think I've had quite enough excitement tonight and I'd like to go home. David, please?"

The officer shook his head, but added, "You should go to the hospital and let the doctors take a look at you. To make sure you're not hurt."

David and Roland again agreed with the officer.

"No. I want to go home." Charlea didn't think she was hurt too badly. Her throat felt tender, bruised, and sore, but she could breathe without pain. A knot was growing on her hand where he'd hit it with the knife butt, but she didn't think her hand was broken. More than anything, she was badly shaken up. Home. She wanted to go home where the familiarity and comfort would help take care of that.

The police officer directed her toward David. "You're a stubborn woman, Mrs. Ludlow. We'll take Leon to jail so he won't bother you again. If by some miracle he bails out, we'll make sure he knows that he's not to go anywhere near to you. If he tries to contact you, call us at once."

"I will," Charlea said. She slowly walked past David, limping on the pavement with her one bare foot as she headed for his car.

David looked at the other men standing there and shrugged. He assured them that he would see Charlea safely home and settled.

Mr. Woodson and the police officer said they would keep a close eye on Leon. Since he would be behind bars, Charlea would have nothing to fear from him.

"I appreciate that," Charlea called back over her shoulder. "Come on, David."

David and Roland bid the other men good night and turned to follow Charlea to the car. She was already there, waiting on them.

"Do you want me to look for your other shoe?" Roland asked.

"No, don't bother." Charlea took her remaining shoe off and threw it across the parking lot where it rolled under another car. She slid to the center of the bench seat, still shaking from the ordeal.

Chapter 12

Roland got in beside her and put his arm around her to comfort her as best as he could while David slid into the driver's seat. David frowned in Roland's direction, but did not stop him.

A wave of relief spread over Charlea as David started the car and began to pull away from the club. The further she could get away from that place, the better she felt.

They were silent for a while, watching the road and the lights go by. Charlea's thoughts were replaying what had just transpired, and she was growing angry with each question that popped into her mind.

"I need to know something," Charlea said at last, looking first at Roland, then at David. "If you know about a 'treasure,' as Leon called it, why would you talk about it in a bar where anyone can hear you? Doesn't that seem a little stupid?"

Roland squirmed uncomfortably. "I didn't know anyone was listening. It was loud in there."

"You didn't want to tell me about it, but then you blabbed about it where everyone could hear. Even over the noise. And obviously someone was listening."

"I didn't blab! I just told David we needed to hurry and find our—treasure. I guess I said it louder than I meant to." Roland hung his head as he realized his part in the incident.

She looked from one man to the other. They seemed embarrassed, but Charlea continued to empty the questions out of her mind. "And whose idea was it to take me out to dinner? Is that the only reason you asked me out, David?"

"Not really. I—" David started to say, but Charlea wasn't through making her inquiries.

"Why didn't you want me to know that you knew each other? What exactly is in that letter?" Getting no response from either man, she shouted, "I want some answers!"

Roland looked at David who said, "Tell her quick, before she pulls her gun out."

Charlea's frustration with both men elicited a heavy sigh. "Where does it say the treasure is located?"

"We don't know for sure," Roland said. "That's why we need you to help us. We need help in finding the right spot to look. And just so you know, I talked David into acting like we didn't know each other. He didn't want to do it, so don't blame him."

Charlea rubbed her eyes as fatigue took over her thinking. "So let me get this straight. You two are using me to accomplish an end. Tonight has nothing to do with being attracted to me or anything like that. The invitation to supper—and lunch—was to get information." Charlea looked at both of them, wanting some sort of rebuttal to her statement, but got none. Her first thoughts had been confirmed. "I knew it was too good to be true." She shook her head. "I am too old for this stuff."

"Look, Charlea," David began, "That's not—"

"Don't bother to explain. I get the picture." Charlea was not in the mood to listen to his excuses. She crossed her arms, indicating the conversation was over.

They drove on without a word between them until they came to the next red light. As the car came to a stop, David turned to look at Charlea. "You're wrong about all the reasons I took you on the date, but I won't try to argue with you about it right now. But let me ask you something. Why did you bring a gun on this date? Am I that threatening? I didn't realize when Bonnie warned me to be a gentleman, she meant you'd gun me down if I wasn't." He waited for her to answer, staring at her with hurt in his eyes.

"I don't shoot people. It's nothing personal, David. I always carry a gun on the first date. A woman can't be too careful." She looked at him and saw that he wasn't convinced. "My dad taught me how to handle a gun for protection. Really!"

"The light's green," Roland said from the other side of the car. He was smiling like an indulgent parent. "Are you going to tell him about the knife in your purse?"

"You have a knife in your purse too?" David asked so startled that he took his eyes off the road while he was driving.

"I keep one with me all the time." She smiled slightly. "I'm a single woman trying to be safe." Then she swung around and glared at Roland. "How do you know I have a knife in my purse? You looked!"

Ignoring her accusation, Roland asked her, "Did your dad teach you how to use a knife?"

"No, my brother did. Never mind that." She turned back to David, who glared at the roadway. "If I hadn't had my gun, Leon would have continued to fight, and he might have hurt you and Roland more than he did. You should be glad I had it."

David sputtered, "Glad you had it? Roland and I were capable of handling the situation by ourselves. We almost had him pinned without your interference."

"My interference! Is that what you call it? I was helping you! I'm the one who ended the fight."

"How many other weapons are you carrying? Got any grenades in your purse?"

"If I'm carrying anything else, I'd never tell you about it," she yelled. She then sat smugly, letting that thought sink in. David stopped at another red light while Roland's shoulders shook with muffled laughter.

David stared straight ahead. "You know what? I think you're the one who's dangerous. Since you're afraid of everything, why did you agree to go out with me tonight? You could've stayed home. Or do you live in an underground bunker?" David chuckled at his own attempt at humor.

"Bonnie told me I had to go, remember? It was her idea, not mine." With that said, Charlea crossed her arms again and stared straight ahead.

Roland exclaimed, "Bonnie? I haven't heard about this."

"Bonnie forced me to come on this date with David," Charlea explained. "I told him no."

"I should have listened to you, instead of her." David's inflection of his voice was rising with his temper.

Roland was chuckling to himself. "She turned him down too. I haven't lost my touch after all. Makes me feel better."

"Oh, shut up!" David shook his head and mumbled angrily to himself. "I'm sorry I asked you out. I would have saved myself a whole lot of trouble if I had just listened to your first answer. I wouldn't have had to wrestle an armed man to the ground. I wouldn't have been interviewed by the police. I wouldn't be sitting here in dirty clothes arguing with a paranoid woman." Angrily he stomped on the brakes at a light that had just turned yellow, throwing the three of them forward. Charlea and Roland braced themselves against the dashboard. Both turned to glare at David who ignored both of them.

"Trying to kill me before you take me home?" Charlea asked like a boxer challenging his opponent right before a bout.

"Let's all calm down here," Roland said, playing the referee. "We need to stop before this goes too far. Can we call a truce?" The anger in the car prevented an answer from either Charlea or David, so he continued. "Tonight, I saw two lonely people having a wonderful time together. You make a lovely couple. David, you told me that you found Charlea refreshing and intriguing. You haven't said that about any woman in years! She must mean something to you." He looked at both David and Charlea, but they were staring straight ahead.

"Tell me you didn't have fun tonight, Charlea, talking and dancing with my brother over there."

"Your brother!" Charlea exclaimed.

The two men exchanged glances. David moaned and shook his head.

"Oops," Roland said with a grimace on his face. "I guess we didn't mention that before. Technically he's my half-brother, but don't change the subject. Tell me the truth. Didn't you enjoy yourself with him tonight?" He looked intently at Charlea.

Without intending it, she felt the corners of her mouth go up slightly as she thought about being held by David while they danced. His nearness, his warmth, his demeanor had reminded her so much of being with Mark, yet she didn't feel guilty for enjoying David's company. She dropped her head in her hands and nodded.

"And, David, we could've handled the situation with that crazy guy by ourselves, but Charlea helped out. That's called teamwork, folks. And the three of us make a great team. So let's work together as a team to solve a mystery! What do you say?" He looked from David to Charlea, searching for some sign of cooperation. "Come on, you two. At least be friends." He paused and got no response. "Be cordial to each other?" Another pause. "Be on speaking terms? Please?" He grinned and laughed and gave Charlea a little hug, then punched David on the shoulder.

Charlea let out a big sigh. "I suppose you're right. I'm sorry, David. I guess I've lived alone for too long and am overly cautious. My brother tells me I'm crazy and perhaps he's right."

David let out a chuckle. "No, you're not crazy. Overly cautious maybe, but not crazy. I don't date very often, so maybe women nowadays arm themselves for dates." He shook his head. "I'm sorry too, Charlea. We really need your help though. I hope we can work together to solve this thing so Roland will get off my back about it. But more than that, I'd really like to get to know you better. Roland's right. I do find you intriguing and charming."

Charlea was very flattered which made her feel happy again. "The ugliness is behind us. I'm safe. You're safe. That's what counts."

"There now, kids, we're all better," Roland said in a whew-glad-that's-over tone. "We're all friends again! And the treasure hunt is on!"

Chapter 13

As David pulled the car to the curb in front of her apartment house, Charlea saw the curtain in Mrs. Butterfield's window move. The mother wolf was waiting for her to get home. A stern lecture awaited her on the other side of the front door.

"I can take care of this part by myself, Roland," David said as he got out and held his hand out to assist Charlea out of the car.

"Don't mind me," Roland called after them. "I'll just take a nap while you two say goodnight. Take your time."

"See you tomorrow, Roland?" Charlea asked him, looking back at him from the edge of the seat.

"You bet. I'll be there. I'll bring David with me too."

David took Charlea's hand and helped her out of the car. She was still a little unsteady on her feet so he grabbed her around her waist to guide her down the sidewalk toward the front door.

To a casual viewer, Charlea's wavering path made her look like a drunken woman being helped to the door. Her shredded dress and lack of shoes and his torn and dirty suit hinted at less than honorable behavior during the evening. A casual observer who didn't know the night's events might get the wrong impression.

And there was a casual observer. Upon seeing them, Mrs. Butterfield exploded out of the front door with her baseball bat cocked and ready for use, rage contorting her face.

"You monster! What have you done to her?" she screamed at David. "Get away from her, you animal!" She ran down the sidewalk waving the bat over her head. The look on her face was unmistakable; she intended to do bodily harm to David.

"Mrs. Butterfield, wait!" Charlea yelled. "It's not what you think!" Charlea jumped in front of David to shield him from the onslaught. Mrs. Butterfield swung the bat to the side of Charlea, trying to hit David. David pulled Charlea out of the way. The older woman held up the bat again and tried to get around Charlea. Charlea yelled at Mrs. Butterfield to stop and yelled at David to stay behind her.

David held her like a shield in front of him. His labored breathing hinted that he was somewhat fearful on how to handle this bat-wielding, mad woman.

Mrs. Butterfield took another swing that both Charlea and David had to dodge. The elderly woman kept swinging, but the target she was aiming for was too quick to be hit.

In the car behind them, Roland's laughter rang through the neighborhood.

Out of breath and unable to take any more swings, Mrs. Butterfield grabbed Charlea's arm and pulled her away from David. "Look at you, poor girl!" She paused to gasp for breath. "Your dress! Did he try to—he didn't—touch you, did he?" She continued to huff and puff from the exertion.

"Mrs. Butterfield! Of course not! Put the bat down and let me explain." Charlea grabbed the bat to take it away from her, but the older woman would not let go.

"I won't let him touch you again!" Mrs. Butterfield jerked the bat out of Charlea's hands and took an angry, if weak, swing at David again. The man dodged easily, but stayed back warily.

David hurried to get behind Charlea again and reached out to touch her shoulder to make sure she stayed between him and the older, bat-waving woman. David spoke from behind Charlea. "You don't understand—"

"Shut up, you ogre! I'll listen to Charlea and then I'll use my bat on you." Speaking softly to Charlea, she said, "Now, dear, don't defend him. He's hurt you and we'll make sure he pays. Let's go call the police." She glared at David who was still holding Charlea between him and the bat.

Charlea put her hand up on the bat. "I've already talked to the police. David's my hero. I was attacked by Leon Reynolds. He was drunk and pulled a knife on me. David risked his life to save me." The older woman shook her head in disbelief so Charlea added, "It's the truth. You can ask the sheriff about it. He was there and took Leon off to jail."

"My stars alive! Leon attacked you?" Mrs. Butterfield lowered the baseball bat. "I guess I'm not surprised. He's been attacking his wife for years, that poor woman." Turning toward Charlea, she sounded very anxious "Dear girl, are you okay? You look terrible!"

"I'm fine, just shaken up and bruised some."

"Are you sure you're not hurt? That drunkard Leon! He's always been trouble!" With her anger redirected for the moment to someone else, David let go of Charlea's shoulder, but still kept her between him and Mrs. Butterfield.

Charlea continued, "I'm here because David saved me tonight. He was a perfect gentleman and has brought me home safely. I have a lot to thank him for." Charlea turned around and pulled David to her side. She felt his muscles tense as if he was ready to run, but Charlea knew the danger was over for now.

"Oh, I'm sorry for misjudging you," the elder woman said to David. "I mean, I saw Charlea and her clothes and thought you might have—" She stepped toward David, holding her hand out. "Please forgive me. I love Charlea and don't want anything bad to happen to her."

"Charlea is fortunate to have such a caring friend. Seeing her like this, I might have jumped to the same conclusion." David smiled like a man just freed from prison and didn't believe it to be true. He reached out to gingerly shake the offered hand.

Mrs. Butterfield shook his hand heartily. "Thank you for taking care of her tonight. I'm very glad you were there." Looking past David, she said, "Who is the other man in your car?"

Charlea jumped in to explain, "That's David's brother, Roland. Roland helped David subdue Leon. They're both my heroes." Smiling, they all three turned to wave to Roland who waved back. He was apparently over his laughing fit and was settling back in his seat to nap.

Charlea put her arm around Mrs. Butterfield and turned her back toward the apartment building door. "Now, if you don't mind, I'd like to end my date on a positive note. If you'll excuse us, I will tell David good night and be in. This has been a long day."

"All right, dearie, but don't take too long. If you need me, just yell. I'll bring my friend with me." She patted the bat as she turned to go.

"Good night, Mrs. Butterfield," David said to her as she left.

Mrs. Butterfield waved over her shoulder and shuffled her way back to the porch. She looked back at them one last time before walking into the building.

"Now we're even," Charlea told David. "You saved my life and I've saved yours."

David laughed, obviously relieved to be out of that situation. "I thought I was a goner. She swings a mean bat. I thought Bonnie was joking about having people come after me if I didn't behave. I was obviously wrong."

"How much you want to bet that she's peeking through the window right now, making sure you mind your manners?" Charlea asked him. A slight movement of the older woman's curtains betrayed the spying eyes behind them.

"Let's give her something to look at." With that, David took Charlea in his arms and kissed her softly at first, but grew more intense as the kiss continued.

Charlea had her arms around him and pulled him as close as she could. She kissed him back with longing and intensity, never wanting him to let go of her. No one had made her feel this way for a long, long time. Not since Mark had held her this way.

Charlea felt something hard push on her side and slide between them. Pulling back from David, she looked down and saw a baseball bat. Mrs. Butterfield put it up against David's chest and pushed him out of Charlea's embrace.

"That's quite enough for the first date. She's not an easy woman, if that's what you're thinking."

"Mrs. Butterfield!" Charlea choked out.

"Ma'am, I assure you, I wasn't thinking…"

"Say good night, Charlea," Mrs. Butterfield said, keeping her eye on David with her bat against his chest. "You can talk to him tomorrow."

"I guess 'Mom' wants me to go in," Charlea said, suppressing a smile.

"I guess so. See you tomorrow?" David responded.

"Yes. Thanks for the wonderful evening, well, except for the fiasco in the parking lot. And I'm sorry for arguing with you on the way home."

"I'm sorry too, and I had a great time…most of the night. Good night."

Like a starry-eyed teenager, Charlea watched him go down the sidewalk as Mrs. Butterfield pulled her inside.

Shutting the door behind her, Mrs. Butterfield made no effort to hide her trepidation with Charlea. "A little over-passionate for a first date, don't you think? In my day, we didn't let a man kiss us until we were engaged. You're old enough to know better."

"Things are different now."

"He'll think you're a hussy and you don't want that. Make him treat you like a queen. That's what my dad always told me. And it's good advice."

"Yes, it is good advice. And he does treat me like a queen."

"Make sure he does."

Charlea didn't want to argue about it. "I'm really tired and I need to clean up. I have to work tomorrow. Good night, Mrs. Butterfield." She gave the older woman a quick hug before going down the hall to her apartment. Inside, she felt like she was floating and wanted to remember every detail of his kiss. She unlocked the door and went inside.

"Oh Mark," she said to the picture on the wall, "what a night! Wait 'til I tell you what happened!"

Chapter 14

Charlea's talk with Mark lasted long past midnight. When she finally slept, Leon's raging face invaded her dreams and she would awaken, shaking in fear. Her hand would go to her throat, her heart pounding as the memory flooded back. Her throbbing, swollen hand was a reminder of the experience. Sleep seemed impossible.

When morning finally came, her body ached with bruises and fatigue, but the impending appointment with David and Roland motivated her to get up. Looking in the mirror, she was horrified to see bruises on her neck where Leon had choked her. Makeup softened them some, but they were still visible. She put on an A-line dress, then picked out a silk scarf to tie around her neck in an effort to hide the bruises.

The place on her hand where Leon had hit her with the knife was painful, blue, and swollen. Other than wearing gloves, there was no way to hide the bruise, and gloves would call attention to it more than not wearing them.

The terror of the previous night haunted her, so she drove to work instead of walking. The car would help her escape quickly if trouble followed her. Upon arriving at the library, she made sure no one was around before she went in. As Charlea reached for the door handle, Bonnie burst out, startling her.

"Are you alright?" Bonnie grabbed Charlea and hugged her tightly. "It's all my fault! I'm so sorry! I should have never made you go. I'm sorry!" Tears ran down Bonnie's face as she clung to Charlea.

Charlea struggled to hold Bonnie up while trying to keep the door open at the same time. This scene could draw attention from those passing by unless she could manage to get Bonnie inside. Leading Bonnie along with tiny footsteps, Charlea managed to maneuver both of them the rest of the way through the backdoor.

"Bonnie, let's go to my office and get some tissues." Charlea led Bonnie into the office and made her sit in the chair in front of the desk. Charlea got several tissues and gave them to Bonnie. "How did you find out what happened?"

Bonnie blew her nose and drew a ragged breath. "Headlines of the paper. It's the feature story."

"Oh no!" Charlea went around the desk and slumped into her chair. "Now everyone knows. I was hoping no one would find out."

"You thought you could keep it a secret?" Bonnie wiped her nose again. "It's big news in town. Are you sure you're okay?"

Charlea nodded. "Everyone in town will come in today, wanting to find out what happened and looking at me like I'm a museum piece on display." She leaned back in her chair and looked at the ceiling. "Why me?"

"Because I made you go." Bonnie's face reddened and puckered as she started to cry again.

Charlea rushed to Bonnie's side to hug her. "Stop it! It's not your fault. Maybe a cup of coffee will make us both feel better." While she made a pot of coffee, Charlea related some of the events of the previous evening, including her conversations with David.

Bonnie interrupted her story. "So, is he married?"

"Of course not. I don't go out with married men." She poured two cups of coffee and handed one to Bonnie. "He's never been married. Two women broke his heart so badly he hasn't been serious about anyone since."

Bonnie took a sip of coffee. "So do you like him?"

"Yes. I wouldn't have stayed there if I didn't." Charlea took a sip of coffee. The memory of dancing with David made her smile a little. "David is a true gentleman, and I had a wonderful time with him—well, most of the time. We got into an argument, but Roland mediated a peaceful ending."

"Roland was there? You mean, *Adonis*?" When Charlea nodded, Bonnie's mouth fell open in disbelief. "Wow! How did you get so lucky?"

"Roland and David are brothers and are here together on vacation."

"Why didn't they tell us that yesterday?"

Charlea wasn't sure how to respond to Bonnie's question. Their cockamamie plan to explore the library had failed miserably and as far as she knew, that was the only reason why they had kept it secret. She couldn't tell Bonnie that. So she lied. "I don't know. It never came up, I guess."

Bonnie sat back in her chair, holding her cup of coffee in both hands. "I'd choose *Adonis*, if given a choice between the two."

Charlea took another sip of coffee and mulled it over. "I don't trust him. He uses his looks and charm to get whatever he wants."

"That would work on me!" Bonnie giggled and drank the rest of her coffee.

Charlea refilled both cups and leaned back in her chair. "He's fun to be around as long as you know what his motives are. That way, he can't use you for his own purposes."

Bonnie threw her tissues in the waste basket and took a sip of her coffee. "Are you okay, Charlea, I mean really okay?"

"I'm still a little shaken, but I'm fine. I'm very sore from falling and the scratches and the bruises, but they'll heal." Charlea leaned across the desk. "I bet the paper didn't say that my dress was ruined in the struggle."

"Not the blue one! That's my favorite of yours."

"Yes, the blue one. And I lost my shoes." Charlea laughed before continuing. "I bet the papers don't say anything about that either." She laughed again. Bonnie's quizzical look and what's-so-funny smile made her laugh a little harder. After a moment, she managed to control her laughter.

"When David took me home, I was a mess. I was barefooted and my dress was torn and I was dirty. Mrs. Butterfield saw me, looking like I'd been rolled. She came storming out of the apartment building, swinging her bat. She thought that he—you know—that he took advantage and..." Charlea could no longer control her laughter. She sat back in her chair and released it.

Bonnie didn't laugh along. "Did she hurt him?"

Charlea wiped her eyes. "No, but she gave him a scare. He knew she meant business, especially after you told him that people would come after him if he weren't a gentleman. I managed to stay between Mrs. Butterfield and David to keep him from getting beaned by the bat. After I got her calmed down and told her the story, she let him alone. And that's the end of the story." Charlea sat back in her chair and took another sip of coffee. The only sound was the ticking of the clock on the wall and the sound of quiet sipping from the two ladies.

Bonnie broke the silence. "Did he kiss you?"

Charlea feigned shock at the question. "Some things are best left between him and me."

Bonnie let out a chortle of triumph. "He did! So how was it?"

Charlea looked off into space, a dreamy expression on her face. "Very nice. Now I've said all I'm going to say. It's past time to open the library." She picked up both coffee cups and went into the ladies room to pour out what was left.

Bonnie was at the door when Charlea came back out. "Was it a passionate one or just a peck?"

Charlea shook her head, indicating that the conversation was over. She walked to the circulation desk and picked up the newspaper. Sure enough, in big letters across the top of the paper: *Local Librarian Attacked Outside Night Club*. A groan escaped her as she thought about the crowds that would come in the library today to see her, asking questions and questions and more questions. She wanted to hide.

"Bonnie, can you take care of the circulation desk today? I already see some movement in our windows, so people are probably lined up to come in. I'd like to hole up in my office, if you think you can handle it."

"I'm not sure they will be happy to see just me. I don't think you can avoid it. You might as well get it over with."

"You're probably right. I wanted to read this before I have to defend myself." Charlea held up the paper. "Roland and David will be here about 10 o'clock this morning to do research. I'll be helping them with it."

Bonnie looked suddenly suspicious. "Research, huh? Whatever you say. I'll hold the fort down while you're 'occupied.'"

Charlea picked up a few books that needed shelving. "If it gets too busy, let me know. I'll help out."

"Let me know if you get too busy with 'research,' and I'll help *you* out."

Their tittering echoed through the bookshelves as Charlea started down the familiar aisles, putting each book in its place. The books were like old friends, and she felt comforted when she ran her fingertips along the spines of the books while walking by them. As her fingers brushed the book spines, gold letters on one particular book caught her attention. There it was, shining like a spotlight on a dark night. *Treasure Island*. She pulled it from the shelf and thumbed through the pages. She hadn't read the book in years, but after last night's events, she wanted to read it again. After David and

Roland left, she'd check it out to herself. She put it back when she heard Bonnie unlock the front door. She quickly put up the rest of the books and dashed toward her office, but stopped in her tracks when she came around the corner of the bookshelf.

Standing in the doorway of her office was Mr. Woodson. "It's nice to see you at work today. I was afraid that you'd be too upset to work."

His voice grated on her already frazzled nerves, causing her to feel slightly dizzy as last night's memories overwhelmed her. His presence, his voice intensified the flashback.

He took a step toward her. "Are you okay? How do you feel?"

Her emotions churned, but she managed to grasp a straw of control. "Yes, I'm fine. Thank you for asking. And thank you for helping me last night." Her throat almost hurt to utter the words, but she continued, "I have a few bruises and scrapes, but am none the worse for wear. Last night almost seems like a bad dream."

"That's good news," he answered softly, almost like he really meant it. "Leon spent the night in jail, but met bail this morning. He's due to be released later this morning. I thought you should know. He has strict instructions to stay away from you, but please keep an eye open for him." He fumbled with his fedora in his hands.

Charlea could hear people making their way around the library. If she didn't get into her office, she'd be inundated by questioners. She was torn between getting into her office where Mr. Woodson would have her cornered or staying in the main library and being swarmed by people. Neither choice was ideal, but she chose the former and pushed past the man blocking her door. She turned just inside and said, "Thanks for the warning. I'll work in the back today, out of sight."

"Good idea. You need to get your budget in order anyway."

A wave from her ocean of anger washed over Charlea and nearly knocked her off her feet. She literally bit her tongue to keep from speaking the words that flashed through her mind. With effort, she managed a nod in hopes of giving him the answer he wanted so he would leave.

In spite of her wishes, he looked around for a moment to make sure they were alone. Drawing closer to Charlea, he said in a low whisper, "You want to tell me what made Leon think those guys had a treasure map?"

Charlea grabbed the door knob to her office and came very close to whamming him with the door. Her grip on the knob would have crushed a tin can. With a voice that would burn paper, Charlea told him through clinched teeth, "We were talking about books we'd read and one of them happened to be *Treasure Island.* You know, buried treasure. Maps. Pirates. Roland and David talked about it at the bar while I was in the ladies room. Leon must have overheard part of the conversation and misunderstood them. He was drunk." Her anger must have made her a better liar, and to her relief, Mr. Woodson seemed to accept it.

"I suppose that makes sense. But, what a dull and strange topic of conversation for a dinner date."

"I'm a librarian, Mr. Woodson. I like to talk about books." Charlea knew from the look on his face what he was thinking: No wonder she didn't date much, if all she talked about were books. Her anger spiked another level.

Mr. Woodson checked his watch. "It's time I got to work. You have work to do as well. I wanted to make sure you were okay."

Charlea was still skeptical about his concern for her, but his offer to leave brought her a measure of comfort. "Thanks for your thoughtfulness. I'll see you at the council meeting next week." Her stomach felt queasy at the thought of the budget and defending it against this man. She knew nothing that had happened would let her off the hook with him where the budget was concerned. He would still be as brutal in questioning her as he had last year.

Mr. Woodson turned to go. He had gone just past the first bookshelf when he stopped and came back to Charlea to say something else. "As your friend, I think it would be a good idea if you avoided those men you were with last night. They seem to attract trouble and you'd do well to stay away from them. I think you can find better company."

A tidal wave of anger swept her out to sea. She released her titan grip on the door knob and used her hand to poke the man in the chest. "Who I associate with afterhours is none of your business. Now, if you'll excuse me, I have work to do." Judging from the frown on his face, he wasn't happy with her answer. He waited for more, but when Charlea said nothing more, he turned and left.

Charlea watched him make his way toward the front door. She did not appreciate his prying into her affairs. She especially didn't like him calling her his friend. As far as she was concerned, there was no friendship between them. They had a tolerated acquaintance for the sake of the library. He set off too many alarms in her head for her to trust the guy. And what did he mean by constantly reminding her to complete her budget? *He plans to be especially cruel in his questioning about it this year*, she surmised. *I must be absolutely sure of my numbers and be prepared for his interrogation.*

As she closed the door to her office, his parting remarks tumbled through her mind, roiling the waves of anger. She didn't want to stay away from David and Roland and had no intention of doing so. At the same time, in the back of her mind, an unwanted thought kept creeping in. What if Mr. Woodson was right and they were trouble? Her life had been predictable and safe before they came, just the way she liked it. In one day, that had all changed. She resolved to be more cautious around them.

Chapter 15

Charlea finished the budget as best as she could. Projected expenditures for the coming year were outlined and ready for consideration by the council. This year's money was not coming out right, but she documented what she could. Perhaps with what had happened last night, the councilmen, other than Mr. Woodson, would be sympathetic and grant her funding requests, including the raise for Bonnie. The risky part would be whether the council would be generous enough to kick in funds to start organizing the museum. That might be too much to hope for, but she would push for it anyway.

Before she knew it, it was time for Roland and David to come. Her heart skipped a beat and the reaction disconcerted her. Only 24 hours had passed since David and Roland had first walked in the door and their presence had already altered her life. A long time ago, Mark had changed her life too. Happy times and good things followed that change, but it ended with a life-altering heartache that still haunted her. Maybe she should back away before that happened again. What would Mark say? He always pushed her to find new experiences. David and Roland were definitely a new experience. Her voice of reason was silent on the matter and her heart was still skipping a beat. Excitement filled her like a sponge soaking up water.

She locked the large ledger in the filing cabinet, along with the proposed budget figures, and straightened up the top of her desk. Rushing to the ladies room, she checked her makeup and smoothed her hair. The last item was to check on Bonnie to make sure all was under control out front.

"Bonnie, how are things out here? Are you busy?" Charlea walked behind the circulation desk. Looking around, she saw several people reading magazines and a few more browsing the bookshelves. Or were they hovering until she made an appearance?

"No, not really," Bonnie said with amusement in her voice. "You seem a little on edge. Calm yourself. I will handle this and you handle the guys. And I mean that literally and figuratively."

"You're naughty, Bonnie." Charlea was embarrassed that her nervousness was so noticeable because that meant that David and

Roland would notice too. "I'll show them around and let them do their research. That's all there will be to it. I'm too sore from last night for anything else."

"And what will you say if they ask you to lunch?"

"I'll say yes. But only to please you and Mr. Wilkerson." Together they tittered which put Charlea a little more at ease.

Charlea glanced at the front door, wondering when David and Roland would get there. Too late she saw several library patrons hurrying over to ask her for details of the attack. In her eagerness to see David and Roland, she'd forgotten to stay out of sight of patrons who might be hovering around, waiting to see her. The last thing she wanted to talk about right now was the attack, but with a saint's patience, she related a few things to them.

Milt, the handyman, came into the library and rescued Charlea from the growing crowd of patrons. She excused herself from them, saying she had to take care of business. As she and Milt walked away, Bonnie gave her a wink.

Milt was excited about being a tour guide for the morning. He had worked in the building when it was a hospital and knew every nook and cranny. Charlea told him about David and Roland, the visiting historical architects, and asked him to show them everything they wanted to see. They were researching the building and were interested in how it was built, any unusual features it had, especially the administrator's living quarters. She felt guilty that lying was starting to come so often and so easily. He accepted her story without question.

Milt left to unlock the basement door and straighten up while Charlea returned to her office to wait for the men. A few minutes later, David and Roland peeked inside the door and greeted her. Roland came in first and hugged her warmly. Roland wore jeans and a button-down shirt with no tie, looking like he expected a casual day. David dressed like a proper gentleman visiting a work site in his slacks, shirt, and sports jacket. Pushing his brother aside, David hugged her as well, hanging on to her a little longer than Roland had. She sensed the sibling rivalry between them and delighted in their competing for her attention.

Pulling away, David said, "You look tired. Did you have nightmares?"

Charlea smiled at both of them. "I'm a little tired, but I'm fine, really. And yourselves?"

David smiled at her and took her hand. "I dreamed about dancing with a lovely woman." With his finger, he pulled down her scarf to see the bruises. "Your neck looks bad. And look at your hand! Does it hurt much?" Roland stepped up behind him to get a closer look as well. Both shook their heads as they stepped back.

"My hand is the worst. It aches."

"Ice." Roland took her hand and examined it like a doctor. "You need to ice it to get the swelling down."

Charlea changed the subject. "Did you see the paper this morning? We made front page news."

"Yes, we saw it when we ate breakfast," David said. "I'm glad there wasn't a picture of us. I'd rather keep a low profile."

"People already know who you are," Charlea told him. "The ones that saw us at the restaurant last night will spread the news like wildfire."

"I suppose so. The small town telegraph."

Charlea stepped behind her desk and sat down. "Mr. Woodson stopped in to see me. Leon is being released this morning on bail. I don't think he'll bother us, but we all need to be cautious."

"Got your gun?" Roland asked with a chuckle in his voice, but Charlea knew he was serious about it. "How about your switch blade? Brass knuckles?"

"I knew my two heroes were coming so I didn't bother with the gun. But one never knows what else I might have concealed." Charlea watched Roland scan her body and she regretted her words. She mentally slapped herself in the mouth.

"You could always have Mrs. Butterfield follow you around with her bat. I bet that Leon character wouldn't bother you with her around. You wouldn't shield him like you did David." Roland started laughing. As the image of last night's battle crossed her mind, Charlea couldn't keep from laughing along. David put his hand over his eyes and shook his head.

"It wasn't funny at the time," David interjected, "but when I think about it now, it must have been a sight!" He began laughing as he mimicked his motions of dodging the bat behind Charlea while Roland swung an imaginary bat at him. All three of them were laughing hard when Bonnie stuck her head in the door to shush them. She waited to see if they would share the joke with her, but when no one said anything to her, she left.

Charlea regained her composure first. "I'm sure it was quite the spectacle. You made a good impression after we got things straightened out. She'll not go after you again, but she'll keep a close eye on you. Both of you." She pointed from one to the other.

Roland put his arm around his brother's shoulders. "We promise to act nice. Now, can we go look for the..." he lowered his voice to a whisper "...you-know-what?"

"Before we go to the basement," Charlea said, "could I ask a favor? I'd like to look at the letter and do a little research of my own. I promise to take good care of it."

David motioned to Roland to comply with her request. Roland pulled it out of the back pocket on his jeans. As he handed it to Charlea, he asked, "I suppose you'll expect a cut if we find the gems, won't you?"

"Of course I do," she said as she put the letter in a file cabinet and locked it. "But I'll keep my part small. By the way, I told Milt that you guys are historical architects, researching old hospitals. Can you pretend you are?"

David nodded. "I took enough engineering classes in college to talk intelligently about it."

"I don't know anything about it," Roland said. "But I'm a good faker. I can take notes or something like that. That might make me look important. I'll keep my mouth shut so he can't tell I don't know what I'm doing."

"Keep your mouth shut? I bet that'll be a first," Charlea muttered, looking sideways at Roland. "Want a pad and pencil so you look the part?" She pulled out her desk drawer and took out a steno pad and a mechanical pencil for Roland.

"That's too girlie for me," Roland said. "Got a legal pad instead? It'd look more official and less secretarial."

Charlea opened another drawer and found a legal pad with a few pages left on it. Roland seemed pleased with his role and the new props.

The three of them left her office and made their way around the staircase to the other side. Library patrons stared at them as they walked by the ends of the bookshelves. Some rose from their seats as if they wanted to join them, but seeing the trio hurry along, they took their seats again. The whispers began, with some loud enough to be heard by all, asking who those men were and where they might be going.

Descending the stairs to the basement, Charlea led the way into the dungy, moldy old room with the low ceiling. The basement walls were stone and the floor was dirt except for one corner that had a concrete pad where the old boiler stood. The place evoked claustrophobia, which is why Charlea hated coming down here so badly. To Charlea, it was the perfect habitat for spiders, which she hated more than anything else. Milt never seemed to mind it.

They found him standing by the boiler, checking it out while he waited for them. Roland and David shook hands with Milt when Charlea introduced them. Feeling safer near the bottom of the stairs where the ceiling was higher and the air was fresher, she watched the men as they began to explore.

"Architects, huh?" Milt asked, still looking at the old boiler. "Why the interest in old hospitals?"

David folded his arms and examined the old boiler with Milt. "They contributed directly to a town's development." He got into character for the charade. "But mostly, we're curious about the construction methods of old buildings. They were usually built to last."

"Not like the flimsy buildings they put up today," Milt agreed. "None of the new ones will last as long and they don't look as good as this one."

"I agree with you. What can you tell me about this one?"

Milt's pride in his building was evident as he talked. He pointed out the detailed stonework and masonry on the basement walls. David seemed genuinely interested in Milt's stories. As Milt guided the two men around the basement area, Roland looked at Charlea and rolled his eyes. She smiled and waved at him, amused at his impatience with the situation.

When she thought Roland had had all he could bear, Charlea called out to the men, "Would you show them around the other floors, Milt, and talk about when it was a hospital? And tell them what was where, like the doctor's offices and the patient rooms."

"I'd be happy to," Milt replied. "I'm glad to have an audience for my stories."

"Great! When you're done, bring them back to my office and I'll take it from there."

"Will do. Come with me, boys." With that, he led David and Roland up the basement stairs to go to other parts of the building. Milt was talking non-stop about the building, and Roland looked back at her as if to say, "I'll get you for this." Charlea followed them up the stairs, relieved to finally be out of that awful place.

Charlea went to her office and retrieved Roland's envelope out of the file cabinet. She looked for marks that might give a clue to its origin. The date stamp was illegible so it was no help. Inside was a letter along with a yellowed newspaper clipping. The letter looked old, although she could not be certain. But one thing was certain: she had seen the handwriting before and knew it to be authentic. That meant that the letter was no hoax.

She read the letter:

> *Dear Robert,*
>
> *How are things at home? I am whole and healthy. We are going through the countryside making sure all the Krauts are gone. We've stayed in castles some nights. They're nice places but very drafty. Reminds me of home.*
>
> *I've collected a bag full of stones, enough to make both of us comfortable for a long time. To the victor belong the spoils as they say. Don't tell Momma or she will make me give them back. I figure it's payment for all I've done for the people here. When I get home, we can hide them in Father's secret hiding place until we figure out how to sell them. It'll be our secret so keep it quiet. Hope to see you soon.*
>
> *Your brother, George*

Opening the clipping, Charlea read how two Williams brothers named George and Robert were killed in a car accident shortly after George returned from the war in Europe. The grief of the family must have been unbearable, especially to have a son survive a war but die at home. The story sent a pang of hurt through her to think about the grief their mother must have felt. At least her son got home. At least his mother knew where her son was. Mark had never come back. Charlea had no idea where he was. The hurt in her heart started to overtake her. She quickly put the letter and clipping back into the envelope and put them in her desk drawer.

Charlea pushed Mark out of her mind. Leaning back in her chair, she thought about the strange situation she found herself in. She knew the stones were real. If Roland hadn't been so intent on keeping his mission a secret, she could have told him that at the beginning. His secrecy had cost him and David extra time and trouble, but provided her more time to be with them. She was excited with the adventure that lay in front of her. Searching for the cache of stones would be refreshing and get her out of the everyday routine.

Bonnie stuck her head in the door and looked around. "No men?"

"They're touring the building with Milt. What's up?"

"Mr. Wilkerson is here asking about you. It's your turn. Or shall you just owe me one?"

Charlea winced and sighed. "I'm sure he read this morning's paper and came to find out what's going on. I'll talk with him and satisfy his curiosity, at least until the guys are done with their tour. That will give me an excuse to cut his visit short."

"I should warn you that there are a lot of people here asking questions. You'll have to talk with them too."

"I knew they would show up. The story in the paper made it inevitable. I might as well get it over with. Give me a minute to pull myself together."

Bonnie nodded and left.

Before Charlea left her office, she locked the letter in the file cabinet, away from prying eyes and sticky fingers. The din from the front of the library was growing as more people gathered to see her. When she walked out of her office, Mr. Wilkerson trotted ahead of the others as fast as his skinny old legs could carry him. He immediately began asking her a string of questions. Was she all right? Had Leon hurt her? Why would he want to hurt her? Was that strange man who came in yesterday responsible for this?

Charlea patiently answered all his questions as other people gathered around to listen to her story. She finally put Mr. Wilkerson's mind at ease. He was genuinely upset over her ordeal and she appreciated his concern. As Mr. Wilkerson finished his inquisition, other people crowded around her to ask more questions,

Gradually changing the subject by mentioning a new mystery book just in, she was able to get everyone talking about books. She recommended the new book to Mr. Wilkerson and gently steered him to the circulation desk where Bonnie checked it out to him. Mr. Wilkerson was still talking as Charlea escorted him to the door and watched him amble down the street toward his home. A few of the remaining crowd followed him out, mumbling among themselves and offering their commentaries to anyone who would listen.

Charlea leaned against the circulation desk and smiled at Bonnie who gave her the thumbs up sign. Charlea's masterful performance had moved Mr. Wilkerson out of there in record time while still handling people's questions. The experience had not been as bad as she thought it would be. Everyone was sympathetic to her and expressed their relief that she was well. Their support bolstered her spirits. Just then, Charlea saw Milt leading David and Roland toward her office. She excused herself from the remaining crowd.

"Bonnie, can you handle things out here? The tour is over and they are in my office. I need to get the guys started on their research in the files upstairs."

"Keep your appointment." Bonnie waved her off. "Don't worry about me. I can handle it as well as you. You just owe me one, okay?"

"Absolutely! A big one!" Charlea said as she hurried toward her office.

"Are those your rescuers?" an elderly woman asked Charlea as she went by. She had watched the men going into her office. "I wouldn't mind being rescued by those two. You're a lucky lady."

"Yes, I am. Thank you," Charlea replied, puzzled at the elderly woman's interest in the two men until she saw the I'm-not-dead-yet smile on the wrinkled face. The two women smiled at each other in agreement.

"So how was the tour?" Charlea asked as she walked in her office. The three men stopped talking long enough to greet her as she came in. Roland slouched in her extra chair, looking like he was bored out of his mind. David and Milt stood talking still.

"Most informative," David replied. "Milt has an astounding knowledge of the building and the people who worked here. He has been very helpful."

"I was able to make enough notes to complete our research," Roland added, not wanting to be overlooked.

Milt beamed, enjoying the praise. Charlea knew he was flattered that others were interested in what he had to say. He shook the men's hands vigorously and thanked them for their time.

"Thank you, Milt. I hope we didn't keep you from anything too important this morning," Charlea said to him.

"No ma'am. I was glad to do it." Turning to David and Roland, he said, "If you boys need any other information, just let me know. I'll be glad to help in whatever way I can." Milt shook their hands again and left to go back to his daily chores.

Charlea closed the door to her office so they could talk in private. She opened the file cabinet to get the envelope. Roland took it and immediately opened it to make sure everything was still there. Satisfied that it was, he put it into his back pocket.

"You can trust me," Charlea assured him as she sat behind her desk. "So tell me, did you find out what you needed to know? I know Milt can ramble on quite a while without stopping."

"We learned a lot," Roland said, getting out of the chair like it had suddenly turned hot. "Milt knew old Doc Williams' sons, Robert and George. He told us that Doc Williams' old desk is the one in the office where you and I looked yesterday. The one with the sink, remember? The desk might have a hiding place in it. Can we go get a closer look?" He finally paused for a breath. "By the way, what did you think of the letter?"

His enthusiasm made her laugh. "After close examination, I believe the letter to be authentic. The story might actually be true. However, I can't help but wonder if someone else has already found the hiding place and taken the stones."

"There's no way to know for sure without looking," David said. He was leaning against the wall across from her desk, watching Roland like a big brother watching a younger brother enjoying new toys.

"We asked Milt about the Williams' family history." Roland said as he flipped through several pages of the legal pad. "He talked about the family's tragedies and how things were after their house burned down. They lived in an apartment for a few months until their new house was built. Then after old Doc Williams died, his wife had to move in with her daughter because money was short.

Doc was not a very good money manager because he frequently forgot to send bills to his patients. No wonder they liked him so much." Roland chuckled to himself. "His wife had to sell their home to have money to live on. If they had found the stones, I don't think she would've done that."

"Probably not. What happened to the family?" Charlea asked.

"According to Milt," David replied, "the daughter and her family left town, taking the mother with them. He didn't know where they went for sure, but he heard rumors that they went out west somewhere to work on a ranch. He made it sound like they had very little money. Maybe they did have money hidden somewhere, but they never knew it."

"It's a sad story. I guess that's reason enough to believe that the stones are still there…still hidden," Charlea said, standing up. "I haven't heard of anyone in the past few years stumbling across a cache of gems. A story that big would have been in the papers. So that must mean we really are on a treasure hunt!"

Roland dashed behind the desk and gave Charlea a hug. He quickly let go of her and stepped back. "Sorry, David," he said. "I forgot myself."

David frowned at his brother.

Charlea liked being hugged by Roland, but she also liked being hugged by David too. She wished David would follow his brother's example, but David made no move. She cleared her throat, tried to get a grip on her emotions, and shoved her thoughts back on track. "Might I suggest as a safety precaution, especially for my sake, that any conversations about this letter and the stones be held only in private places where no one else can overhear. I don't want to go through another episode like last night."

"Nor do we," David said in response. He was still frowning at Roland.

Roland seemed uncomfortable under David's glare. "I agree. Let's make a pact to keep this between the three of us," he suggested. Roland put his hand out, Charlea put hers on top of his, and David put his on top of her hand. "This signifies a pact between the three of us," Roland began, emoting in a solemn voice, "that none of us will speak in the presence of others about the letter or the stones. Any of us who violate this pact will forfeit his or her share of the stones and possibly face bodily harm from drunks."

"And old ladies with baseball bats," David added.

"And old bats with bats," Roland improvised.

Charlea gasped. "Mrs. Butterfield would come after you if she knew you called her an 'old bat,' and I wouldn't protect you. You'd deserve it."

They all dropped their hands after Roland's who-me look spread across his face. Charlea got the keys and went to the door.

"Let's get back to work. You should go upstairs to look at the old doctor's desk."

The trio hurried out of her office to the foot of the stairs. As they went behind the velvet rope across the stairs, Charlea looked across the library. More people had come in and were watching their actions intently. She knew as soon as she turned her back, the whispering would begin as each individual would offer differing interpretations of their actions. Her reputation as a straight-lace librarian was crumbling around her.

She ran up the stairs behind Roland and David, hurrying them along. She led them to the administrator's office and opened the door. The walls had mahogany paneling that would be beautiful if it were cleaned up. Sunlight tried to make its way through the dirty window to light the surface of the roll-top desk. Lots of elbow grease would transform this room into a showplace for the museum. She knew Milt would relish seeing it returned to its former glory.

David looked around the room while Roland began digging through the drawers in the roll-top desk. Charlea put back whatever papers or things Roland dug out while he continued to search for hiding places.

"So Milt confirmed this was Dr. Williams' office? It's so small!" she said as Roland pulled one drawer completely out to examine the bottom and sides of it. "Not much room for seeing patients."

"That's what he said," David replied as he looked along the wall for hidden compartments. "Sometimes he slept on a cot in here when things were really busy or he had a touch-and-go case. Milt told us where they built their new house, so if we find nothing here, we can go look there."

"The old man had a wealth of information," Roland said as he rummaged through another drawer. "And he seemed willing to give more, if we asked him. Nice guy, but he talks way too much. He certainly likes to be the center of attention. I don't like being around people like that." David and Charlea exchanged glances, smiling at each other behind Roland's back.

Charlea shuffled through the papers Roland put on top of the desk. "If someone comes in here while we're looking, what will you tell him? You can make something up, can't you, David?" she inquired.

"Yes, of course. Don't worry, we'll handle it. Come on, Roland, let's move this cabinet away from the wall."

While the men moved furniture, Charlea went to get rags to clean off the dust and grime. When she returned, she found David and Roland struggling to slide the large hall tree away from the wall enough to see behind it. David took off his jacket and hung it on the back of the chair. Their muscles were accented by the taut shirts across their backs and arms, straining with the large, heavy piece of furniture.

"What are you doing?"

Charlea jumped as Bonnie's voice startled her from behind. "You scared me! What's wrong?"

Bonnie looked at the two men who had stopped their work. "We can hear loud scraping noises downstairs and everyone is asking what's going on. I came to investigate. So what are you doing?"

David stepped forward, pulling out a handkerchief to wipe his face. "We are examining the materials used in the building. These mahogany walls are beautiful and I'm not sure we can get this kind of material any more. I wanted a better look."

Bonnie looked confused, then shrugged. "That makes sense. Just so you know, the more you three are seen, the more people are curious. So unless you're ready to answer a lot of questions, you're drawing too much attention to yourselves."

"I'm sorry," David said, putting his handkerchief back in his pocket. "We'll try to keep the noise down. Thanks for letting us know."

"Um, Charlea," Bonnie said, "Look at your dress." Charlea looked down and saw she was covered with dirt. She tried to wipe it away with her hands. "Bonnie, we should both get back downstairs. I'll be there after I freshen up in the bathroom."

Bonnie nodded and excused herself from the work scene.

Charlea handed the men the rags she had gone for. "You're on your own for now. I'm supposed to be working, not treasure hunting, and I can't do my job in dirty clothes."

"It wouldn't look good to your library customers. You should just supervise then," David said.

"But how can we look around without making noise? We need to move this stuff away from the walls," Roland looked a little worried.

"Do what you need to do as quietly as possible. If anyone asks, we'll say that you are doing 'detailed' research." Charlea smiled at the two men. "And now the supervisor says get back to work."

"Slave driver," Roland muttered.

"I'll take over downstairs and let Bonnie go to lunch," she told them. "It's almost noon. I'll be back later. Check for loose baseboards. And I emphasize the word 'loose.' A hiding place has to blend in so it's not too obvious. Consider a secret place in the furniture as well. The letter wasn't specific to the building."

"Yes, ma'am," Roland said factiously. "We'll keep that in mind."

"Just trying to help. Let me know if you need anything." Charlea left the men to their searching.

"Sorry I'm late," she told Bonnie when she got to the circulation desk. "Why don't you go to lunch?" Charlea looked down at her dress and wiped a missed spot of dust from it.

"What about your guests?" Bonnie asked as she handed a stack of books to a mother and her small child.

The mother looked at Charlea in an odd way, then took the books and left, hanging tightly onto her child's hand. Bonnie handed Charlea a roll of masking tape to help get the dust off her dress.

"They can handle their research without me. I thought you'd want to take a break for a little while." Charlea wound the tape around her hand and began to brush her dress. The last of the dirt disappeared.

Bonnie rushed off while Charlea turned her attention to the circulation desk. Few wanted to check out books, but everyone wanted to ask questions. Although she was not in the mood for it,

Charlea answered all the questions as every patron in the library crowded around her. She began wishing Bonnie would get back from lunch soon. She wanted out of the crowd and away from all the questions, both legitimate and misinformed.

Time crept by as people came and went, but the crowd hovering around Charlea never seemed to thin. She thought she recognized members of the garden club who must have cancelled their meeting for today to come question her. City Council members and firemen and business owners stood in line, listening intently as she answered questions. Mrs. Dunwoody with her red beehive hair was there, also listening intently. Most were regular library patrons. The rest of the crowd was curious spectators who wanted to hear the latest gossip topic. As the crowd around her turned over and new people joined in, Charlea repeated the events with as few details as she could. Her southern genteel upbringing wouldn't allow her to tell them to go away and leave her alone, although it was what she really wanted to say.

In an instant, the buzz and discussions stopped as if a switch was turned to off. Scanning the group for the source of the uneasy silence, her eyes stopped where the crowd was parting to reveal what she feared most. In the doorway stood Leon.

Chapter 16

Leon was wearing the same clothes he had worn last night, still dirty and torn from wrestling with David and Roland. Terror swept through Charlea and her knees started shaking. She quickly looked to see if he had a knife in his hand. Seeing none brought her little comfort since he was a powerful man who wouldn't need a weapon to do significant damage. Surely, with all these witnesses around, he wouldn't hurt her. As he strode slowly toward her, Charlea stepped back until her back was against the circulation desk. Several mothers picked their children up and rushed out the door.

Leon stopped a few feet in front of Charlea, his eyes narrowed by hate. He glared at her, but said nothing at first. The silence fed her fear. Would he attack? Involuntarily she sidled to her right to put more space between them.

"You're spreading lies about me," he snarled like a cornered animal. "I know I was drunk, but I know what I heard." He stabbed a dirty finger in her direction. "Those two men know where there's a treasure, and I think they should share it with the rest of us."

To her own amazement, Charlea spoke with an unwavering voice, "Leon, I told you last night. They were talking about a book they read. *Treasure Island*, remember? You misunderstood what they were saying. There's no evidence that there's a treasure anywhere around here. Don't you think someone would have found it by now if such a thing existed?" Once again, she hoped that she was a convincing liar.

"Then why are them strangers here? Tell me that, missy!" Leon was starting to get agitated and he shifted from foot to foot as if preparing to pounce.

Charlea knew she needed to keep him calm. She looked around at the crowd who were watching her, waiting for her response to Leon. No one seemed afraid. They seemed more curious than anything. She wondered why no one went to get the police. Likely no one wanted to miss some detail or fight or whatever might occur so they remained, forming the walls of this hostile arena.

"Mrs. Dunwoody, would you go to my office and call the police?" Charlea urged the woman.

"Stay where you are!" roared Leon. He pointed at Mrs. Dunwoody who shrunk back. The only phone was in Charlea's office and he would catch anyone who ran for it. For now, the showdown was a draw.

"My friends are doing research on this building to, to—" Charlea's mind raced to find a reason for their research "—to write a book on historical buildings in the state. We have museum materials that they are looking through." Her heart was pounding in hope that he would buy the story.

"So why was you at that club last night with them? You're helping with them find the treasure, ain't you. Why else you hanging around with them. You looking for that treasure so you can grab it and skip town. I say you should share it with all of us!"

Charlea was getting angry with Leon and with everyone who kept challenging her right to go out with someone. She was no simpering girl who needed to justify her actions to others. She didn't have to answer to any of them. Her growing ire helped allay her fears. "I was there because one of them asked me out and I said yes. The other guy just happened to be there. They are friends so we left together." Feeling empowered by growing confidence, she stood a little taller.

Leon looked uncomfortable, like he'd just noticed that other people were standing there watching him. His eyes scanned the crowd, maybe looking for a friendly face. The scowls of the people around Charlea made him back away slightly. "I want you to quit telling people that I'm crazy." Leon's voice was getting louder and angrier.

"Ask anyone here if I said anything to imply that you are crazy." Charlea and Leon both looked around the crowd and saw several of them shaking their heads.

One of the elderly men defended Charlea. "She has said no such thing, Leon. Not while I was here."

Leon shuffled nervously while he looked around to others in the crowd, then back to Charlea. He pointed at her and said, "Quit talking about me in front of the whole town. I'm not crazy! I know what I heard and they was talking about finding a treasure—"

"Is there a problem here?" Charlea heard David's voice to the side. She was relieved to hear him, but also a little irritated because she had regained control of the situation on her own. She would have ended this confrontation by herself with a little more time.

Leon and the crowd spun toward David's voice and saw both David and Roland standing there, their clothes dirty from the morning's activities. David stood with his arms crossed, waiting for an answer. Roland's fists were clenched and he stood ready for a fight. The crowd murmured amongst them as Leon set himself against the two men.

For a moment, his eyes flashed recognition and fear, then they narrowed again in hate and rage. "You two started this. I heard you talking. I know what you said!" He spat the words at them.

"I think you should leave before you get yourself into more trouble," David told him calmly, pointing to the door. When Leon made no move to go, David added, "Charlea, go to your office and call the police. Didn't they say they wanted to know if he came around?"

"Yes, they did," she answered firmly

Leon fumbled with something in his pocket. David and Roland tensed, ready to spring. The crowd backed away from Leon, giving the men room to rumble. Seeing the response, Leon changed his mind and pulled his hand out again.

Roland lowered his fists a little. "If you're smart, Leon, you'll leave here now and not come around Charlea again. I'm sure the nice people here don't want to see anything violent. Anyone here want to see men fighting?" The crowd murmured "no" together.

Slowly backing toward to the front door, Leon said, "I'm leaving, but this ain't over. I'll be watching you!" He pointed at David and Roland before spinning around and going out the door, leaving the people in the library staring after him.

When Leon disappeared from sight, the crowd turned in unison to look at Charlea. She slumped against the circulation counter behind her, relieved that the confrontation had ended peacefully.

Mrs. Dunwoody rushed up, grabbed Charlea's arm, and patted the back of her good hand. "You were so brave, Mrs. Ludlow. I would have fainted dead away if he came for me."

Other people gathered around Charlea, asking the inevitable question: was there really a treasure somewhere in town? What had Leon heard that made him think there was?

Charlea resisted the urge to pull her hair out. "There is no treasure!" she said more loudly than she intended. "Leon overheard a conversation about *Treasure Island*. Somehow the word 'treasure' got stuck in his head and he won't let it go."

Mrs. Dunwoody turned and pointed at Roland, "You! Do you know where there's a treasure? Word is that you've been acting strangely around here. Just what are you up to?"

Roland looked surprised. "No, I don't know where a treasure is! I'm doing research, that's all."

Mrs. Dunwoody gave a skeptical snort.

"It's true," Charlea moaned, her head spinning with guilt for lying and the effort it took to keep up the ruse. "They are only doing research on the building. Please believe me." Charlea rubbed her forehead. *Yes, please believe me because I'm tired of explaining all these lies.*

Bonnie, who had come in the back door just after Leon entered, quietly told the people in the crowd that the show was over. She asked if anyone wanted to check out books while she moved them along. The silence was broken with the growing din of comments from the crowd, talking over what had happened and their speculation on whether there was a treasure or not. Several people shook Charlea's hand and complimented her on how bravely she had handled the situation. A few slapped David on the back and thanked him for taking control of the situation. One-by-one, everyone left the library except the four who were working there.

David took the arm of the still stunned Charlea to help her to her office. She found herself leaning on him more than she thought she would as he helped her to her chair behind the desk. He picked up the phone, dialed the operator, and asked for the police station.

Charlea put her face in her hands, trying to get a grip on her emotions. Her temporary confidence had given way to uncontrollable trembling. She wanted to cry, but she feared she might never stop so she fought the urge with all her might.

The doubts began to cloud her mind. Did she handle the situation as well as she should have? Did people believe her when she told them there was no treasure? Would Leon ever believe her? Maybe she should have emphasized it more. She desperately wished she could think faster on her feet, a personal weakness she had never overcome.

Charlea desperately wanted her life to return to its normal serenity. But today, her place of quiet learning and peaceful reading space was ruined. All because a drunken shell of a man had overheard talk of a treasure. A treasure she had to keep refuting, yet she knew existed. A treasure that was turning her into a liar and a hypocrite.

David hung up the phone and knelt down beside Charlea. "It's going to be okay," he told her, rubbing her back to comfort her. "The police will pick up Leon and take him back to the station."

Charlea put her arms around David. She was thankful for his presence and his words comforted her. She was still trembling slightly and fighting the urge to sob on his shoulder, but the fear was slowly receding. His arms were strong and sheltering around her.

"I'm embarrassed by the whole situation," she told him. "I should have handled things better. I should have—I don't know—I could have insisted that he leave or something or—I don't know! Now what will happen to my library? What if people quit coming? What if they are scared to come?"

David let go of her and moved his hands to her face. He put his face very close to hers. "People love to read and they'll keep coming. You'll see. You handled yourself just fine, Charlea. Most women wouldn't have had the courage to stand up to him like you did. You're a brave woman."

"I don't feel very brave. In fact, I was scared to death, but hoped with so many witnesses, he wouldn't do anything."

"You were right. He knew he didn't stand a chance with that many people watching him. Good thing Mrs. Butterfield wasn't here or she wouldn't have let him leave in one piece." He was smiling at her now and she couldn't help, but smile back a little. Then he pulled her toward him and softly kissed her on the lips and her face.

"Ahem." Roland cleared his throat as Bonnie peered over his shoulder. "Sorry for interrupting this touching moment," Roland gave his brother a wink as he continued, "but the police are here. You want to talk to them out front or do you want them to come in here?"

Charlea pulled away, embarrassed to be caught in such a position in her office. "Please have them come back here. I've disturbed library business too much today as it is." She tried to smooth her hair down and straighten her clothes.

Bonnie stayed behind while Roland went to get the police. "No one's in the library right now, so I can stay with you. Are you all right?"

"I'm fine, just shaken. Again." Charlea was tired of telling people she was fine. She wasn't fine. She was an emotional mess, her hand hurt, and she wanted everyone to go away so she could cry it out of her system. But, being a proper Southern woman, she dredged up a little more strength to continue her masquerade for a while longer.

Roland escorted the police officer to Charlea's office where he, David, and Charlea all told their stories. She was tired of talking about Leon and wanted the nightmare to end. Just turn the clock back or ahead; she didn't care as long as this ordeal was over. She wanted her library and peaceful life back.

After the police left, Charlea, Bonnie, David, and Roland returned to the deserted library area. Word of the confrontation had no doubt spread like a pandemic throughout the town and people would be avoiding the library for a day or two. The paper would print another front page story about the battle between the librarian and the town drunk. No doubt the article would portray the library as too dangerous for the general public, hinting vaguely that people should avoid it for a while. Mr. Woodson would love that! And people would too—everyone except for Mr. Wilkerson. Dear Mr. Wilkerson would come. And Mr. Woodson.

As if thinking of the devil somehow summoned him, Mr. Woodson came storming in the front door. "I heard what happened. Is everything okay here?" he asked, studying her. He frowned at the two men sitting with her, but said nothing to them. "I need to know exactly what happened here. We could be talking about a crime on city property."

"Everything is fine," Charlea explained to him. "Leon made a spectacle of himself in a room full of people. Nothing happened, other than harsh words being thrown around. No crime was committed. David and Roland were here and got the situation under control...again."

Mr. Woodson eyed the two men suspiciously. "Yes, well...I suppose we owe them a debt of gratitude for always being in the right place at the right time. May I speak to you alone, Charlea?"

"Certainly. Let's step into my office." Charlea led the way, finding her seat behind her desk, putting a buffer between her and his advances, should he decide to make them. She also felt weak in the knees. Too much excitement for one day.

Mr. Woodson closed the door and spun around, furious at her. "I thought I asked you to keep some distance between you and those men. Who are they? Friends of yours? How do you know they aren't the ones causing the problems?"

Charlea immediately felt defensive, but tried to stay calm. "Yes, they are friends of mine, visiting for a few days, and doing research on this building's architecture. They spent the morning with Milt who gave them a tour of the building." His expression was so skeptical she urged him, "Go ask Milt, if you don't believe me."

Mr. Woodson shook his head. "It's not that. It seems odd to me that since they've been here, you've been assaulted twice."

Charlea shrugged her shoulders. "Assaulted once. Threatened once. By one person. That's all it is. Or bad luck, depending on your point of view."

"All the same, I think you should steer clear of them. In fact, I think it best if you told them to go home. Tell them their research here is over."

Charlea stood up and leaned on her desk. "Mr. Woodson, this is a public facility, and I will not turn away anyone who comes here to do research. They are museum customers, and I will help them however I can as required by our charter. Beyond that, I may work for the city, but you cannot tell me who I may or may not keep company with. Those men are my friends, and I'll continue to associate with them if I so choose. Now if you'll excuse me, I have work to do." She walked to the door and opened it for him, signaling their conversation was over.

Mr. Woodson frowned and lightly rapped her desk with his fist. He made no move to leave and rapped the desk a second time, harder. "Very well, Charlea. May I suggest that you take a few days off work—at least until all this dies down. The publicity is not good for the library. If Leon comes around again, I don't want you here. Take a little time off to let things settle, and in a couple of days, the furor will pass. Take the rest of the week off, courtesy of the city."

Charlea pondered his words and realized he was right. She needed to get away from the library for the sake of people feeling it safe to return. The library's reputation as a safe haven could be restored with her out of the way for a while. "Perhaps you're right. I'll finish out today which will give me time to find someone to help Bonnie while I'm gone. Then I'll take tomorrow off. Surely, by Monday, the hubbub will have died down."

Mr. Woodson seemed satisfied with her solution. "Three days away from here will do you good. Do you have someone in mind to help Bonnie? If not, I'll ask my wife to come down and help."

Charlea had no intention of asking Mrs. Woodson to help at the library. She was renowned for being a busybody and carrying tales back to her husband and the town council. "Thanks, but no. I have someone else in mind, someone who is already familiar with our procedures. But I'll keep your wife in mind just in case." Charlea was lying again and hoped that Mr. Woodson couldn't tell.

Mr. Woodson moved toward the door to leave. "I'll check on the library while you're gone to make sure everything is running smoothly. And I'll call you at home to make sure you're safe."

"There's no need to call me at home. I'll be fine." Charlea smiled, still holding the door for him. She hated his interference in library business, but she was in no position to argue with him. She'd give Bonnie advice on how to handle him when he did show up.

Mr. Woodson strode out to the circulation desk and announced, "Charlea will be taking the rest of the week off until things settle down a little. Bonnie, you'll be in charge. My wife is available to help you, and I'll help out in any way you need."

"I will arrange for someone to come help you, Bonnie," Charlea interjected quickly. An uncomfortable silence followed.

"Charlea, if Mr. Woodson thinks his wife should come…"

"Bonnie, I already have others in mind who are familiar with how we do things. I will arrange it."

Mr. Woodson seemed frustrated with the rejection, but acquiesced. "Yes—well—I'll be off then," he said as he headed toward the door. He glared at Roland and David as he left to make sure they knew of his disapproval. He started to say something to them, but then thought better of it. He walked quickly out of the library, slamming the door behind him.

"If looks could kill, you'd be reading our obituaries in tomorrow's paper," David said looking at the closed door. "I get the distinct impression that the guy doesn't like us."

"Your uncanny observation of the obvious is astounding," Charlea joked. "No, he doesn't like either of you at all. He warned me that I should stay away from you. You're trouble, he says."

"Do you believe him?" Roland asked.

Charlea laughed and sat down beside him. She still thought of him as *Adonis*, despite everything. "Good sense says I should. I was leading a nice, peaceful life until the day you walked in the door. That's when the trouble began." She dared not say more lest Bonnie find out that they had all been lying to her about their purpose for being there.

Roland took her hand, raised it to his lips and gently kissed it. "Some may call it trouble. Some call it excitement and adventure. A chance to meet new and beautiful people. Instead of following good sense, you should follow your heart. You seem like a person who doesn't follow her heart enough."

Charlea was mesmerized by his eyes. The eyes of *Adonis*. He was right: she did not often follow her heart. She was too sensible and rooted to do that. That's why she lived in a nice safe place, working a job that was structured and predictable. This was her comfort zone, with little risk in daily living. And there was no adventure. Adventure scared her, but it also intrigued her.

Behind her, Charlea heard David clear his throat, or give a low growl; she couldn't tell which. Bonnie gave a long sigh, evidently moved by Roland's tender speech. The sounds helped her break free of the spell Roland had cast over her. Charlea felt her blood racing through her and her face reddened.

"Fun and adventure are a matter of perspective. Architectural research is fun for some, but dull for others." Charlea was trying to subtly remind Roland not to say too much in front of Bonnie. She hoped he would get the hint.

Roland caught on, looking a little embarrassed that he had almost revealed their secret. He sat up straight in the chair. "Of course, you're right. Not everyone is as interested in architecture as I am. I forget myself. If you'd rather sit home and watch soap operas, I won't make you feel guilty for wasting your life."

Bonnie laughed out loud. "Charlea? Watching soap operas? That'll be the day! She won't quit reading books long enough to watch television more than fifteen minutes—except when movies are on with Cary Grant or Tony Curtis." She got up and went behind the circulation desk.

"You have a weakness for handsome men?" David asked Charlea. Jealousy tempered the tone of his voice and the loaded question made Charlea squirm.

Bonnie rescued her. "All women have that weakness, honey. Charlea, you should listen to Mr. Woodson. Why don't you get out of town for a few days? Go somewhere. Do something fun. Give things here time to settle down a little. I'll help these guys with their research."

Charlea shook her head. "I don't run away from problems. I'll make myself scarce for a while. Maybe I'll explore the field of architecture for a few days. I'm sure we have books on the topic." Turning to David, she smiled and said, "Would you mind if I helped you with your research?"

David had been quiet, seemingly lost in thought. Charlea noted a slight look of sadness about him and wondered what it meant. He didn't answer her question, but sat staring at the floor. Roland reached over and punched his brother to get his attention.

"Do I take your silence as a no?" Charlea asked.

"I'm sorry. What?"

Charlea looked at Roland and Bonnie, unsure about whether to ask the question again. Roland nodded, so she repeated, "I asked if you would mind me helping you with your research."

"That would be nice. Thank you."

"Why don't you go home now," Bonnie told Charlea. "I can handle the library without you."

Charlea thought a moment. "I'll ask Mr. Wilkerson to come help you. He knows the circulation desk routine and could take care of it while you do everything else. You wouldn't have to worry about him. He would love the opportunity to make a few extra dollars and visit with everyone. You could be busy. People may come in expecting me to be here."

Bonnie thought about it and nodded. "He's a good choice. He can handle the circulation desk without much oversight. I think that's a great idea!"

"Good. I'll call him this afternoon. If he turns us down, we'll find someone else. What about Mrs. Butterfield as a backup? She'd probably do it for free just for the chance to keep an eye on things."

"The two of them would keep order in this place, that's for sure. Can we afford both? You haven't finished the budget, so I wonder about that."

Charlea felt miffed. Why did everything always go back to the budget? "Yes, I can manage it. I'll get them both. Bonnie, if Mr. Woodson comes in, let him look around, but don't let him boss you around. The library works quite well without his interference."

"But he's on the town council. He's doing his job."

Bonnie is defending him again, Charlea thought. *I don't understand why, but as long as library services aren't interrupted, I won't argue about it now.* She went to her office to make phone calls. She hadn't taken many days off during the past year. She might actually get some rest and forget about Leon.

She had just picked up the phone to call when David and Roland walked in. She'd forgotten about them with her excitement in finding substitutes. David turned to close the door behind him so they could all talk privately. Charlea motioned for one of them to sit in the chair in front of her desk. She set the phone down and sat back in her chair.

"Got a plan?" David asked as he sat down.

"Actually I do," Charlea told him. "You can finish looking around here today. Roland, you said Milt told you where the Williams built their new house?" Roland nodded. "I'll get the address from your notes. Tomorrow I'll go by the courthouse and look up who owns the place now. That way, if you find nothing here, we'll know where to look next. I'll make arrangements to look at the Williams' house. By the way, did you find anything upstairs?"

"Not yet," Roland told her. "We're still looking through the desk. We were slowed down when we heard Leon's voice."

"He won't be back and Bonnie is busy, so you shouldn't be interrupted. That way you'll be busy someplace other than where I am in case Mr. Woodson decides to come around again."

David cleared his throat and looked at Charlea earnestly. "Charlea, how much do you know about Woodson? I get a bad feeling about him."

"I don't know him well. I don't like him, but I have to work with the man. He's instrumental in funding the library."

"I think you should keep him at arm's length, especially now. Something about him doesn't set right with me."

"I agree with David," Roland added. "The guy is a jerk. He's hiding something."

Charlea agreed with both of them. "Jerk or not, he's one of the leading citizens of the town. Most people have a lot of respect for him."

"He has them fooled," David replied. "We just want you to be extra careful. We can't be there to protect you all the time."

"I will, I will." Charlea rolled her eyes. "Now, why don't you finish your architectural research upstairs." The two men looked at each other. Roland shrugged his shoulders and then turned to go. David sighed resignedly and followed him.

Charlea dialed Mr. Wilkerson's number.

Chapter 17

Charlea walked into her apartment, relieved to be home at last. She took off her scarf and laid it and her purse on a small table by the door. On her way to the sofa, she kicked off her shoes, letting them lie where they fell. She stretched out on the sofa and looked at the TV console in the corner next to her personal library. The picture over the TV was crooked, and she made a mental note to straighten it when she got up. A floor lamp hung over an overstuffed chair, the perfect place for reading.

Exhausted, she closed her eyes and let memories of the day flood over her: her confrontation with Leon, Mr. Woodson's warnings about David and Roland, David and Roland's warnings about Mr. Woodson. She was in the middle of opposing factions, all because of a silly letter that Roland won in a poker game. She felt apprehensive about the turn of events with Leon, but soon Roland and David would have the stones and go home. Things would return to normal after that. She relaxed and let the stress drain away.

As she lay there, there was a knock on the door. She tried to get up, but her legs did not respond. Her arms and legs were so heavy that she could only move them inches. Turning her head, she watched the door open by itself, revealing Leon in the doorway with a murderous grin on his face. He said nothing as he slowly began to move toward her. A knife blade glinted in his hand. She tried to scream, but no sound came out of her throat. As panic gripped her, she saw David step in the doorway behind Leon. Her hero! He would save her!

David lunged at Leon and tried to take the knife away from him. He shouted at Charlea to run, but as hard as she tried, she could not get up off the sofa. In their struggle for the knife, Leon and David moved closer to her until they were almost on top of her.

As the two men struggled over the knife, she tried in vain to get up. She saw the glint of the knife just before Leon pushed it into David's stomach. David grabbed his belly as the blood began to flow. He looked at Charlea as if to ask for help, then fell to the floor face down. Leon stood over David and laughed in triumph. Slowly, he turned and started toward Charlea again. Her heart pounded and she broke out in a sweat as Leon leaned over her. She tried to scream—

Charlea jerked upright on the sofa, gasping for breath. Finding her voice, she let out a guttural scream. Wild-eyed, she looked all around her. Everything was in place in her neat apartment. No Leon. No David. No blood. Only a dream that seemed so real that she had trouble believing it was not.

Leaning back on the sofa, she fought to catch her breath and calm her pounding heart. She was covered in sweat, completely drained of energy, and shaking uncontrollably. Summoning what strength she could, she stumbled to the bedroom and took her clothes off. She decided to shower, to wash away the dream and the terror that came with it. After starting the water in the shower, she took the bobby pins out of her hair. Looking up, she couldn't help but stare. The mirror showed a woman, bruised and scared. She stood there until the steam obscured her reflection.

The shower felt good, washing away the sweat and the dream. She scrubbed her body with a washcloth until her skin turned red. The moist heat and massaging of the water against her body rejuvenated her.

After her long shower, she put on her robe and returned to the living room, grabbing Mark's picture off the wall on the way. The photograph showed Mark, handsome in his uniform, in front of an American flag, with a slight smile on his face. His smile of pride, Charlea called it. He was proud of his service to his country. She propped Mark on one side of the sofa against a pillow and sat on the other end. Drawing her knees up under her chin, she sighed and ran her fingers through her wet hair.

"I wish you were here to tell me what to do." She felt tears sting her eyes and she blinked them back. "Remember the guy that threatened me with a knife that I told you about? He came in the library today and threatened me again. This time he didn't have a knife, but he is still after me." A tear rolled down her cheek. "Mark, I'm scared." She began to softly cry.

"Mr. Woodson wants me to stay away from David and Roland. But to tell the truth," she paused a moment and began to play with the hem of her robe as a smile turned up the corners of her mouth, "I really enjoy being with them. I'm even attracted to them both. Are you shocked by that?" She stared at the picture as if waiting for a reply,

"You're gone, but I wonder. Do you ever think of me? I dream of you at night, only to have the light of dawn snatch you from my arms, leaving me to face another day alone. I made a vow to be faithful to you, until death parts us. Has death parted us? Or are you still out there somewhere?" She cried softly.

"Being with David and Roland, I realized how lonely I am. I haven't spent my heart on anyone but you, and now you're not here to take it. Is it all a waste of a good heart?" She contemplated the question, but no answer came. The tears came faster and she let them flow unimpeded. The clock on the wall counted off the minutes while she sobbed, alone in her apartment in front of a picture of her husband. She cried about her dream. She cried about what had happened to her the last couple of days. She cried about her continuing loneliness.

When the tears emptied her emotions, she leaned back on the sofa, stretching out her legs. Wiping her face, she smiled at Mark's picture. "Thanks, honey. I feel better now. Everything will all work out somehow."

She got the picture and held it to her breast. She got up and went to the small kitchen where there was a small table against one wall with two placemats on it. Setting Mark's picture on the countertop, she went to the refrigerator to take out her supper's ingredients.

"Remember how we used to fix omelets together?" she asked as she diced vegetables. "I'd cut up the ingredients and you'd whip the eggs and cook them. Now I do it all. You would think that after 12 years, I wouldn't mind doing things alone. I should be used to it by now.

"I love the freedom to make my own decisions. I have no one to answer to. Control of my own life, it's the ultimate freedom." She began to chop onions and tomatoes, although her hands were shaking. "I am in control. I am in control. I am in control," she said, trying to convince herself of its truth.

Whipping the eggs into froth, she turned to Mark's picture. "I'll enjoy this gemstone adventure while it lasts and then the peace and quiet will return." She dumped the eggs into the frying pan and added the onions, tomatoes, mushrooms, and cheese. "Some of the circumstances are scary though. This thing with Leon is unnerving. I know, I'll call Richard and talk to him about it. He'll help me out. Thanks, Mark, you always have good advice for me." She turned her omelet. "Yes, dear, I'll be careful." She turned her omelet out on a plate and took it and Mark's picture to the table. She said grace and began to eat.

After the dishes were done and Mark was back in his place on the wall, Charlea called the operator and gave the phone number to her brother's office in Dallas. She guessed that he was still there since he liked to put in long hours. On the third ring, a familiar voice answered.

"Still at work, I see," Charlea started. "You really spend too much time there."

"Someone's got to run the family business," Richard answered back. He laughed when he realized who it was. "I'm glad to hear from you. Gives me a chance to put my feet up and take a break. So how are things out in the boonies?" A man of money, he felt she had lowered her status when she had taken the librarian job. A woman of her upbringing should be in a nice apartment in Dallas, making money by managing business affairs.

"Things are buzzing. Have you ever heard of a man named Roland Parker? He showed up here with a letter saying there were 'stones' hidden in a secret place and needs my help to find them."

"Seems like I've heard that name before." Charlea could hear the smile on his face. "Seems to me that he's a waiter at my favorite restaurant. So are you going to help him?"

"I hope to, but he was overheard talking about a 'treasure' and has brought some trouble down on us. And he brought his brother with him."

Richard's voice changed with concern. "His brother? I don't know that guy. What kind of trouble is he in?"

Charlea sat on the sofa and twisted the phone cord as she explained the events of the past two days to him. He gasped when she told him about Leon holding a knife to her throat. She stressed that David and Roland had protected her and would continue to do so. For some reason—she didn't know why—she didn't mention Mr.

Woodson. Richard had enough to think about without that extra worry.

"I'll leave first thing in the morning and be there tomorrow afternoon. I don't want you mixed up in this anymore. I should have known that Parker wouldn't be able to handle the job. Can you trust his brother? I'll check him out for you."

"Richard, I can't believe you did it again! I wish you wouldn't do that!"

"Do what? I don't know what you're talking about." Richard laughed. "I'll run a check and let you know what I find out."

"Don't bother. I trust David completely. And I don't want you to come. It'll mess everything up. Please, let me see this thing through. This project shouldn't take more than a day or two to finish, and then they'll be on their way. Things will go back to normal after that."

"Charlea, if you're in trouble, I have to come. Until then, I want you to be really careful. Watch your back. I'm on my way."

"Please don't come," Charlea pleaded with him. "I can handle this." Charlea was growing tired of pleading with him. "At least give me one more day to get this worked out. Please! I don't need you to fight this battle for me."

A long silence hovered between them. "You have until Saturday afternoon. Get them the information they want and get them on their way. You can contact them later if you want to continue the relationship. Call me every day, more than once if you can. I want to know everything that's going on. I can be there in a few hours if you need me."

"I promise to call. Tonight, I needed to hear your voice and its calming influence. Thanks for being there for me. But listen to me. This has to be the last time you do this for me—and don't deny your part in this. You know what I mean. I hope this one doesn't come back on you in a bad way. You take too many risks."

"What are brothers for? I love you, sis."

"I love you too, big brother. I'll talk with you later." Charlea hung up the phone. Richard always made her feel better. He seemed to be in charge of everything when she felt like she wasn't.

While she was reading, the phone rang. Startled by the sudden sound, Charlea knocked a glass of iced tea onto the floor. She took a moment to regain her composure, before she could tiptoe around the mess on the floor. Sitting on the sofa, she reached for the phone, but before her hand closed around the receiver, the image of Leon flashed through her mind. His parting words of "I'll be watching you!" echoed in her ears.

A shot of fear ran through her. In an instant, a few possible callers went through her mind, but her thoughts kept returning to Leon. She decided it was time to confront him and tell him she was calling the police again to ask them to keep him in jail. Then he would surely leave her alone. When she picked up the receiver, her anger controlled her voice.

"Hello," she barked like a German Shepard given the command to sic. She didn't want Leon to think she was scared of him.

"Charlea?" David's voice brought instant relief to her tension. "Are you all right? You sound strange."

"Thank goodness, it's you," she said, patting her chest to calm her pounding heart. "I thought it might be Leon calling."

"I'm sorry to scare you, but I wanted to make sure you're okay. Do you need me to come over and keep you company for a little while?" He sounded hopeful that she would say yes.

Charlea was flattered by his offer and was ready to have someone with her through this long evening. But a man in her apartment? Alone? Mrs. Butterfield would have a fit about them not having a chaperone. Feeling rather excited about time alone with David, she decided to disregard what Mrs. Butterfield thought.

"I would love for you to come over. I'm feeling rather jumpy tonight. You would help take my mind off things."

"Great! Shall I bring ice cream? There's nothing like ice cream to calm the nerves."

"Sure, I'd love it!"

"Give me about 20 minutes. But wait! What about Mrs. Butterfield? I can't defend myself against a baseball bat if I have ice cream in my hands."

"If you come within the hour, she won't know you're here because her favorite TV show is on and she hears nothing until it's over. I'll escort you out when you leave. I'll be your bodyguard for a change."

"Great! I'm on my way!" He hung up before she could reply. She laughed as she hung up the phone. Mrs. Butterfield had certainly put the fear in him.

Charlea went to the bathroom to freshen up. There it was, in the mirror again: that color in her face and twinkle in her eyes. David's effect on her. She smiled and felt the weight of her troubles lift off her shoulders. She thought about changing into something dressy, but decided against it. Casual was appropriate. She slipped on a pair of slacks and a blouse and combed her hair. On her way out of her bedroom, she stopped to look at Mark's picture and blew him a kiss.

She picked up her purse and shoes that she had kicked off when she had come in and fluffed the pillows on the sofa. In the kitchen, she put up her now dry supper dishes and set out bowls and spoons in anticipation of David's arrival. With everything in place, she paced her apartment.

Soon there was a gentle rapping at the door that signaled David's arrival. Her dream of Leon flashed through her mind, along with another stroke of fear. Charlea looked through her peephole to make sure it was him. It was. She flung open the door.

"Hi!" Charlea greeted David warmly and he gave a quick kiss on her cheek. "Let me take that." She took the cold paper bag from his hand and locked the door behind him to make sure no one else unexpectedly came in, friend or foe.

"I forgot to ask what flavor of ice cream you like best. I brought vanilla and chocolate syrup," David said. "I figured I'd cover more bases that way." He followed her into her small kitchen.

"I love vanilla," Charlea replied over her shoulder, noting how considerate he was. "Ice cream, any flavor, has always been a weakness for me. Shall we dish it up?" Charlea handed David the scoop and let him dish it out into bowls while she opened the can of chocolate syrup. She poured a generous amount of syrup over her scoops and, when David requested it, did the same to his.

Taking the bowls in to the living room, they both sat in the middle of the sofa. They toasted each other with a spoon of ice cream. Laughing, they dug into the rest of their bowls.

"What would Mrs. Butterfield say if she knew I was here?" David asked before taking another bite.

Charlea let her mouthful of sweet stuff slowly melt before answering. "I'm sure she would find it outrageous. No proper woman entertains a gentleman in her room unchaperoned. But enough about her. How about some music?" Charlea asked David as she put her bowl on the coffee table in front of them.

"That would be great." David was very relaxed.

A large stereo console was next to the sofa. Charlea slid the side doors open to look through her large collection of albums. Pulling out a few of them, she held each one up for David to see and let him choose: Johnny Mathis, Elvis, the Lettermen, Frank Sinatra, Kingston Trio. She started the albums playing and sat back down on the sofa. Finishing off the last of their ice cream, they sat back and shared stories like old friends.

David told her more about growing up on a farm with a little brother named Roland who followed him everywhere. Charlea laughed at the many stories of trouble that seemed to follow the two boys. Little had changed in adulthood.

"Would you like to dance?" David put his empty bowl on the coffee table, stood up, and held out his hand for hers.

"I'd love to," Charlea said extending her hand out to his. "But let's move this to make more room." She pointed to the coffee table that held their empty bowls. David took one side and Charlea took the other to move the table out of the way. He held out his arms and she moved quickly into their grasp.

Holding her close, he spun her around and she laughed out loud. He swayed her back and forth and down into a dip. His face was very close to hers and she felt the urge to kiss him. He must have felt the same thing because he raised her up and kissed her hard as they stood in the middle of the living room.

The phone rang and Charlea jerked away in response to the unexpected noise. David, feeling her tremble, held her closer. She looked up at him. "I should answer that."

"Are you afraid it's Leon?"

"If he's smart, he'll leave me alone. The question is, is he that smart?" Charlea sat on the sofa and slowly picked the receiver up to answer. "Hello?" she answered feebly. Disgust with her weak answer filled her. She needed to show strength, regardless of how she really felt. She cleared her throat. "Hello," she said again, much more firmly.

"Charlea?" Mr. Woodson asked, "Are you alone?"

"Am I what?" she stuttered, flabbergasted that he would ask such a question. "Why do you need to know that, Mr. Woodson?" Charlea immediately grew angry that he would call her, much less ask such a thing. She looked at David, who was frowning.

"I don't want anything to happen to our town's librarian," he replied, sounding facetiously sincere.

"How does being alone guarantee that?"

Politician-smooth, he tried to change the conversation to safer ground. Mr. Woodson stuttered, searching for words. "I didn't mean to imply anything—untoward. I meant, are you safe?"

Suspicious of his motives, Charlea wondered why he cared if she was alone or not. He must know more than he was letting on. She took a gamble and asked, "Mr. Woodson, are you having my apartment watched?" A pregnant pause fell on the other end of the line.

Furious, she yelled into the phone, "Because if you are, then I will file a protest or a charge of stalking or something. My private life is outside the realm of your authority."

"Not if it concerns the integrity of a public servant," he replied, angry that she had discovered his spying.

"Is my integrity being threatened?" Charlea stood up, a reflection of her rising anger.

"You may be keeping company with someone who is involved with illegal activities."

"Illegal activities? Of what nature?" Charlea asked, uncertain on whether to believe him or not.

Mr. Woodson was silent.

Charlea grew impatient with his nonresponse. "I think I have a right to know," she demanded.

He didn't answer immediately, but paused long enough for Charlea to wonder if he was searching for a reasonable lie to tell her. "Investigations are on-going."

"Well, until charges are filed or allegations proven, then they are baseless accusations. You call your goon or whoever you have spying on me and tell him to leave me alone! Get your nose out of my private life, Mr. Woodson, or I'll consult a lawyer about suing you on the grounds of harassment." Charlea started to hang up on him, but decided to wait and see if Mr. Woodson had an answer for her. She put the receiver back to her ear.

The long silence on the other end of the phone made her wonder if he had hung up on her. "My apologies. Your welfare was my only concern. Good night." With that, he hung up on Charlea.

Charlea slammed her phone receiver down.

"That was Mr. Woodson," she told David, wringing her hands as if to wipe them clean.

"So I gathered," he replied. "The weasel is having you followed, is he?" He went to the window and peeked through a part in the drapes to see if anyone was skulking around or sitting in a car watching the building. Apparently whoever was watching Charlea had left or was well hidden.

Turning away from the window, he clinched his fists. "I'll go get Roland and we'll pay him a little visit to get things straightened out." He headed toward the door.

Charlea hurried to him and grabbed his arm. "No, don't. He is a very powerful man in town and not one to be trifled with. Leave him alone. We only need a day or two to complete our work and then—" Charlea paused, not wanting to continue. "And then you and Roland will go home and it will be over." A lump formed in her throat that pushed a tear of anger, frustration, and fear down her cheek. Too many things were happening for her to be left alone, too much for her to bear by herself. She didn't want David to leave yet because she didn't know if she could face Mr. Woodson or Leon alone.

As if he were reading her mind, David took her in his arms and held her tightly. His strong arms around her were very comforting and she felt completely safe. She clung to him while fighting back the tears. She was determined not to cry. She could not show weakness. She had to be strong.

Why is this happening to me? She thought. *What if Mr. Woodson was right and David was not who he said he was?* The sensible voice in the back of her head grew louder and louder until she couldn't ignore it any more. She needed control. Control of her life. She pushed away from David.

"This is nuts!" She paced around the room, flailing her arms.

David looked suddenly scared.

"This is crazy! What am I thinking?" She stopped and looked at David for a long minute. "I have known you a little more than 24 hours and we're acting like we've known each other for years. You're a stranger to me! And Roland is more of a stranger to me than you are. How is it that I'm tangled in your affairs, but I'm the one being spied on?"

David let her rant and rave without saying a word, shrugging his answers to her questions.

"I don't know either," she continued. "I haven't done anything wrong!" She paused long enough to spear David with a look. "Actually, neither have you. Have you?"

"No, we haven't," David said meekly as if afraid to interrupt her speech.

"So why are we the bad guys in this?" She began pacing again and continued, "I think I'll bow out and let you and Roland do whatever it is you need to do. Anyone with a lick of sense would do that and be better off for it. In fact, I think that's what I'll do." *There, she thought, I'm back in control of my life. I just wish he didn't look so forlorn standing there while I'm making good sense. It clouds my judgment.*

There was a long silence between the two of them, with only the sound of Johnny Mathis singing, "I'll Never Be Lonely Again" filling the room. As he sang the words, Charlea realized she could not say those words. She glanced at David. She was pushing away someone who could make those words come true for her.

"Charlea," David began uncertainly, "you're right. I'm sorry about everything that's happened. Roland and I, we never meant to bring trouble to your door. Please believe me. We would have never—"

Charlea felt her anger melting away. "I believe you," she whispered.

David seemed not to hear or didn't want to stop. "Roland won this stupid letter in a poker game and it made him crazy to chase it down. He didn't want anyone to know about it, but then he said too much at the bar that night. He's the one who started all this trouble." David shook his head and smiled. "It's so hard trying to keep him on track sometimes. He goes overboard with everything he does."

"He seems like the impetuous type."

David laughed. "You have no idea." A serious look came over his face like a thunderstorm moving across the land. "It's crazy to chase the dream of precious stones. I don't know why I let him talk me into this. But looking at the evidence of the past two days, Roland and I are not good for you. As much as I don't want to, we'll go and leave you in peace." He looked at Charlea who was still standing in the middle of the room.

"You know what my biggest regret is?" He walked over to her. Taking her face in his hands, he looked at her tenderly. "I came to this town looking for a treasure. I found one. My treasure is not gems or gold. You are my treasure." He kissed Charlea as though it would be the last time and wanted to sear it into their memories for all eternity. Charlea melted into his embrace and let the kiss quiet the sensible voice in the back of her head.

Urgent knocking at the door broke the spell. Charlea jerked away, instantly afraid of whomever might be on the other side of the door.

David pushed her behind him, shielding her from whatever threatened her.

The pounding on the door continued until Mrs. Butterfield's voice reverberated through her door. "Charlea, let me in!"

David caught her by the arm before she opened the door. "I need to get behind you!" David said, releasing the built-up tension. "Look through the peephole to make sure she's alone."

Charlea looked and turned to him with her eyes wide. "She's got the bat and she's looking for you!"

David took a step back, dread clearly showing on his face.

Charlea let out a gotcha laugh. "I was just kidding! She's alone. And there's no bat."

David took another step back anyway.

Another knock sounded and Mrs. Butterfield yelled again, "I know he's in there! Let me in now!"

Charlea opened the door and Mrs. Butterfield raced into the room, looking around. "Has he hurt you? You haven't given him money, have you?" She looked around wildly, and spotting David standing several steps away, she snarled at him, "Why are you here?"

"Why—what? I'm not—what are you talking about?"

"If you got nothing to hide," the elderly woman growled as she walked up to him, jabbing David in the chest, "why did you sneak past my door?"

"You have a bat and aren't afraid to use it on me."

Charlea pushed her way between the two. "I asked him to come here, Mrs. Butterfield. Why are *you* here?"

"Mr. Woodson said he was a criminal who is trying to dupe you out of your money. Either that or he is going to rob the library. He better not try it. Not as long as I'm around." Her narrowed eyes and fixed jaw gave off the essence of a wolf protecting her pup.

"When I saw his car out front, I called Mr. Woodson. He asked me to let him know whenever one of those men was around. I've been watching, but he"—Mrs. Butterfield pointed at David— "must have sneaked past my door. Mr. Woodson said he'd take care of it, but then he called back and said I'd better get down here right away." She looked from Charlea to David and back again. "Are you all right, Charlea?"

Charlea put her hands on her hips. So that was it. Mr. Woodson was using Mrs. Butterfield to spy on her. She gave the floor a how-dare-he stomp.

Mrs. Butterfield pulled Charlea's arm to lead her to the kitchen. She whispered, "Charlea, how can you be so blind about this man? Tell him to get lost and look for a nice man somewhere else. I have a very nice nephew who is—"

David, upon hearing their conversation, walked into the kitchen area. "Mrs. Butterfield, I'm here because I like Charlea and I hope she likes me. I'm not a criminal and I'm not after Charlea's money. I have a job with an electric company in Dallas that pays well. Here, I have proof."

"David, you don't have to—" Charlea began, but David held up his hand and cut her short. He pulled a work ID card out of his wallet and showed it to Mrs. Butterfield.

"Want more proof? Here's my pass to the city zoo, here's my library card." He turned to show it to Charlea as well. "Here's my driver's license with my picture on it. Here's a picture of my nieces, my oldest brother's girls. And here's a nephew, another brother's son. Aren't they beautiful?" He held out the picture for both women to admire before putting everything back into his wallet. "Let me think. What other proof do I have on me?"

"That won't be necessary," Mrs. Butterfield replied somewhat hesitantly. "I guess I believe you. But not entirely. Why would Mr. Woodson say you're a criminal if there is no truth to it?" She studied David as if she could read his mind.

"He's determined to discredit David and Roland," Charlea told Mrs. Butterfield who would not take her eyes off David. "For some reason, Mr. Woodson doesn't like them. I don't know why, but he doesn't. David and his brother Roland are good, decent people, and I consider them my friends. They are visiting for a few days, doing research at the library. Historical architectural research. Money has not been mentioned. "

David mused, "Maybe Woodson is upset with me dating Charlea. I don't know why, him being a married man and all. It couldn't be that he's jealous or anything, could it?" The question lingered in the air.

"That's absurd," Charlea said firmly.

But Mrs. Butterfield agreed with David. "Could be. He sounded like a jealous lover. His wife drives him crazy, so maybe he's looking around."

Charlea shook her head. "His wife drives everybody crazy."

The tension left Mrs. Butterfield's face and she laughed. "That she does! I don't know anyone who likes to be around her. He must feel the same way. He made a move on you in the past, didn't he, Charlea?"

"Want some ice cream?" Charlea asked Mrs. Butterfield, moving to more pleasant conversation. "David brought some over tonight. We've already had some, but if you twist our arms, we might have more along with you."

"I'd love it, but three's a crowd." She moved toward the door to leave.

"Don't be silly. We were talking about the research he and Roland are doing. We should stop talking about work."

"Research?" Mrs. Butterfield asked, looking around. "With music, and furniture pushed back out of the way?"

"It's our own special research method," David said, winking at Charlea.

"David, can you get the ice cream and chocolate?" Charlea pulled out more bowls and dished the scoops. She got a folding chair and they all sat around the little kitchen table while they ate.

Charlea was the first to break the silence. "I'm relieved to learn that you're Mr. Woodson's spy."

Mrs. Butterfield was embarrassed. "I'm sorry, Charlea. He told me that David was a criminal who wanted to extort money from you. And I believed him."

David pushed his empty bowl back and said, "Mr. Woodson called Charlea tonight and we didn't know how he found out I was here."

"It scared me to think Mr. Woodson might be lurking around somewhere outside," Charlea told the older woman. "That would have been creepy. At least now I know the spy is a friend." She smiled at Mrs. Butterfield.

"It may be worse than you think," Mrs. Butterfield said uncertainly, "I saw Leon and Mr. Woodson together this afternoon at the drug store. They sat in the next booth while I was enjoying a lime fizz. They were talking about things, like how Leon could keep an eye on you without being seen."

"What?" Charlea knocked her bowl across the table where it teetered on the edge just before David pushed it back on the table. "I'm being spied on?" She rushed to the living room window, pulled back the curtain, and looked out. Black. All she could see was black and a distant street light.

David came up behind her and shut the curtains. "You can't see out your windows when it's dark outside, but whoever is out there can see in here clearly. I'll go outside and look around."

"No!" Charlea and Mrs. Butterfield said in unison.

"I don't want you running into Leon, if he's out there," Charlea said, grabbing his arm to keep him from leaving. "He might hurt you this time."

Mrs. Butterfield motioned for them to sit down. "I told the sheriff about what I heard and they will patrol this area more often. That will probably keep Leon at bay. He's had enough trouble with the law lately so he won't want to catch their attention anytime soon."

"I hope you're right, Mrs. Butterfield." David sat again and mindlessly folded his napkin in funny ways.

Charlea pushed her bowl away. "Mr. Woodson wants to know who is coming here and where I go. He's probably after that supposed treasure that Leon keeps harping on." She and David exchanged quick glances. "He's made Leon his flunky to do his dirty work."

David rubbed his chin with his hand. "If Woodson thinks Mrs. Butterfield is keeping track of you here, it's likely Leon isn't around the apartment. Leon will be watching you when you're away from the apartment. So I don't think you need to worry about him outside your windows here."

"I never thought about that," Mrs. Butterfield said thoughtfully. "I'll keep up the ruse so there's no need for Leon to watch you here. Mr. Woodson will still think he's got everything covered." The elderly woman looked nervously from one to the other. "Charlea, you know that I love you like you were my own daughter and I want what's best for you. You being alone and all, I worry about you."

David leaned across the table toward the elder woman. "Mrs. Butterfield, I am very fond of Charlea, maybe even falling—" He stopped and looked shyly at Charlea, apparently saying things that he didn't intend to reveal yet. "She is an amazing woman, like no one else I've ever met. I was worried about her too, so I came tonight to make sure she was doing okay." Turning to Charlea, he took her hand and looked at her like a man finally overcoming his fears. "And to spend more time with you because I can't seem to get enough of your company."

Charlea was overwhelmed and surprised at his emotions. She knew she was very fond of him, but she hadn't been sure that her feelings were reciprocated. A faraway thought of Mark gave only the slightest ting of guilt. Happiness swept over her like a waterfall, washing away her loneliness for a moment.

Mrs. Butterfield looked away, but not before Charlea saw tears glistening in the older woman's eyes. She cleared her throat and said, "I'm happy for Charlea. You seem to be a fine man and I'm glad to know it." She patted Charlea's hand. "She's needed someone for a long time." She fumbled in her pocket for a tissue and finding one, wiped her eyes.

The three of them sat in silence while Mrs. Butterfield pulled herself together.

"So what should I tell Mr. Woodson when he calls me? He asked me to find out what was going on and report back to him. We need a good story that he'll believe. I'm sure we can come up with something."

A knowing look passed between Charlea and David. Now that Mrs. Butterfield had become a double agent, she could keep them informed on what Mr. Woodson was doing. The advantage would be theirs. But first, they had to devise a story to keep him at bay.

Chapter 18

In her little kitchen over the next hour, they concocted a story about how Mrs. Butterfield heard Charlea and David arguing and that David had left in a huff after Charlea said that she never wanted to see him again. That might give Mr. Woodson incentive to leave her alone. To give credibility to the story in case Leon was watching, David would storm out the front door of the apartment house when he left and Charlea would slam it after him.

While they were visiting, Charlea asked Mrs. Butterfield if she had known Dr. Williams and his family.

Mrs. Butterfield sat back in her chair and looked thoughtfully into the past. "Yes, I remember him. He was totally devoted to the townspeople and doctored all of us at one time or another. His wife was a strange woman who kept to herself most of the time and wasn't very sociable. She was totally devoted to their children, even when they were older."

"What happened to them?"

She frowned. "A lot of tragedy is associated with that family. They lost their home in a fire, but they rebuilt a lovely house, the large one out on the end of Sherwood Street."

Charlea and David exchanged glances. That house must be the one they were looking for.

"They say a workman died while building the house and that it's now cursed. The curse must have been true because later they lost their two sons in a car accident. I think one had just come back from the war in Europe. I suppose it's better to die at home than on the fields of war, but it's tragic either way. Their deaths tore the doctor and his wife apart. Mrs. Williams started drinking so heavily that she never got out of bed. Doc Williams died of a heart attack a year later. All that happened was just too much for him, losing his sons, his wife and her problems, and all the hospital money problems."

Charlea empathized with the wife and could understand why she started drinking. She had considered it when news of Mark had come. "What happened to Mrs. Williams?"

"She left to live with relatives. She just up and left one day. No one ever heard from her again. They say the house is still full of their stuff, but people have looted the place. They say it's haunted, that Dr. Williams and the boys still move around there."

"Who owns the house?"

Mrs. Butterfield shook her head. "I'm not sure. Perhaps the family still does, wherever they are. Or maybe it sold. Why are you interested in Dr. Williams?"

Charlea answered, "David and Roland are doing research on the old hospital building and his name came up in some of the papers we found. We were curious about him."

With that, they got up from the table and put their bowls in the sink. Charlea refused their offers to wash the dishes, saying she would do them in the morning.

As they walked into the living room, David looped their conversation back to its beginning. "Mrs. Butterfield, I am afraid to leave Charlea alone tonight. What if Leon is watching outside? Maybe I should go out and look for him."

"No, don't do that. He'll know we're on to him. I'll keep Charlea safe. She'll stay with me tonight."

Charlea jumped in. "I'm not going anywhere tonight except to bed. It's scary thinking about him being out there, but I won't let him scare me out of my home."

"I can stay here with you," Mrs. Butterfield offered.

"No! There's no need. I have my gun by my bed. I'll be fine."

David shook his head and moved to speak, but Charlea held up her hand. She was done discussing it.

Mrs. Butterfield added, "I have large rose bushes under all the windows to keep out prowlers. Her curtains will be fully closed so no one can see in. Don't you worry about her. I will keep a close eye out."

Mrs. Butterfield hugged David and he kissed her on the hand, a gesture that left her flustered. She rehearsed their plan one more time. When David left, she would watch through her window so Leon, if he was there, could see that she was paying attention to the situation. After that, she would call Mr. Woodson and give him their story.

Charlea quickly shut the door after the older woman shuffled away to her own apartment. She'd been anxious for her to leave so she could ask David about something weighing on her mind. "Did you really mean what you said a while ago, I mean, about, um, being fond of me? Or was that just an act for Mrs. Butterfield's benefit?" Her heart was pounding, but she had to know.

"I'm no actor," he said, coming closer to her, "and it was not for her benefit. It was for yours." Once again he took her face in his hands and she put her arms around his waist. "You are an amazing woman, and I really want to get to know you better." He kissed her gently. "How about one more dance before our parting argument?" He smiled at her, still holding her near.

The last record was on the turntable and Frank Sinatra crooned a slow song. Moving his hands around her waist, David pulled Charlea closer and moved around the room. She rested her head on his shoulder, smelling his shirt and feeling the warmth of his body. She could feel his muscles moving and contracting. Her back felt warm where he rubbed it as they danced.

She looked up and saw that he was looking at her. For a lover's eternity, they stared into each other's eyes, alone in the universe of their own. She willed time to slow down so she could memorize every detail and relive it all later. The song came to an end, but they kept holding each other close. Neither wanted the moment to end. Until Mark's image flashed through Charlea's mind, breaking the spell.

Pulling away, Charlea told David, "It's going to be hard to argue with you after this. Could you help me out by doing something annoying?"

"Roland thinks I'm annoying all the time."

"Seems to me that Roland is the annoying one. He's so stuck on himself. Doesn't it drive you crazy to hang around him? I mean, he's all charm and no depth."

"You're insulting my brother and my best friend! He's a deep person. You don't know him very well or you wouldn't say that." His tone was rising as well as the volume.

"You could do better. You're the sensible one, right? He's impetuous, out of control. The troublemaker. You said it yourself." She winked at David, hoping to take the scowl off his face and make him understand why she was saying these things.

It worked. The light bulb came on for David. "How dare you say such things about my brother! He came to your rescue last night and this is the thanks he gets? I think you're the one with the problem here."

"Oh yeah, he was real brave, waiting until you had things under control before he came in. He let you do all the dirty work and then tried to take credit for it."

"He got cut for you!"

"He's a gutless wonder that lives on your shirttail." Charlea opened her door and started out into the hallway. David followed her out.

"I can't believe you said that. You don't know what you're talking about, you, you old hag!"

Charlea swung around, with a glare in her eyes. This was getting a little too close to home. David smiled and winked at her, but 'old hag' was terminology that a wink of the eye would not soothe. "Old hag! How dare you call me that! You are the biggest jerk I have ever been around. I want you out of here now!"

"Don't worry! I'm going! You're on your own. Don't expect Roland or me to help when you get into trouble again."

"Don't worry, I won't. You've been nothing but trouble since you got here. Goodbye and good riddance!" She blew him a kiss before they opened the door to the apartment house. "Go or I'll call the police!"

David walked outside and turned to shake his fist at her. She slammed the door hard and leaned on it. She hoped that their performance was adequate to fool anyone watching. She gently rapped on Mrs. Butterfield's door and it was quickly opened. Charlea slipped in.

"How was that?"

"Lovely. If I didn't know better, I'd say that you two really had an argument." She looked questioningly at Charlea. "Did you?"

Charlea shook her head. "I don't like being called an old hag. That one hurt."

"I'm sure he didn't mean it." Mrs. Butterfield gestured her toward a chair. "He seems a lovely man, dear. I hope you hang on to him. You light up around him. Could it be love?"

"It's too soon for that."

"Maybe it's love at first sight."

"I don't believe in that. Love takes time to develop. You have to get to know each other and…"

Mrs. Butterfield snorted. "Nonsense. Gerald and I fell in love on our first date, and we were married for 42 years. Some people are meant to be together, and there's no use in wasting time getting to know each other. That takes a lifetime, because there are always new things to discover about each other." She sat in her chair and wistfully gazed at Gerald's photo on the coffee table. "I still miss him."

Sitting in another chair, Charlea gazed at the ceiling as if looking into heaven. "I still miss Mark. I feel guilty about how I feel when I'm with David. When Mark went off to war, I told him I'd be here for him when he got back. He never got back, and I'm still waiting."

"He rests in another place, dear. Your wait was over a long time ago. He's not coming home."

"Yes, I know, but I made a promise."

Mrs. Butterfield got up and walked over to Charlea. Putting her hand on her shoulder, she said, "Let it go. Mark is gone and it's time to move on. You've grieved long enough. Don't let any more of your life slip away. David seems like a nice man. Open your heart and see whether or not he belongs there."

Charlea took a deep breath to work up the courage to ask a sensitive question. "Mrs. Butterfield, when a woman gets older, things begin to…" The right words weren't to be found so she made hand gestures instead.

"Things get saggy, baggy, and waggy?" the older woman asked. She laughed when Charlea nodded. "Yes, they do, don't they? Not to worry, dear. If a man loves you, it won't matter. My Gerald didn't care about things like that."

"If it doesn't matter, why do so many men chase younger women? Even older men like young women. How can someone my age expect someone like David to find me attractive? In that way, I mean."

"Love is blind, Charlea. Even for that. He's not eternally young. Time weighs on him too."

Charlea took Mrs. Butterfield's hand and held it to her cheek. The elder woman was giving good advice and Charlea should listen to it. David was a wonderful man, but the sensible voice in the back of her head was warning her to take it slow and easy. "You're a dear, Mrs. Butterfield, and you're right. I'll give David a chance and see what comes. Now if you'll excuse me, it's been a long day and I'm really tired. I think I'll turn in for the night."

Both women jumped when the phone rang. They knew who it was. Evidently, Leon was watching the apartment and had called Mr. Woodson to report that David had left. Mrs. Butterfield motioned for Charlea to leave. "I know what to do and say. You go and let me handle it."

"No, I want to stay and hear what he says."

Mrs. Butterfield nodded and answered the phone from her comfortable chair. "Hello? Why no, Mr. Woodson, I'm not in bed yet. As a matter of fact, I heard that man leave just a little bit ago. He and Charlea were having quite an argument and were calling each other names. What was that?" She paused as he asked a question. "I saw him leave in his car, so I'm sure he's gone. Charlea slammed the door when he left which is how I knew he was out of the apartment house." She paused again. "Yes, I went to talk with her, but she wouldn't tell me anything. She just kept saying that he was a jerk and she never wanted to see him again." She paused. "Yes, that's what she said. I really don't think you have anything to worry about. Maybe she's come to her senses." She paused. "Yes, we can only hope that's the case." She looked at Charlea and winked. "Yes, I'll keep you informed if he ever comes around again. I'll keep a close eye on Charlea and let you know if anything changes. Good night." She hung up the phone. "He's such a jackdonkey."

Charlea laughed. "I completely agree with you. Did he say anything else?"

"Nothing that you couldn't have figured out. He hopes that you have come to your senses and that those guys will leave town tomorrow."

"Maybe our story will placate him for the time being. I must get to bed, and you have a busy day tomorrow. You'll be at the library, remember?"

"Oh my, yes, and I'll enjoy it too. I'll keep an eye on things there for you. What will you do?"

"I have errands to run and groceries to buy. Nothing strenuous. If I keep moving, Mr. Woodson won't be able to find me. If I see Leon following me, I'll call the police."

"Let me know where you are, in case something goes wrong." Mrs. Butterfield looked worried.

Charlea gave her a hug. "Of course. Don't worry about me. I'm fine. Now get some rest."

Charlea entered her own apartment just as her phone started to ring. If it was Mr. Woodson again, she would hang up on him immediately. She sat on the sofa, picked up the phone, and softly said, "Hello?"

"Everything okay?" David's voice comforted her when she realized who it was. She breathed a sigh of relief.

"Yes, it's fine. Mr. Woodson called Mrs. Butterfield right after you left. Leon must be watching from somewhere and called him. She told him the story and he apparently believed it. He's relieved that I won't be seeing you anymore. Things seem to be going according to plan."

"So what will you do tomorrow?"

"While you and Roland are at the library, I'll go to the courthouse to see who owns the old Williams house. When I find out, I'll contact the owners and get permission to go inside. If the house is the one I think it is, it's abandoned, so there shouldn't be a problem with exploring it. I'll try to be back here by lunch if you want to call me."

David sighed. "Just go to the courthouse and back, okay? I'm worried about you."

Charlea reclined on the sofa, relaxed and enjoying the conversation. "But you'll worry anyway, wherever I am."

"Yes, you're right." Charlea could hear Roland talking in the background.

"What's Roland saying?"

"Here, I'll let you talk to him." There was a pause as David let Roland have the phone.

"Hey gorgeous, did you have fun with my brother?" Roland, ever the charmer. "No, don't tell me or I'll be jealous. Tomorrow we'll finish going through the desk. Any suggestions on where else we should look?"

"I hope to have permission to enter the Williams house by afternoon. Until then, you're on your own. Just don't tear anything up without fixing it."

"Thanks, Charlea. Do you still want a cut if we find them?" He paused, waiting for an answer, but Charlea only laughed. "I'll take that as a yes. We'll discuss the percentage later. Will we see you tomorrow?"

"We'll know after I visit the courthouse. The less I'm around you right now, the better. I suppose David filled you in on Mr. Woodson."

"Yeah, the jerk is having you followed. If I catch him, I'll strangle him."

"Please! No death threats on town council members. You guys get some rest and I'll do the same."

"Right. David wants to tell you good night. Good night, Charlea. Sweet dreams." There was another pause as Roland gave the phone back to David.

"Will you sleep well tonight? No nightmares I hope."

"I have Mrs. Butterfield guarding the door for me. I have pleasant memories to relive before I fall to sleep. Sleep well yourself, and I'll talk to you tomorrow."

They said goodbye to each other. Charlea sat back on the sofa. *What a day*, she thought. *I can't go through too many like this and keep my sanity.* Getting up and going into the bathroom to get ready for bed, she looked at herself in the mirror. Her eyes were brighter, and she felt younger than she had this morning because David had made her feel that way. She loved being with him. Somehow, she would find a way to be with him tomorrow in spite of Mr. Woodson and Leon.

Finishing up, she went to her bedroom and changed into her pajamas. Pulling the covers back on her bed, she paused. She usually went to say good night to Mark, but tonight, her thoughts were of David. Maybe it was time to move on. She got into bed and lay there, thinking of the feel of David's arms around her and the feel of his lips on hers. A sweet warmth surged through her. With a smile on her face, she turned over and went to sleep.

Chapter 19

The county courthouse was in the middle of town. Its 19th century architecture distinguished it from the newer surrounding buildings. Massive oak trees shaded the lawn and provided a cool place to sit on a hot day.

Charlea found a parking spot not far from the front door. She looked around before leaving the safety of her car and then rushed through the large doors. Her steps echoed down the hallway as she walked to the records office. Giving the excuse of researching material for the museum, she asked for land ownership records.

After the lady brought her the deed book, she turned the pages until she found the address that she needed on Sherwood Street. The property had been sold to a corporation. No surprise there. A corporation she knew, so permission to enter the house was no problem. *Adonis* would find his treasure before the house was torn down to build a new housing subdivision or shopping center or some other development project.

Closing the deed book, she carried it back to the clerk for filing. Making her way back down the hallway, she saw several people staring at her, no doubt full of questions. She smiled at them and said hello, but she didn't stop to talk. Quickly glancing around for signs of Leon or Mr. Woodson, she dashed to her car, got inside, and locked the doors.

Her next stop was the grocery store because she needed a few things. She took the route past the library where she saw David's parked car. Their plan was in action. If the men found what they were looking for, that would be the end of it. If not, she was fairly certain they would find what they were looking for in the old house. Then they would go home. Her heart sank. She'd be alone again. *How*, she wondered to herself, *could I let this happen to me in such a short time? Was Mrs. Butterfield right? Have I fallen in love?*

Turning a corner, she drove into the parking lot of the grocery store. With her mind on David, she forgot to look around before she got out of the car. Inside the grocery store, children darted here and there while their mothers tried to keep them in check as they shopped. Several of the children recognized her from the library and smiled and waved at her. Their mothers grabbed their hands and led them quickly away. Their reaction upset Charlea. She wasn't the villain, but was being treated as one. She quickly gathered her groceries.

At the checkout, the sacker seemed nervous, glancing sideways at her while he bagged her things. Charlea credited it to the stories circulating around town about her. He put her bags in the cart and followed her toward the door.

"Miss Parker, can you wait a minute?" the teenaged bagger said in a troubled voice.

"Is there a problem?" she asked.

He did not look at her, but stared at his feet. Clearing his throat, he said uncertainly, "I read the story in the paper about what happened to you the other night. And—well—when I took out groceries for another customer a little bit ago," he looked up at Charlea, "I noticed Leon Reynolds sitting in a car out on the far side of the parking lot. Well, ma'am, I thought you should know."

Charlea must have paled when she heard the news. She spun around to peer out the large windows of the store.

The young man reached out to touch her shoulder as if to steady her. "Are you okay?" he asked with genuine concern.

"Yes, I'm fine," she lied. Charlea thought for a moment. "Have you seen his wife in here? Perhaps he brought her to the store?"

"No ma'am, I haven't seen her, but she might have come in while I was busy. I can go look for her, if you want."

"No, don't bother."

Looking at the young man next to her, she smiled. He was a nice young man, tall, on the verge of manhood. She really appreciated his thoughtfulness toward her. "Thank you for warning me about him. You're escorting me out to my car, right?"

The young man stood a little taller and prouder. "I'd be glad to provide protection. If he messes with you, I'll step in."

"I don't think he will. Too many witnesses. Thank you, I feel safe with you."

They walked through the door and headed for Charlea's car. She stared at Leon so he would know that she was aware of his presence. He slumped down in the seat of his rusty truck when he saw her looking. A sickening feeling enveloped her, knowing that he was following her.

The young man put the few sacks of groceries in the back seat of her car while keeping a close eye on Leon. After he put in the last bag, he opened Charlea's door for her. "Ma'am, I really think we ought to call the police and tell them about this. Do you mind? I think it would be best."

As Charlea got into her car, she nodded and said, "You're right. At least they would know about it. Can you do that for me?" She stuffed a couple of dollars in his hand. "Thanks so much for the extra service and bravery. You're a true gentleman."

He put his hands on his hips, then dropped them to his sides, fidgeting like he didn't know what to do with them. "I'll be here if you need to come back. Just ask for Alan."

"Thank you, Alan."

Alan smiled and waved at her as she drove away. She watched closely in her rearview mirror, but never saw Leon's truck follow her out of the parking lot. Taking no detours, she went straight to her apartment and parked in her reserved spot behind the building.

She looked around carefully before unlocking her car doors. Seeing no one, she got two bags of groceries out and quickly trotted to her apartment. As she went in, she wished she hadn't bought so much because there was another sack in the car. That meant one more trip outside. Seeing Leon had unnerved her so much that she dreaded leaving the security of her apartment.

Leaning against her apartment door, she summoned her courage and went out to get the last sack. She peeked outside the back door of the apartment building, and seeing no one, ran to her car. Unlocking the car door, she grabbed the last bag and ran back into the apartment building. Once in the hallway, she unlocked her apartment door and slipped inside. Her heart was pounding and her breath came in gasps as she leaned against the door.

Turning to lock the door behind her, she moved the bag to her other arm and noticed that the loaf of bread that had been in the top of the bag was gone. She clawed through the other sacks. No bread. Had she already put it away? She looked in the breadbox. Nothing. Disgust filled her as she realized she must have dropped it on her mad dash to the door.

Slumping into a kitchen chair, she argued with herself about whether she really needed the bread or not. Her morning toast was lying in the driveway, so she needed to get it. She tried to summon her courage one more time, but this time, there was no courage left in her. She would eat oatmeal instead.

Charlea shut her eyes tightly until the threat of tears subsided. She would not be made a prisoner in her own home. The bread was hers and she would go get it. Feeling calmer, she opened her eyes again and looked around her apartment. Everything was familiar and comfortable. Her heart was beginning to slow down and calmness returned. She went to the door, turned the doorknob and stepped out into the hall.

"Mrs. Ludlow?"

Charlea jumped at the sound of the man's voice behind her and spun around ready to fight. She found herself face-to-face with Mr. Calhoun, one of her apartment neighbors, who was holding her missing loaf of bread. She leaned against the wall, breathing heavily with her hand over her pounding heart.

"I'm sorry I startled you," he said, looking over his reading glasses at the end of his long nose. "Mrs. Butterfield will be mad at me for giving you such a scare. She told me to keep an eye on you. She'll kill me for giving you a heart attack." The slightly pudgy older man seemed more concerned with Mrs. Butterfield's wrath than Charlea's current physical state.

Charlea shook her head and said, "I think you've taken ten years off my life, but I won't tell if you won't." She opened her door and motioned for Mr. Calhoun to follow her in. Mr. Calhoun set down the loaf of bread on the kitchen countertop while Charlea sank onto the sofa.

"Can I ask why you were running from your car to your apartment? Were you being chased?" Mr. Calhoun timidly took a seat in her overstuffed chair. Noticing he still had his reading glasses on, he put them on top of his head.

"Just in my imagination." Mr. Calhoun looked confused so she explained, "I saw Leon Reynolds tailing me at the grocery store."

Mr. Calhoun sucked in a quick breath, indicating that he knew Charlea's story. "Is he out there now?" he asked as he got up to look out the window. He pulled back her curtains and surveyed the area.

"I don't think so, but it spooked me so bad to see him that I panicked. When I got home, I was afraid he was still following me. I hurried so fast to get in my apartment that I dropped my bread. I was working up the courage to go back outside."

"I don't blame you. After what you've been through, I'd be prone to panic as well." He pulled the curtain closed again and sat back in the chair. "Sorry to know all your business, but between the papers and Mrs. Butterfield, everyone knows what's going on. Not to mention that I've seen that gentleman coming to your apartment. Are you sure you should be seeing him?"

Charlea was not in the mood to discuss this topic again. Why didn't people mind their own business and leave her alone? The whole town wanted to butt in her private affairs and offer opinions on the matter. But rather than debate the issue, she smiled with saccharin sweetness and said, "He's a friend that needs my help with a research project. That's all there is to it."

"But the argument last night—"

"Can you do me a favor?" Charlea interrupted him to change the subject. "Would you mind going outside and see if you can spot Leon? I would feel better knowing that he's not around."

"I don't mind at all. In fact, I usually go for a walk this time of day anyway."

"I really, really appreciate your help."

"Mrs. Butterfield will check on what I did today. Now I can give her a good report."

"I'll put my groceries up and tend to some business while you're gone."

Mr. Calhoun adjusted his bowtie and ran his thumbs behind his suspenders. "What kind of research are you helping with?"

"My friend is researching historical architecture similar to our library's building. With research, one thing leads to another so he is looking at all aspects, the buildings, the people involved. Did you know Dr. Williams who worked there long ago?"

"He was my mother's doctor when I was born in the building where you work. Mother trusted no other doctor."

"So you knew him pretty well?"

"He was a hard man to get to know. He worked incessantly, was completely devoted to all his patients. I think his wife resented that. Their sons were killed in a car accident—did you know that?"

Charlea nodded.

"His wife went crazy and left him. He died not long after that."

"I read about the accident. On another note, I also read that their house burned down and he rebuilt another. Do you know where it is?"

"Yes, it's that old haunted house at the end of Sherwood Street. It's falling down. They should raze it before someone gets hurt in it."

"Did he design it?"

"Rumor was that his wife did. But I'm sure he had a hand in it. Would your friend be interested in that?"

"Yes, I think he would. He can look for similarities between the two buildings and how they were laid out."

Mr. Calhoun nodded thoughtfully. "Makes sense. So what does he plan to do with all this research?"

"Write a book." Charlea was surprised at her instantaneous spirit of cleverness. "That's usually what people do with research."

She went into the kitchen and started putting her groceries away, hoping Mr. Calhoun would get the hint that it was time for him to leave. Instead, he followed her.

"Perhaps he'll give an autographed copy to the library," he said to her as he reached in the paper bag and handed her a few grocery items to put away.

"I'd hope so. It's the least he could do after all we've done for him." She closed the refrigerator and turned to face Mr. Calhoun.

The widowed man had recently retired from the banking business, and she guessed that he was as lonely as she was. "So how is retired life?" she asked, trying to change the subject.

"Aimless. And I'm bored. I need something else to do. Nothing full time. Just something to fill a few hours a day."

"Why don't you volunteer at the library? We're always looking for someone to read to the kids in the afternoon story times. Or perhaps you would enjoy organizing things for the museum. I need help with it and can't afford to pay anyone. Aren't you a history buff?"

Mr. Calhoun seemed flattered that she remembered. "Why yes, I am. What do you need done for the museum?"

"Everything. Someone needs to sort through boxes and files and catalog what's there. We need to do that before we can organize displays. My problem is there's no funding for the museum, but I hope with cataloging items and making progress, we'll be able to persuade the city council to fund it. I've been hoping for volunteers to step up and help with it."

Mr. Calhoun thought about it a moment, then began to nod his head. "That sounds intriguing. And it would give me something meaningful to give back to the town." His demeanor took on a smile. "That was a very lucky loaf of bread I found on the sidewalk outside." He laughed and turned to go. "Charlea, seriously, if you need help with anything, please call me."

"Thanks so much, Mr. Calhoun. I appreciate it more than you know. Call me next week, and we'll get you set up at the library."

Mr. Calhoun turned toward the door. "I will. I'll take that walk now and have a look around. I'll be back in a little bit to tell you what I saw." He left, leaving Charlea alone with her groceries. She immediately went to the door and locked it. Alone at last!

Chapter 20

Mr. Calhoun reported back later that no sign of Leon was found. When he left, she turned on the radio and fixed herself a small lunch, listening to the noontime news. The news was depressing. The body count with the escalating war in Southeast Asia left her mourning with those who would get the bad news. If Mark were around, she knew he'd be sent off to that action. If it hadn't been Korea where he was lost, it might have been this war.

Not wanting to think about war with all that was going on in her life, she switched to a channel with music. The sounds soothed her and turned her thoughts to more pleasant topics. She wondered what David and Roland were doing and wondered how Bonnie was managing with Mr. Wilkerson and Mrs. Butterfield at the library. Surely they would be helpful and not a problem. As soon as Mrs. Butterfield got home, she'd go find out how things had gone.

Charlea busied herself with household chores, but she had little motivation to do it. Her mind kept returning to David so much that she got little done. She longed to hear the sound of his voice and wished he would call her.

Checking the time, Charlea suddenly remembered that she had not called for permission to enter the Williams house. She made herself comfortable on the sofa before dialing the number. A secretary answered the phone. Charlea identified herself and asked for the president of the company. After a few moments, a familiar voice came on the phone.

"Hi Sis!"

"Hello, Richard. It seems that your company owns the old Williams place here in town."

"You don't say," he said with mock surprise.

"I am calling on behalf of two researchers who want access to the building for research. May we have your permission to go into the house? Nothing will be harmed. We are just looking for information."

"Will you be accompanying the gentlemen while they look?"

"Of course. I want to see the treasure too."

Richard was silent for a moment, but Charlea could feel him smiling through the phone line.

"Permission is granted by this corporation for you and whomever you choose to enter the Williams house to do whatever research you deem necessary. You may keep anything you find." He paused for another moment to change the tone of the call. "And how are things with you? Any more trouble?"

Charlea relayed what had transpired since she had talked to him last night, about the phone call from Mr. Woodson, seeing Leon at the grocery store, and Mr. Calhoun helping her out. They spent a while on the phone, talking of what Charlea needed to do if more trouble arose. Richard once again said he would come to help, but she refused to hear of it. As long as David was around, she felt safe. Once he and Roland left, the threat would be over.

They talked more, just small talk between siblings. After they hung up, she felt better. All her business had been taken care of and she could tell David and Roland that they had permission to go to the Williams house. The final piece was in place.

She was wishing David would call and tell her how things were at the library when the phone rang. An increasingly familiar twinge of fear went through her. That fear made her hesitate until the third ring before she picked it up. "Hello," she said timidly.

"Charlea, it's David. Are you okay? You sound funny."

Charlea felt her heart skip a beat at the sound of his voice. "I'm still a little nervous about answering the phone."

"Any trouble today?" Charlea could hear the concern in his voice and it thrilled her to know it was there.

"Not much. I went to the grocery store and saw Leon sitting in his truck in the parking lot. He didn't follow me home or make any move to contact me. Mr. Calhoun, my neighbor, checked around the neighborhood to make sure he was nowhere around. And the coast was clear."

"That's good to know."

"Have you and Roland found anything this morning? How did things go? Any trouble there?"

David laughed. "One thing at a time. Roland and I looked through the office thoroughly and found nothing. We moved everything back to where we found it. Mr. Woodson came in about mid-morning and poked around some, talked to Bonnie for a little while, and then went his way without too much fuss."

"I guess he was making sure things were going smoothly. Did she tell him to leave her alone?"

"Not that I heard. They just talked and he left."

Charlea rubbed her forehead. Bonnie apparently knew how to get along with that man better than she did and that bothered her. What were Bonnie and Mr. Woodson planning? How Bonnie would take over after Mr. Woodson had her fired for embezzlement? Charlea shook her head, refusing to believe that Bonnie would do that to her. "Anything else?"

"Mrs. Butterfield flirted with Roland, which was really funny to watch. Mr. Wilkerson was talking to everyone who came in the door. I think he was having the time of his life."

Charlea laughed again. The library patrons were getting his larger-than-life treatment.

"They may want you to be gone more often," David said with a smile in his voice.

"I wouldn't doubt it. Does this mean that my job is threatened?"

"No, not at all. Lots of people asked about you and were told that you decided to take some time off. People care about you and miss you. What did you find out about the old Williams house?"

"A corporation owns it. I talked with the president of the company and we have permission to enter the house and poke around. I told him we would not harm anything."

"And he didn't ask more questions about what we're looking for?"

"None at all. He didn't seem concerned. Perhaps he has too much on his mind to think much about it. Or he knows it's an old fire trap with nothing in it. Either way, he said yes. We'll go in, get our business done and leave. Should be simple."

"Should be, but nothing up to now has been simple. Shall we go out there this afternoon? It's still early and I think Roland is anxious to get out there."

"We might as well. Shall I meet you out there?"

"We'll pick you up since we don't know how to get there."

"But we're not supposed to be seen together."

"The place is probably deserted so no one will see us. We could pick you up in the alley behind the apartment house. No one will see us."

Charlea mulled it over. "I guess that will work. Please make sure that you're not followed by anyone. What time will you get here?"

"Roland and I can be there in about 15 minutes. Can you be ready that quickly?"

"Yes, I think so. See you then." Charlea hung up and proceeded to get ready. She slipped into a pair of slacks and a blouse. She grabbed a larger shirt to wear over the other one to hide her revolver that she'd strapped to her waist. She hoped not to use it at all, and she really hoped that David and Roland wouldn't ask if she was carrying it. They wouldn't be happy about it, but she didn't care.

She decided not to carry her purse, so she put her driver's license and a little money in her pocket and stuffed a small switchblade in her bra. They wouldn't ask about that and she certainly wouldn't let them know it was there. She ran a brush through her hair and put a scarf on to keep it out of her face.

"Bye, Mark," she said as she sped by his photo on the wall. "Wish me luck." She left the radio on to suggest to her neighbors that she was home. She quietly opened the door and looked around before stepping out. Sneaking down the hallway, she slipped out the back door. She didn't see David's car, so she stood behind a lilac bush where she'd be hidden from view. Before long, she saw his car turn down the alley so she stepped out from the bush into view. David pulled up beside her and Roland got out to let her in. She slid across the front seat next to David and Roland quickly got back in. Speeding away, they left the alley and turned onto the street.

"You're looking gorgeous again today," Roland said as he put his arm around her, just like the last time they had ridden together in David's car. The gesture brought a dirty look from David, but Roland didn't move it.

Hoping to get David's attention switched to something else, she inquired, "You weren't followed, were you?"

"I'm sure we're not being followed," David said. "We took the back streets where there were few cars to watch." Looking back in his mirror, he added, "And I don't see anyone around now. Let's stop worrying and enjoy the afternoon."

"Let's do," Charlea said. She felt like she could relax a little and enjoy the moment, sitting in the car between two handsome men.

The radio was tuned to a station that played the new long-hair rock and roll. A Beach Boys song came on and she began to keep beat to the music, surprised that she found the music appealing. Her mood was catching and soon David and Roland were keeping beat to the song as well. When Roland began singing along, she knew who set the radio to that station.

While they drove across town, Charlea pointed out where David needed to turn. They kept mainly to the residential areas to avoid the chance of being spotted on main thoroughfares. The trip was a little longer, but none of them were eager for the ride to end. With the music and laughter, she forgot to give directions.

"Oh no! We missed a turn." They were headed out of town, going the wrong direction. You need to turn around and go back the other way. Take the first left and go east for a couple of miles."

A little further down the road, there was a wide spot. David exclaimed as they approached it, "Watch this!" He spun the steering wheel and the car took a hard turn, throwing Charlea against Roland. She landed against his chest, face to face with him. The inertia pressed her body and her face against his. Her mouth was almost against his. Her heart pounded as she felt his breath on her face and realized he was going to kiss her. Just as his lips touched hers, she felt a hand grab the back of her collar and yank her away.

"Sorry about that," David said as he let go of her collar. "I should have given you more warning to brace yourself." He had not noticed that his brother had almost kissed her.

"You were lucky this time, David," Roland said. "I caught Charlea before she went flying out of the car."

Charlea kept looking at Roland who smiled and winked at her. She glared at him, making it clear that she did not want him to say any more. Disappointed at not finishing the kiss, she was glad at the same time. She had no time for a triangular love affair.

"Thanks for that, buddy," David told Roland. "I'd hate to lose the only one in the car who knows where we're going. That's the first left, you said, Charlea?"

"Right."

"Huh?"

Charlea felt nervous sitting between them. She loved David. The thought surprised her. *How could I love someone I've known only one day?* she wondered. *The feeling isn't logical. How can I love David and yet be attracted to Roland? Surely it's not true love, just infatuation. No matter. Enjoy the moment.* She let the warm, pleasant feeling David created permeate her heart like soothing hot chocolate on a cold winter day.

Roland bumped her arm and pulled her out of her fantasy. She glanced at his handsome face. He was so charming that any woman—young, old, married, or single--would be attracted to him. What I feel for him, she reasoned, was hot and lusty. The feel of his lips touching hers, his closeness, warmed her blood like an electric shock.

She turned to look at Roland and then at David again. They were both singing along with a Beatles song, oblivious to her inner turmoil. She would die of embarrassment if either one of them could read her mind. She would definitely have to go to church on Sunday and pray about it.

Sunday. The day after tomorrow. They would be gone and her life would return to normal. A pang of regret filled her. Pushing it away, she reminded herself that right now, in this moment, she was the luckiest woman in the world, sitting between these two extraordinary gentlemen on a lovely day. She laughed out loud and beat the song's tempo on the dashboard.

Chapter 21

They drove past new housing developments that were gradually replacing the farms. At the end of a long narrow lane, in a small pasture on the edge of town, sat the target of their search, a two-story dilapidated house, dreary and gray. The paint had long since flaked off and the windows were either gone or boarded up. From the looks of it, the stories of it being haunted were true.

David turned off the radio as they drove up the overgrown driveway. Grass scraped the bottom of the car as they went along. Upon reaching the house, he turned off the motor, and they sat in silence staring at the old house. Charlea shuddered involuntarily. David reached for her hand and squeezed it.

"What are we waiting for? Let's go!" Roland got out of the car and headed toward the house.

"You might want to be careful on that old porch," Charlea called out after him as David helped her from the car. "The boards might be rotted and break under your weight."

Roland paused momentarily, surveying the porch. He tested the boards with each step and looked back at them and smiled. "Seems sturdy enough. Come on!" He was like a little boy, excited to explore new territory and search for treasure. The front door opened after he gave it a shove. Charlea and David came up behind him as he went inside.

Immediately the smell of dust and mold hit them. They stepped into a large foyer that had a staircase across from the door. To their right was a large room, probably the living room. Broken pieces of furniture, coated with thick layers of dust, were strewn around. Charlea shrunk up against David after she spotted spider webs hanging around the room. Spiders terrified her and she hated being anywhere near them. David looked at her questioningly, but didn't speak. He put his arm around her and led her further into the dusty room.

"Where should we start looking?" Roland was already prowling around the room, looking for clues to hidden spaces. He picked up a loose board and used it to poke various points on the wall and around the fireplace.

Trying to forget about the spiders she felt were creeping nearer, Charlea replied, "I don't think it's in here. He'd have wanted someplace more private and didn't have much traffic. A home office perhaps. David, let's you and I see what the main floor rooms look like. Roland, why don't you go see what's upstairs?"

Roland stared at her, irritation plain on his face. "Do you always take charge of things?"

"Yes, I do. Why?" Charlea smiled at Roland and, not waiting for him to answer the question, left the foyer with David behind her.

Charlea and David went down a hall to push another door open and peer inside. This smaller room was completely empty, giving no hint of what it was previously used for. A broken window let in the afternoon sunlight where it shown on faded carpet flooring. The wood paneling had bent nails sticking out of it. Walking around the edges of the room, David quickly surveyed the walls for any indication of a loose panel or crack that might lead to a hidden compartment. Finding none, he turned back to Charlea who was still keeping a sharp eye out for spiders.

"Ready to look in another room?"

Charlea nodded and hurried back into the foyer. They saw Roland's footprints on the staircase and could hear him walking around upstairs. At least she hoped it was his footsteps they heard. She stayed close behind David, hanging on to his shirt. They went into what was obviously a dining room. The top of a large table was sitting on the floor and a broken chair was pushed against one wall. Looking through another door, they found the kitchen.

While David looked around the dining room, Charlea went into the kitchen. The cabinets had their doors ripped off, exposing bare shelves with mouse droppings in them. To the left, there was another door. Making her way slowly over to it, Charlea gingerly opened the door, hoping nothing jumped out at her. The door creaked when it opened, revealing a large pantry. She heard the scurrying of mice as they scrambled to find cover.

"See anything?"

Charlea jumped and let out a short scream. Completely unnerved, Charlea spun around to face David, her eyes glaring. "Don't do that!"

"What? I didn't mean to scare you. I thought you heard me."

Charlea leaned against the wall of the kitchen. Suddenly realizing what she was doing, she jumped back quickly, repulsed by the filthy surroundings. As she brushed her clothes off, she told him, "Just give me a little warning. Find anything in the dining room?"

"Nope. What about here?"

"I don't think a man would have a hiding place in the kitchen. In Dr, Williams' day, the kitchen was a woman's domain, not a man's. The stones must be somewhere else."

They went back into the foyer. Roland was making his way down the staircase, looking at the walls and steps as he came.

"Find anything?"

"No. You?"

"Just a bunch of bedrooms. The master bedroom is easy to spot, but I didn't see anything there."

Charlea reiterated, "I wouldn't expect a hiding place to be in the bedroom. It would be too risky. Someone might find it inadvertently."

"You seem to have all the theories. What next, boss?" Roland was eyeing Charlea, waiting her instructions. David crossed his arms and leaned against the wall supporting the staircase. They heard a creak and the wall gave way a little, revealing a small camouflaged door that opened under the staircase.

"I think we should concentrate our efforts there," Charlea said smugly, pointing at the door. Roland shook his head as he came down the rest of the stairs to join them. David pushed the door a little further but it did not open enough for them to enter. Roland joined him and both men pushed on the door. It wouldn't open any wider and there was no light to see inside.

"Don't we have a flashlight in the trunk of the car?" Roland asked David.

"I think so. Should one of us go get it?"

"Why don't you? I'll get this door open while you get the flashlight. Besides, you have the car keys."

"I'll give you the keys. I think it's in the trunk in the tool box."

"Since you know where it is, you go."

"I found the door. You go get it."

"You go. It's my letter."

At the end of her patience, Charlea put an end to the argument. "I'll go! Give me the keys and I'll find the flashlight. Don't find the treasure without me here. I want to protect my cut."

"Don't argue with her, David. Just do it." Roland was acting like he was scared of Charlea. David pulled out the car keys and she grabbed them, leaving the guys to pry at the door.

Walking into the sunlight and fresh air, Charlea was glad she'd volunteered to get the flashlight. The old house depressed her. Perhaps it was the reputation of the house being haunted. Or it was the story of the workman who died that made it an unhappy place. Whatever the case, she felt like an intruder inside a house that wanted to be left alone.

Opening the car's trunk, Charlea rummaged around until she found the flashlight. She looked at the neighborhood around her. The lot surrounding the house was covered with tall grasses and shrubs. The trees along the edge of the lot were in dire need of pruning. Trash was strewed across the yard. Neglect was evident all around.

As she walked back to the house, she could hear the guys talking, but she couldn't make out their words. She couldn't resist the opportunity to hear what they talked about when she wasn't around. Partly out of curiosity and partly out of sneakiness, she stepped quietly across the porch to eavesdrop, stopping out of sight.

"She's definitely not your type," Charlea heard David say. "You prefer young, firm, sexy women. She's a librarian, Roland! Hand me that board so we can get some leverage on this door." She heard Roland's footsteps as he walked a few steps, stopped, then walked back to where David was still working on the door.

"I know, but this old girl's got some spunk. And courage too. Most women her age wouldn't have handled the attack that well."

Old girl! Charlea thought. *Women her age!* She was no spring chicken, but she certainly wasn't an old girl! She felt her anger level start to rise.

"She's too old for you," David said out of breath from prying the door. "Wrinkled, soft, starting to gray. Remember what you said when we got here? That librarians are frumpy and—what was it?—frigid. Frumpy and frigid. That's definitely not your type." The sound of grunting drifted out to the porch where she stood. "Can you get your hand behind the door to see if something is blocking it?"

Charlea had to put her hand over her mouth to keep from crying out. David's words hurt her to the core.

"The old girl's not your type either. You wouldn't like someone who is frumpy and frigid any more than I would," Roland replied. "But I guess when you've been single for so long, you'll take any woman who shows some interest. Right?"

Charlea flinched. A loud cracking noise echoed through the empty house as they worked on the door. She heard more straining and crackling as wood splintered.

"I'm the oldest," David said. "Why don't you back off and let me take care of her. I don't mind older women." A pause passed between them. "There's got to be something behind this door that's blocking it."

"I can't see or feel anything."

She heard the sound of more grunting and cracking wood as they exerted force against the door.

"Why should I let you take care of the old girl?"

Charlea's anger spiked as she heard that phrase again. Not only was she mad that Roland would refer to her in such a way, but she was mad at David for not reprimanding him for using it.

David's voice interrupted her thoughts. "Because I don't trust you with her. You're too cold with the ones you discard. You'd hurt her feelings. That would break her heart. And her heart might not be able to handle it."

"I am not cold."

"Yes, you are. I've seen it many times." A loud crack gave the sign of success. "Hey, I can feel something against the door. I think I can reach it and move it a little." The sound of manly straining drifted outside like the sound of fingernails on a blackboard. "I think we've got it! Where's Charlea with that flashlight?"

Hearing her name, Charlea stepped quietly back down the porch. Her heart ached from the hurtful words spoken and the anger they caused. She wiped the tears running down her face as she got to the edge of the porch. Old girl! Frigid and frumpy! Charlea chided herself for being a fool, for believing all of David's endearing words to her last night. *Mr. Woodson was right after all*, she thought, *David and Roland are using me to find the stones. As soon as they have them, they will be on their way, laughing at me for being such a sap.* She couldn't wait until they found what they were looking for and got out of her life. She hated them both!

"Charlea? Is there a problem?" David had walked up behind her. Not wanting him to see her tear-reddened eyes, she continued to stare out into the surrounding bushes. *Yes!* She shouted silently in her mind. *There's a problem! You and Roland are no good, shallow, deceitful, lying jerks!* Feeling the car keys in her hand, she thought about driving off in the car, leaving both of them here. They deserved it. She was so filled with hurt and disappointment that her only thought was to get away from them as quickly as possible. But at the last second, she changed her mind.

Charlea didn't turn to look at David, but spoke in a whisper to him over her shoulder. "I thought I saw someone over there, but I can't be sure. There's too many hiding places in the bushes."

David took her by the shoulders and guided her to the front door. "Get inside and stay there until we have a look around. Roland! Charlea thought she saw somebody out here. Let's go have a look around."

Roland popped out of the front door, looking concerned. Both men walked down the front porch scanning the surrounding areas for signs of movement. Charlea went inside the foyer, but stayed by the door. She didn't like being in the old house by herself. Too spooky to be comfortable here.

Then she remembered the treasure and curiosity took over. Walking to the little door under the stairs, she pushed on it and shined the flashlight inside. Shelves and a jumble of items were illuminated, but all Charlea could see were the myriad of spider webs around everything. She jumped back and turned off the flashlight.

"All we found was a dog prowling around," Roland said, stepping inside the door. "That's probably what you saw. Let's keep our fingers crossed that we'll find the stones so we can get out of here." He took the flashlight out of her hand and walked over to the little door.

David turned Charlea to face him and hugged her. "Are you all right? You seem so jumpy." He pulled back and looked at her closely, but she kept her head down. He genuinely seemed concerned.

Still hurting from what she had overheard, Charlea smiled faintly. "Yes, yes, I'm fine. Why don't you help Roland? I'll keep an eye out." She pushed him away and turned toward the front door to keep watch.

Roland had the flashlight shining on something behind the little door. "Wow! Come look at this, David. It looks like bootleg in here. One of these kegs fell against the door and that's why we couldn't get in. The old doc must have been a boozer! Or needed a little extra cash on the side."

David crowded inside the small room behind Roland and chuckled. Curiosity turned Charlea around and she went to peer into the dark room beneath the stairs. In the glow of the flashlight, she saw several small wooden barrels and a host of bottles scattered around. A barrel must have fallen against the door, blocking it until Roland moved it out of the way. Tucked inside some of the wine racks were papers and small books. Forgetting about the spider webs, Charlea reached inside the wine rack and pulled some of them out. The room was too dark to read in, so she took the books out to the foyer to read them in adequate lighting.

The books appeared to be ledgers of household expenses and the papers were letters to Dr. Williams. The museum would be the perfect place to archive these documents. Richard wouldn't mind her taking them to include in the museum collection. She could also report the day's events to him.

"Hey! Look at this! I think this is it!" The excitement in Roland's voice resonated throughout the house. "I think this is it!" He let out a yell that shook the shutters.

"Quiet down or the whole county will know we're here!" David was obviously excited about it as well. "What did you find? Let me see."

Charlea put down the papers and books and rushed to the doorway. The men were huddled together, looking at something. Charlea stood on her tiptoes to peer over their shoulders, and saw that they indeed had found what they were looking for. In Roland's hand was a pile of sparkling gemstones of all colors.

Charlea gasped at the sight of the beautiful stones. "So they really did hide a treasure." She looked at both men and smiled. "And you found it!"

Even in the meager light, the gems twinkled brightly, casting colorful stars around the small room. They counted three diamonds, three emeralds, two rubies, two topaz, and four amethysts. Some large stones and some small. Glistening in the beam of the flashlight. Roland poured them back into a small leather bag and put it in his pants pocket. They stepped out on the porch and brushed off their clothes. The sun was getting low in the sky.

"Do you think anyone heard Roland shouting?" Charlea asked. In the distance, a dog perked up his ears, looked at them, then trotted off. Nothing else within earshot could be seen.

"No one seems to have heard," David said. "Come on; let's get out of here."

Charlea stood on the porch and watched the two men as they walked out to the car, talking and laughing, slapping congratulations on their backs. Dread and anger filled her. They paid no mind to her. They'd completed their mission and no longer needed her. The end of the adventure had arrived. *Who*, she wondered, *would be the one to—how did David put it?—take care of me?* She decided to make it easy for them.

"I suppose you'll be going home now," she called out to them. "Don't worry about me. I can deal with Mr. Woodson and Leon. I'm not afraid of them. I'll be fine..." Her voice trailed off as the lump in her throat choked it off.

The men turned and gave her a puzzled look.

"What?" David asked.

With effort, she swallowed the lump in her throat. "I said don't worry about me. I can take care of myself. It will be nice to have things back to normal after you're gone. Roland, you really must control that mouth of yours. I'd hate for you to cause this much trouble for someone else."

Roland's jaw fell open, stunned by the sudden attack. "You can't blame all that on me!"

"Yes, she can!" David added as he came to her defense. "She's right. Your big mouth got us—no, got her into this mess with Leon and that jerk Woodson."

"I never said anything to him about the stones."

"But," Charlea argued, "he heard you talking to David about it! I saw the two of you talking at the bar that night. Leon overheard you. Mr. Woodson was there that night too. My life was peaceful until then and now it's...it's chaotic. Leon is stalking me and Mr. Woodson is after me constantly."

"That's not true! Besides, Woodson wasn't near the bar. How did he find out?" Roland pointed at Charlea. "She told him. She's setting us up. She wants the stones for herself. I bet she has told them where we're staying so we'll get robbed. Or—"

"Me? Setting you up? That's absurd. Why would I have myself harassed for a handful of gemstones?"

"It's so clear to me now. You're a librarian. You crave excitement and attention from men, something you only read about in books. You found an easy way to get it. You want our treasure so you can buy yourself a man somewhere."

Charlea was furious. "You're the ones who came into my library, pretending not to know each other. You're the ones who tried to deceive me from the beginning. You used me to get what you want, then will throw me away like a used rag." Her heart's distress poured out, and she couldn't hold it back any more. "You two have brought me nothing but trouble. Go home and leave me alone!" The moment the words spilled out, she regretted saying them.

Roland was speechless.

"Do you really feel that way?" David asked dejectedly.

Charlea opened her mouth to answer, but no words came out. She had saved them the trouble of dumping her.

David spoke softly. "We'll leave first thing in the morning." He took a step toward the car, then turned back. "I know what it is. It's the stones! They are making us say things we don't mean. The love of money is truly the root of all evil. So let's all calm down. Roland and I will take you out for supper tonight and celebrate the success of our mission. We couldn't have done it without you."

The calm tone of his voice dissolved her anger. Another lump was forming in her throat, but she managed to speak before it got too large. She wanted to shout, "No!" But—and she couldn't explain it to herself—she wasn't ready to let them leave her life. Yet. But after hearing what they had said, they couldn't leave fast enough. The conflicting emotions tossed inside her. "Sure. I guess so."

David nodded. "Shall we go?"

"I want to get the papers and the ledgers I found in that room." Charlea went back into the house and picked them up. Looking around her, she couldn't help wondering what the walls would say if they could talk. Once there was a happy family in this place. Tragedy and heartaches had torn them apart. Now it had torn her and David apart. All that was left was dust and faded memories. The house was as empty as her heart felt. Maybe it was really cursed. She shuddered as something cold had brushed past her. Quickly, she turned and went back outside.

"Let's get out of here," she said as she walked quickly past Roland and David. They followed her to the car. Getting in, David started the car, turned it around, and started down the rough driveway.

Chapter 22

"We never decided what your cut is, Charlea," Roland whispered across the booth in the dimly lit restaurant. The waiter had just left with their orders. "Should we discuss it now?"

"Here?" David asked, whispering as well. "I think the topic would best be handled in other, more private places." He looked to Charlea to support the idea. She nodded.

Roland looked at the nearby tables. The restaurant was not crowded, and no one was sitting near them. Most important of all, there was no sign of Leon or Mr. Woodson.

"No one will hear us here."

"Let's not take the chance," Charlea said. "I don't want anything else to happen before you leave. I guess we can go back to my apartment after dinner and discuss it there. I have ice cream in the freezer." The men agreed.

Roland lifted his glass. "Here's to a great partnership, the three of us," he saluted David and Charlea with his glass. "And to our ability to find what we are looking for." Roland cheerfully clinked his glass against David's. They turned to look at her. Not wanting to bring talk about how she was feeling, Charlea picked her glass up and toasted the others.

"Will you miss us when we're gone?" Roland asked Charlea.

She wasn't sure what to say to him. In spite of how much they had hurt her feelings, she would miss them after they left. Her loneliness would overwhelm her and she'd be left talking to a picture on the wall. But the afternoon's overheard conversation left her unsure whether to reveal her true emotions to them or keep them hidden. She really wasn't sure what those emotions were. Love and disgust were all mixed together. Chaos. That's what it was.

"It's been one of the oddest few days I've ever experienced. I suppose life will return to normal after you leave." She smiled at them, but then looked away so they could not read the emotions on her face.

David seemed uncomfortable. "Look, I'm sorry we've caused so much trouble. It was never our intent to cause you any pain or hurt." Roland squirmed in his seat, but didn't interrupt David.

"I thought...I mean..." David sighed. "You called us your heroes. We've been through a lot together. I really like you. I was hoping we could keep in touch." He took her hand in his. "I thought we had something special."

It was Charlea's turn to squirm in her seat. They'd called her an old girl, frumpy and frigid and she couldn't forget about that. She didn't want to give them the satisfaction of knowing she'd fallen for one of them—no, both of them. She tried hard to act indifferent, but it was increasingly difficult to do so. Still averting her eyes, she concentrated on David's warm hand closed around hers. They were waiting for her reply. Much to her relief, the waiter brought their salads and she was given a few more moments to think of what to say.

"I suppose there is a bond between us, like rescuers and victims have. We should keep in touch. I would really like that." She took a big bite of her salad, signaling that she was through talking.

David looked dejected and it broke Charlea's heart to see the hurt in his eyes. Perhaps she'd been wrong about him and he really cared for her. She looked at Roland who was looking at David with something like pity in his eyes. He just shook his head and began eating his salad. Charlea fumbled with her salad, separating the ingredients into piles on her plate. She desperately wanted to change the subject. The silence at the table was almost too much to bear.

"I wonder how it went at the library this afternoon," Charlea said, forcing cheer into her voice.

"I'm sure it went well," David said between bites. "Mrs. Butterfield would make sure everyone stayed in line."

Silence fell over the table again. The waiter came by and picked up their empty salad plates. Charlea felt very uncomfortable, not being able to say what she was feeling. She looked down at her hands, wishing the time would pass quickly and she could hide at home. The waiter brought their entrees and they began to eat.

"This is ridiculous," Roland burst out, laying down his fork. "Charlea, do you have any feelings at all for David? He needs to know because he's crazy about you." He leaned closer to her. "Or could it be that you're in love with me instead?" He looked closely at her, a twinkle in his eye, searching for the slightest response.

Charlea rolled her eyes in disgust at his narcissism.

"Roland, you talk too much," David spat out at him. "Don't put her on the spot like this. It's none of your business."

"No, it's time for the truth to come out," Roland said. "We don't have much time left, and it's time she made a choice." Turning back to Charlea, he asked, "So who is it? Him or me?"

Charlea looked from one man to the other. "I have no feelings for either one of you, other than friendship."

"You're a liar."

"Roland!" David cried out, but then was embarrassed by drawing too much attention to their table. The men took a few bites, attempting to blend in with everyone else. Minutes passed while they ate and hoped people would go on with their business.

Roland finally broke the silence and the tension. "Let me rephrase that. I don't believe you." He turned to David and asked, "Better?"

"Only a little. Charlea, this afternoon we were having a great time, singing in the car, looking through the house, excited about finding the you-know-what. Then all of a sudden you started giving us the cold shoulder. We want to know what's going on." He leaned closer and whispered, "Is it about your cut of the stuff?"

"No!" Both men were waiting for more, but Charlea was in no mood to discuss the issue.

David grew impatient. "I thought you were a person who says what's on her mind. And frankly, before I go home, I want to know what I've done or what Roland's done to turn you into this, this tight-lipped—"

"Watch it," Roland warned.

David took a deep breath and nodded at Roland. "Charlea, what's wrong?"

Charlea knew there was no way out, and she'd have to admit that she'd eavesdropped on their conversation. She took a deep breath and began. She told them how she stood out on the front porch listening to them while they tried to open the door to the secret room. Choking back the tears, she repeated what she'd heard them say and how it made her feel old and used. Once the floodgates opened, she poured out all that was in her broken heart.

David looked at Roland. "We said that?"

Roland groaned. "I remember part of it. We were just messing around."

Charlea's anger immediately flared up. Embarrassed over revealing her deepest feelings and the lack of apology on their part left her infuriated. She wanted to throw her plate across the table at Roland and dump her drink on David. She fought the impulse to get up and leave.

"Gee, Charlea," David said, "I had no idea you were listening. You misunderstood what we were saying. It's not nice to eavesdrop, you know."

"So now it's my fault?" Charlea asked angrily.

"No, that's not what I'm saying," David said trying to calm her down. "I meant that you didn't hear everything. You heard things out of context." He looked to Roland for help, but Roland was so amused by this confrontation that he was no use to David.

"You called me an old girl who is frumpy and frigid. What's to misunderstand about those descriptions?"

"Charlea," Roland said, "it sounds like to me that you're a little sensitive about how old you are. Am I right?"

"I heard you talking about dumping me because I was so old, so useless, so past...everything." Her voice broke as she choked back tears. Her worst fear was happening; she did not want them to see her cry. Grabbing her napkin to daub her wet eyes, she shook her head and said, "I'm fine, so don't even ask."

"Charlea, darling," David began as he reached for her hand. She yanked it away. He and Roland exchanged glances, then began to smile at each other.

"How dare you two laugh at me," she snarled. She scooted around the side of the booth. "Let me out! I've never met two more calloused men in my life. Move!"

"No," David said, "I'm not going to let you leave this way." Neither man would let her out of the booth.

"I know when I'm being laughed at."

"We're not laughing at you." David looked at her tenderly, but she looked away. "Give us a chance to explain. Let us have that much more of your time. Please. It's not what you think." David suddenly seemed a little nervous. "You see, both Roland and I are crazy about you. We really are."

"I don't believe you." Charlea looked from one to the other. They both looked at her and nodded. She rolled her eyes and moved again to leave. Roland grabbed her arm and held her in her seat.

"It's true," Roland said. "It's been that way from the first time we met you. You turned me down and went out with David. You broke my heart."

"You're telling me that you were attracted to a 40-something year old woman? I find that hard to believe. You're like 'Adonis.' You can have any woman you choose."

David moaned. "Please don't call him that."

Roland shot David a dirty look, but continued with Charlea. "I was attracted to your beautiful eyes. After spending time with you at the library, I found the rest of you attractive too, so I asked you out. That wasn't part of our plan, but I wanted to be with you, and I was hurt when you told me no. I'm not used to hearing that from a woman." He stuck his lip out pouting.

"I bet you don't hear 'no' very often."

He laughed. "True. I've never had trouble getting dates. Now David, on the other hand, doesn't date much. I decided to be noble and let him have you. I figure when you're tired of him, it'll be my turn."

"You're taking for granted that I will get tired of David and that I'd go out with you afterwards. You are also taking for granted that I would let it go beyond this point anyway. So your plans for me are full of holes."

"Maybe. Maybe not. I know you have feelings for David and I know you're attracted to me. Don't shake your head. You can't deny it because I know it's true."

Charlea's face reddened. "You are full of yourself," she said.

"You're not the first one to tell me that."

Charlea couldn't pull her eyes away from Roland. He picked up her hand and kissed it very tenderly. David immediately cleared his throat.

"Roland, back off! I let you run off with the last one, but I won't let you do it again. Charlea, I'm so sorry for what we said this afternoon. It was dumb of us to talk that way. Please, forgive me and say you care for me." He took her other hand and kissed it tenderly.

Overwhelmed, Charlea pulled both of her hands back. "Knock it off, you two! Finish your supper." She cut a slice of her steak and ate it. Both men followed her example. She swallowed and asked David, "What do you mean you let him run off with the last one?"

The two guys focused on their plates, eating much faster than normal. Charlea kept staring at David, waiting for an answer. He sighed and set his fork down. "Remember when I told you that I was left standing at the altar? When my fiancée ran off with my best man?" Charlea nodded. "Roland was my best man. He's the one who ran off with her."

"Him? He ran off with the woman you loved? And you don't hate him for that?"

Roland explained, "His girlfriend was after me the whole time they were dating. She would find any excuse she could to be alone with me. I told David about it, but he was in love with her and didn't believe me. Oh, she liked him well enough, because he had a good job that would provide her with status and the material things she craved. But she couldn't keep her hands off me. On the day of the wedding, David was in the next room when she found me and tried to seduce me...again. I left with her to save him from making a huge mistake." Judging from David's pained silence, Charlea knew that the episode still hurt.

"What happened then?" Charlea asked.

"I dumped her off at her apartment and told her to get lost. She hurt my brother, so I didn't want her either. She was a waste of female flesh."

David finally spoke up. "I was grateful that he showed me the truth. I was headed for a miserable fall. I was deeply in love with her and I thought she loved me. Instead, she made a fool out of me and I resented that. I was determined to never feel that kind of hurt again."

"You're a very special woman, Charlea," Roland said. "You're the first woman he's trusted with his heart since then. That's why I decided to let him have the first chance with you."

The story melted Charlea's heart. In some ways, David led as lonesome a life as hers. She stared at him for a bit, admiring the handsome line of his face. He was cultured, well mannered, and considerate of others. What kind of woman would turn away from that? His fiancée must have had rocks in her head, Charlea thought. A strong longing swept over her, washing her away from any doubts she had earlier. The feel of his arms around her, his lips on hers as her heart beat faster...

David interrupted her thoughts. "So do you believe us now? You have stolen both of our hearts. What you heard this afternoon was two brothers fighting over the same woman, each trying to discourage the other. It was childish of us and hurtful to you. I apologize for what we said."

Charlea took his hand this time. "I don't know what to say."

"Just say you like me. I'll settle for that...for now."

Charlea smiled and squeezed his hand tighter. "I really like you, David." She leaned over and gave him a kiss on the cheek.

"Ah, love," Roland said. "I'm not only Adonis, I'm Cupid too."

Charlea laughed at his egotistical view of himself. "Let's finish our dinner and get out of here. We are drawing too much attention to ourselves."

They glanced around at several sets of eyes on them. Charlea saw no sign of Leon or Mr. Woodson, but there was an unexpected face in the bar watching them. "Have them put my leftovers in a box please. I need to visit the ladies room." David let her slide out of the booth and she headed toward the back of the restaurant. Looking back to make sure the two men couldn't see her, she slipped into a dark corner.

"Pat, what are you doing here? Where's Richard?" Charlea asked. Pat was Richard's employee and best friend, who often ran important errands or conducted business affairs in Richard's place. Charlea liked Pat because he was honest and straight forward with her.

Pat set down his hardly touched drink. "Nice to see you too, Charlea. Richard's at your apartment."

"He's where? Why is he there?" Charlea was frantic. "He said he'd give me until tomorrow afternoon to get this straightened out. Please, call him and tell him to get out. We're going there and I want him gone by the time we arrive. If they find out he's here, it will ruin everything!"

"Richard's worried about you and he wanted to make sure you were safe. He received troubling information about this Woodson guy. Turns out he's a very dangerous man."

"How can that be? He's on the city council and a respected businessman in town."

"He's also a hopeless gambler up to his eyeballs in debt. He has some tough scoundrels after him to pay up or else. He may be after the stones to pay off those debts."

"But he doesn't know they exist for sure."

"He's desperate enough to take the chance that they do."

The puzzle fell into place. Mr. Woodson wanted the stones to save his own skin. No wonder Mr. Woodson had taken such an interest in Leon lately. If Leon followed Charlea, he might find out where the stones were. If Mr. Woodson wanted the stones that badly, he'd stop at nothing to get them. David and Roland must get out of town as quickly as possible.

"Where are you and Richard staying?"

"At the Towers Hotel."

"Good. Roland and David are staying elsewhere. Tell Richard to stay out of sight until they leave in the morning. Until then, don't let anything happen to them. Do you understand?"

"What about you?"

"I'll lock myself in my apartment. With Mrs. Butterfield guarding the front door, I'll be safe enough. After they start home, tell Richard to come over and we'll talk."

"He won't be happy with that plan."

"It doesn't matter. I don't want them finding out who I am. They won't understand why I didn't tell them. Please don't ruin this. Please, Pat, convince Richard to stay out of sight."

"I'll try, but don't be surprised if he does what he wants to."

"He usually does, but I think everything will turn out for the best if he just stays low. The main thing is to make sure my new friends don't get hurt."

"Whatever you think." Pat looked around. "People are getting suspicious. You'd better go."

Charlea shook his hand. "Talk to you later." She turned to go and ran into David and Roland. "I'm ready. Let's go." She hurried away without introducing them to Pat.

"Who was that you were talking to?" David asked after they got outside.

"He is a contributor to the museum. I intended to call him about some financial matters, but hadn't done so yet. I thought it was a good time to ask him about it." Charlea felt a twinge of guilt as the lie came out.

"You never seem to stop working."

"I take advantage of opportunities as they come up. Shall we go to my apartment for ice cream?" Charlea nervously looked around the parking lot before stepping away from the safety of the restaurant's front door. She saw nothing unusual, but nevertheless hurried to David's car. The two men stuck close to her side.

"We made it without trouble," Roland commented as David unlocked the car doors.

"Let's get out of here."

David tossed Roland the keys. "You drive this time," he said. He held the door for Charlea who slid across the seat to the middle. David got in beside her, put his arm around her, and drew her near. As he kissed her softly, Roland turned up the radio and began singing along with the songs. He tried to be inconspicuous.

"Keep an eye out for someone following us," Charlea said to Roland. "See anyone?" She turned around in the seat to look out the back window.

"No, I don't," Roland said, eyeing the rearview mirror. "Should there be? Do you know something we don't?"

"I'm paranoid, I guess." Charlea didn't want to alarm them, but she wondered if she should tell them what she knew about Mr. Woodson. If she did, she'd have to tell how she found out and that would spoil their fun together. No, she'd risk keeping them in the dark since Pat and Richard would be watching their backs. The less David and Roland knew, the better.

"You seem nervous," David remarked.

"I never thanked you," Charlea began, "for saving me the other night. You could have run, but you stayed to help. Thank you for risking your safety for me."

"Running off was never an option. We're not that kind of men."

"I know you're not. I didn't mean to imply…"

"You're welcome," David said. "If it happened again, we'd do the same thing. Will you be all right after we leave? I hate to leave you with Woodson still after you, but I think he will leave you alone after we're gone. Our presence seems to be what is setting him off."

Charlea forced a laugh. "Don't worry about me. Between Mrs. Butterfield, Mr. Wilkerson, and Bonnie, there will be no trouble. I only need time between me and this strange week. After that, everything will be back to normal. And Mr. Woodson will have other things to pursue."

Chapter 23

Arriving at the apartment, Roland parked the car and they got out. Movement in Mrs. Butterfield's curtains betrayed her spying as they strode up the walkway together. When David waved, the small part between the curtains quickly disappeared. She was standing in her doorway when they walked in the door.

"Charlea, can I talk with you privately for a moment?" the older woman asked.

"Yes, but let me put my purse away." Charlea hurried down the hall, leaving the men to visit with Mrs. Butterfield. Unlocking her apartment door, she prayed that Richard was gone. Not seeing his hat on the sofa, she knew the coast was clear. Breathing a sigh of relief, she left the door open for the men.

Charlea went back down the hallway. Mrs. Butterfield bid the men good-bye, then took Charlea by the arm, pulled her inside her apartment, and shut the door.

"Your brother was here looking for you. He looked worried. What's going on? And don't give me no stories."

Charlea sighed and sat on the arm of Mrs. Butterfield's tattered chair. "Yes, I know he's here. He heard about the trouble and decided to come check on me. It's nothing, really. He's worried the same way you are and came to see for himself. After Roland and David go home, I'll enjoy visiting with him in person rather than over the phone."

"Don't you want him to meet David and Roland?"

"Not right now. I will later on."

"Well, I for one am glad he's here. I feel better knowing your family is watching out for you. You take too many chances, Charlea. You need to be more sensible."

Charlea stood and started toward the door. The door handle was in her hand before she remembered. "I haven't had a chance to talk to you about your day at the library. Did you enjoy it?"

Mrs. Butterfield immediately broke into a grin. "Oh yes, I had a wonderful time being there and seeing everyone. Mr. Wilkerson keeps everyone entertained with all his stories. He read to the kids and they loved him."

"That's great! I'll have to keep him in mind for story time in the future." Charlea hated to ask, but she had to know. "Did Mr. Woodson come around at all?"

"Yes, he was there twice. He and Bonnie went in your office to talk, but I don't know what about. Bonnie wouldn't tell me."

A secret meeting? About what? The budget? Bonnie didn't know anything about that. "How long did he stay?"

"An hour the first time. The second time, he stayed for half an hour or so. He and Bonnie went upstairs for a little while, then he left in a hurry."

"Did they have words?"

"No, I never heard them argue."

"That's strange. I didn't think she liked him. What business would they have together?"

"I'm not sure. She seemed troubled. Maybe he upset her."

"If he did, I'll deal with him on Monday. Until then, I have visitors to entertain." Charlea turned the door handle to leave, but Mrs. Butterfield called her back. The elder woman took Charlea's hand and squeezed it.

"Charlea, those are nice men and I know you like them, but please be cautious."

Charlea straightened the watch on her wrist. Defending David and Roland was getting tiring, but she didn't want to speak in anger to the lady who cared so much for her. "They are really nice gentlemen and we've had lots of fun together. Their company has been a nice change of pace for me. They are leaving in the morning. Roland has to go back to work tomorrow night. After they're gone, no one will need to worry anymore."

Mrs. Butterfield patted Charlea's arm in a motherly way. "And none too soon. Still, if you need help handling them, you call me. I have my bat here by the door."

Charlea smiled and nodded. "I'll remember that." Charlea hugged Mrs. Butterfield and left. She hurried down the hall to her apartment where she found David in the kitchen dishing up ice cream and Roland putting records on the stereo.

"I hope you don't mind us making ourselves at home. We started the party without you," David said from the kitchen.

"Of course not," Charlea replied smiling. "Sorry it took a little longer than expected."

"What did the old bitty want?" Roland asked coming into the room. "Did she offer you her bat to keep us in line?"

"Yes, she did, but I turned down the offer. I can always go back and get it. Do you think I'll need it?"

"We'll behave ourselves," David said, coming into the room. "Here, have some ice cream before it melts." David handed her a bowl, then one to Roland.

As they sat around the kitchen table, Roland talked about going back to work at the restaurant until he found out how much the gems were worth. The appraisal would determine his future actions.

David stopped Roland before he could go on. "Before we start divvying up the stones, are we sure we can keep the stones? Technically, we found them on someone else's property. Doesn't that mean the stones belong to them? I'm not a thief and don't want to be accused of being one."

"Finders keepers!" Roland slammed his fist on the table. "They're ours!"

Charlea patted Roland's fist and tried to unclench it. "You will have to trust me on this one. The property is owned by a corporation that intends to tear down the house. We rescued the stones from destruction. They are yours to keep. You won't be labeled a thief."

David shook his head in doubt. "But are you sure about that? It doesn't seem right."

"I'm certain. The treasure is yours. No doubt about it." Charlea smiled and took another bite of ice cream.

Roland let out a laugh of victory. "One thing is for sure, I'm going to get my own place. A nice apartment would be good. An ex-wife wouldn't get the apartment in a divorce."

"What's my cut?" David asked. "I should get at least one third of them."

"I'm the guy who just lost everything in a divorce settlement. I need it more than you do."

David chuckled. "Love, for you, has been expensive."

"Love's not expensive. It's the death of love that's expensive."

"Death of love?" Charlea asked. "Why do they say that true love never dies?"

"Maybe true love never dies," Roland replied, "but the regular kind does. At least that's been my experience."

"That's nonsense. Love is love and it doesn't die. Maybe what you experienced wasn't love."

Roland shrugged and took another bite.

David finished his ice cream, then said, "You need to find the right woman, not just *any* woman. I'm waiting for the right woman and she will cost a lot less than several of the wrong ones."

"Advice from a lonely old man with nothing but his job to keep him happy."

David growled. "How did we get on this subject? Let's change it."

"Can we talk about your share of the cut?" Roland asked Charlea, following David's stated desire. "I need to know how nice of an apartment to get." He pulled the small bag out of his pocket and poured out the gems. They sparkled in the kitchen light as they rolled across the table. The beauty of the stones with their rainbow colors was breathtaking. They picked up individual stones and held them up to the light, delighting in each one.

"I don't want a cut. You can have them all," Charlea announced.

"You can't be serious," Roland said disbelieving. "I was fooling around when I said I didn't want to share them. Look, there're fourteen stones. You helped find them. At least take two or three."

"Thanks, but no. They're all yours." She pushed them away from her.

"Why?"

Charlea pushed back from the table and folded her arms. "I don't want them. I have a nice apartment and live quite comfortably. I'm sure you'll put them to good use. Just remember to sell them to a reputable dealer and not some fly-by-night outfit. And don't sell them all in one place. You'll get more if you spread them out."

"How do you know?"

"I read."

Both guys seemed satisfied with her answer. Together, they put the stones back into the bag after holding each one up to the light once more. Roland tied the top closed and stuffed them back into his pocket.

"If I were you, David," Charlea said, "I wouldn't let Roland out of my sight. Or have him divide the stones between you before he gets his own apartment. Otherwise, you might never see him again."

"I'd hunt him down like a dog. I'm not like you. I want my share!"

"Come on, old girl, let's dance," Roland said. Charlea shot him a fiery look, but he ignored it. He grabbed her and pulled her close, swung her around and pulled her close again. He spun her out and she ended up in David's arms.

"May I cut in?" he whispered in her ear. "He's trying to steal you away from me again."

Charlea laughed. She had no intention of resisting the flirtation of either man. Charlea danced with David, then Roland. Only two days had passed since she met them, yet so much had transpired to bond them together as friends. Two days that had changed her. But, as with all things, time passed and brought with it what she had been dreading. The hour was late and they must go. Heaviness weighed her heart down as they got ready to leave.

"You have my phone number, right?" Charlea tried to keep a cheerful demeanor. Standing near the door, she fidgeted with her blouse, smoothed her hair, wrung her hands, and shifted her feet to keep from showing her unease. That lump in her throat was trying to get bigger and she was fighting it.

"Yes, and your address. I promise, I'll stay in touch," Roland reassured her. But she was looking at David. And he was looking at her.

Roland kissed Charlea on the cheek. He made her heart skip a beat and butterflies fluttered in her stomach. She wished he didn't have that distracting effect on her.

Roland touched the side of her face with his hand to get her full attention. "Charlea, you are an amazing woman. Don't let anyone ever make you believe otherwise." He kissed her other cheek. Turning, he winked at David and said, "I'll wait in the car, but don't hurry." He left, closing the door softly behind him.

David pulled Charlea to him and lifted her face to his. He kissed her gently at first, them more earnestly. She wanted to remember this moment. How his lips felt against hers, his taste, his smell, and the warmth of his body. She moved her hands across his back to hold him as close as she could. She made it a vivid memory so she could relive it, feel it, taste it and smell it over and over again. She never wanted this moment to end, but time stops for no one, no matter how badly she wished it.

She pulled away from him. They stared at each other for a long time, not saying anything. David touched her face and a tear trickled from her eye. He gently wiped it away.

"I will miss you," she said quietly. "It will be lonely around here without you. I..."

"It's not good-bye, Charlea. I'll be back and I hope you'll come to see me too. We're more than friends, aren't we?" He looked at her earnestly. "Please say we are."

"Yes, we are."

He smiled at her. "Good. I should go. It's late and we're leaving early. I'll call you when we get home."

"Please do."

He kissed her softly and turned to go. With a glance back, he pulled the door shut behind him. Charlea went to the door and leaned on it, trying to feel his presence on the other side. Being with David had reminded her of how long it had been since she'd been loved by a man. She stood there for a long time, hoping he would come back to her. His knock never came and, sighing, she turned away. The burden of loneliness was upon her and it felt like the weight of the world. She took Mark's picture off the wall and held it against her chest. Walking to the sofa, she threw herself on it as the tears came. Her quiet sobs echoed around the empty room.

After her tears and despair emptied out, she put Mark's picture on the other end of the sofa. His twinkling eyes stared out at her. He seemed so close that she could imagine him sitting there. He would tease her about crying so much lately. *Get a hold of yourself*, he would say. *You don't like the way things are going? Take charge and change it.*

"You're right, Mark. Things need to change. If you came home right now, I'd love you as much as the day you left. I will always love you, but, after all these years, I found someone else to love. He reminds me of you in many ways. I feel at home with him, just like I felt with you. Would you mind if I found someone else? Would it hurt you? I would never want to hurt you."

The phone rang, interrupting her conversation. Maybe it's David. Maybe he missed her too much to wait until tomorrow.

"Hello," she said, expecting his warm voice to respond.

"Charlea, this is Bonnie."

"Bonnie? Is something wrong? I was just about to crawl into bed."

"I'm sorry to bother you, but there's a problem at the library. One of the water pipes broke and books are getting wet. Can you come and help clean up?"

"When did this happen? What happened?"

"Milt happened to stop by and found the leak. He called me first, but I can't handle it alone. I'm sorry to call so late, but we need to save these books."

"Yes, of course, I'll be right down."

"Thanks, Charlea. I've unlocked the back door so park back there. I'll leave the back light on."

Charlea hung Mark's picture back on the wall and hurried into the bedroom to change into a blouse and slacks. Tired from the long day, she was not looking forward to cleaning the mess up tonight. She thought of Leon and Mr. Woodson and put her small revolver in a holster that fit in the small of her back under her shirt. As an additional precaution, she put a knife in her bra. She grabbed her purse and left her apartment.

Chapter 24

Pulling up behind the library, Charlea saw that Bonnie had left the light on like she had said. Cautiously, she looked around before getting out of her car and slipping inside. The familiarity of the surroundings put her at ease. No lights were on, except for the one shining from her office door. The floor was dry and all the books were in place. No sounds of water dripping. Alarms began to go off in her head.

"Bonnie," Charlea called out, "are you here? What's going on?"

"I'm in your office, Charlea."

Charlea slowly made her way toward the door and looked in. Bonnie was sitting behind her desk, nervously tapping a pencil on the desk.

"Bonnie, I don't understand. Where's the water?"

"Charlea, I—" Bonnie looked at something behind Charlea and then looked down as if she was ashamed of something.

"Perhaps I can explain."

Charlea recognized the evil voice. Mr. Woodson. Adrenaline immediately shot through her body. For a moment she was terror-stricken, but she quickly regained control. Spinning around, she stood up straight and squared her jaw.

"What are you doing here? Do city councilmen help dry books out?"

"It was a false alarm. I needed to see you here alone to discuss city business without any distractions." Mr. Woodson walked around Charlea to her desk and picked up the ledger with her budget work in it. Somehow, he had retrieved it from her locked file cabinet. "After close examination of your work, I find that you've been skimming library funds for yourself. The city—more importantly, the law—takes a dim view of those who use public money for their own profit."

"That's a lie! I've done no such thing!"

"I expected you to say that. Criminals always deny their wrongdoings. Books are easily altered. Anyone as intelligent as you can fix them to hide things from honest people." He picked up the pencil that Bonnie had been tapping, erased an entry and changed several numbers. "It's not that hard to do. A few changes here or there and the money goes where you want it to." He stood up and crossed his arms. "Very convenient."

Charlea glared at him. "You're lying. I'm not doing it. You are! You're the one doing the skimming since you seem to know so much about it. Paying off your gambling debts, Mr. Woodson?"

He stiffened slightly as if the words stung him a little.

Charlea continued for Bonnie's benefit. "You've been stealing city money and want to frame me for it. No wonder you were so eager to get a look at this year's budget proposal. You needed to work out how much more you could take without drawing attention to yourself."

Mr. Woodson turned to Bonnie who was still sitting behind Charlea's desk. "Bonnie, she's wrong so don't listen to her. Thank you for your assistance with this matter. The city will reward you for reporting the financial discrepancies at the library. And you will be in line to head this institution after Charlea is dismissed. I'm sure your family will appreciate your new status and larger paycheck."

"But sir, I didn't..."

"No matter. You've done what I needed you to do."

Bonnie looked from Mr. Woodson to Charlea, clearly not knowing exactly how to react or what to do. "What you needed me to do?"

Mr. Woodson's eyes narrowed. "You brought Charlea to me. Now we can set things right."

Bonnie picked up the phone and dialed zero. Mr. Woodson grabbed the phone and slammed the receiver down with such violence that Bonnie jumped up from the desk. "What are you doing?"

"You said we would call the police when she got here."

"Plans change, sweetheart."

Bonnie opened her mouth to say something, but changed her mind. Her shoulders stooped, hinting at her shame for betraying her friend. "Charlea, I—"

"He's an evil man, Bonnie." Charlea glared at Mr. Woodson. "Go ahead and take the library money. We'll give you a six hour start before we call the police. Just go."

Mr. Woodson laughed. "My business here is not finished yet. I'll go when I'm good and ready."

"Fine. Stay here if you want. Bonnie and I will be leaving." Charlea motioned for Bonnie to join her and they tried to push their way past Mr. Woodson, but he shoved Charlea back toward the desk.

The shadow of a large man filled the doorway which made Bonnie stop abruptly. The smell of liquor wafted through the room. Mr. Woodson's accomplice, Leon, had arrived.

Charlea was profoundly afraid, and she nearly jerked out her gun right then, but Bonnie was in the way. Her hand froze with indecision. She decided to bluff. Maybe if he thought she wasn't intimidated, he'd let her go. "What's really going on here? You know I haven't been fixing the books, and it would be extremely hard to prove so in a court of law."

Mr. Woodson walked behind her desk and sat down. He looked pleased with himself as his plan came together. "Charlea, do you know that the curtains in your living room don't come completely together? That someone looking through the small parting can see your kitchen table? And that earlier tonight, at your kitchen table, there was a pile of gemstones worth a great deal of money?" He waited to see what kind of reaction Charlea had.

Bonnie gasped, turning to look at Charlea.

Show nothing, Charlea thought to herself. *He's looking for a reaction. Don't give him what he wants.*

Not getting a reaction from her, Mr. Woodson continued. "It seems that you and your two new friends have been treasure hunting and actually found one. How much of it did they leave for you?"

Bonnie spoke softly with wide eyes, "There really was a treasure? You lied about it?"

Charlea said nothing. She would not give Mr. Woodson the satisfaction of drawing a reply or defend herself from Bonnie's accusation.

"From what was seen through the window, you didn't get anything. You let them have it all. You surprise me, Charlea. I know what you make here and it's not that much. Why didn't you take some of them?"

It was becoming increasingly difficult for her to keep her composure around this monster. If he intended to hurt her, she had the revolver and the knife. If she had a few seconds, she could reach her revolver, but from where Mr. Woodson and Leon were, either one could get to her if she went for it and use it against her. She needed to put more space between them.

"We're leaving now. Leon, move!" Charlea turned and pushed Bonnie ahead of her. Leon pushed both of them back. Mr. Woodson stood up and leaned against the side of Charlea's desk.

"You're not going anywhere! Don't you want to hear the rest?" He looked at her with evil eyes, intent on controlling Charlea. "You don't need those stones, do you? I've done some of my own digging and guess what I found out? Seems the librarian in our little town is really an heiress to one of the largest fortunes in the country."

Charlea looked quickly away. Her secret had been discovered and he would no doubt use it against her. She didn't need to look at Bonnie to feel her disbelieving gaze.

Mr. Woodson crossed his arms. "I thought about ransoming you for the gemstones, but I can't take a chance on how much those losers value your friendship. Maybe they wouldn't think you were worth it." He had a lecher's smile. "Maybe, if you'd let them in your bed, they might be willing to give them up. But I know you. You're too straight laced for that."

Charlea slapped his devilish face, hard, with the strength of a woman that wasn't going to take it anymore.

Fire flared in his eyes as he raised his arm to strike her with the back of his hand. For a long instant, he stood there with his hand raised. He looked beyond her and seemed to relax a little before he sat in her chair and put his feet on the desk. He pulled a cigar out of his pocket and lit it.

The urge to flee overwhelmed Charlea. She grabbed Bonnie with one arm and tried to push Leon aside with the other. Bonnie pushed on Leon too. Between the two of them, they made Leon stumble backwards. He grabbed Bonnie's head and slammed it against the door frame. Bonnie fell to the floor in a heap. Charlea dove to catch her, but Leon grabbed her hair with one hand and the other held her around her waist, holding her tightly so that she was helpless.

"Remember, Charlea?" Leon jerked on her hair so hard it felt like it was being pulled out. "You called me a liar. Now we know that you're the liar. You'll pay for that." Leon pulled out a knife and held it to her throat again. "This time there's no one here to help you.

You carrying a gun again? It was strapped to your thigh the last time."

Mr. Woodson got up and came around the desk. "I'll look for it," he said.

Having this monster touch her was so repulsive that Charlea let out a scream and struggled to break free. She shoved Mr. Woodson backwards with her foot, slamming him against the file cabinet behind him. She tried to loosen Leon's grip. Leon quickly moved his hand to cover her mouth and she felt the knife cut into her skin. A hot trickle of blood slid down her neck onto her blouse. The sensation convinced her to quit struggling. Her opportunity to escape may come later.

"If she resists, cut her more," Mr. Woodson said, standing and rubbing the back of his head. He continued to feel her thighs, then moved his hands up her body. When he felt the revolver in the small of her back, he laughed with delight.

"Ah, here it is." He pulled it out and put it into his suit coat pocket. "That's better. No miraculous escapes this time." He leaned against her desk. "And now, I must insist that you come with us. You're a valuable commodity and I need you to get money from your brother. I can double my profit. Get the gemstones and a ransom. You're worth a lot to your brother and his pockets are deep. And odds are he'll pay it to keep you alive. I've got nothing to lose at this point."

He took a handkerchief out of his pocket and wiped the blood that was running down her neck. "This ought to convince him that I'm serious about it. I'll send it to your brother and tell him there'll be more bloodshed unless he pays." He turned away to find an envelope for the stained handkerchief.

"By the way," he said over his shoulder, "do your boyfriends know that your brother is the one that planted those gems? That he has so much money that he finds men he thinks his sister will like and lures them in your direction with the promise of hidden treasure? I'm sure they'll be interested in knowing that they were played for fools to entertain you for a few days."

Charlea, through her terror, felt her heart drop. How did he find out about that? David and Roland would never forgive her for what Richard had done. She had nothing to do with it. Richard had set it up and she'd played along. They were proud men, and this insult would be too much for them to forgive. This revelation would be the end of her relationship with them. Her body began to shake in response to the flood of emotions that ran through her. She struggled, but to no avail.

Mr. Woodson seemed delighted to know that he was breaking her down. He tsked and walked closer. "You've been a bad girl, Charlea. They'll drop you like a hot potato. You'll never see them again." He looked at her, up and down, like a piece of meat. "What about me? I can show you a good time, for the right amount of money." He tittered as he said that and anger welled up in Charlea.

"So what do you have to say?" He motioned for Leon to take his hand away from her mouth. Leon moved his hand from her face to her hair, where he grabbed it tightly. "Come now, Charlea," Mr. Woodson railed at her, "you and me. Want to give it a try?"

She spat at Mr. Woodson. "Never!"

Mr. Woodson wiped her spit from his face. "You'll run with those two losers and not me? You'll regret it."

"Leave David and Roland out of it. And let Bonnie go. I know about your gambling debts, you creep. If it's money you want, then I'll get you money. But leave all of them alone!"

"Leave them out of the fun? Not a chance! I need them. You stole library funds to pay for a couple of gigolos from Dallas. The papers will have a field day with it. An old maid librarian with secret desires found a way to fulfill them at the taxpayer's expense. The accusations will be the end of you and them." He shook his head. He enjoyed his power over her.

Mr. Woodson walked over to her and said in her face, "You see, I hate you as much as you hate me, but I need you. You have everything I want. Money. I don't understand what makes someone walk away from wealth and power to live a useless life in a small town."

His cigar-tainted breath was so bad, Charlea almost gagged. She kicked out at him to make him step back. "I live here because I make a difference. Satisfaction is not found in how much you have, but in how much you give. But you wouldn't understand that. You're too greedy to think of anything beyond your own desires."

Mr. Woodson feigned a tear, then laughed in her face. "How touching and noble! Such self-sacrifice! You're right about one thing. I don't understand. Those with money don't understand what it's like to live without it." She shoved him, but the man barely moved a step backwards, grinning at her feeble efforts. Furious, she lashed out with her foot again, connecting in the man's stomach. He doubled over, his breath whooshing out all at once and he staggered backwards to fall against the desk, gasping in shock. He held up his hand to strike her, but stopped.

The hate in his eyes was piercing, and she knew that he would hurt her any way he could. Leon pulled her hair so hard that she cried out.

Woodson walked over to her desk and pulled out a cloth and a bottle. He poured liquid from the bottle onto the cloth. "You seem restless, Charlea. Maybe a little nap will help you relax. I need to call your brother so he can start getting my money together."

Richard! He was not home so Mr. Woodson would not be able to reach him. Charlea thought of him in the hotel just a few miles away, unaware of what was happening to her. Why hadn't she taken the time to call him before she left her apartment? No one knew where she was and wouldn't miss her until tomorrow. A lot could happen to her before then.

Behind her, Leon snickered and held her head back, holding tightly on her hair so she could not move her head. Mr. Woodson held the cloth tightly over her mouth and nose so that she could not breathe except through the cloth. She fought him as hard as she could when she realized the odor as chloroform. Not knowing what they intended to do to her while she was unconscious brought on a new wave of fear. She struggled harder against Leon, but could not break his hold. As darkness swept over her, she heard their evil laughing echoing through her office. She went limp and fell to the floor.

Chapter 25

The fog clouding Charlea's mind slowly began to dissipate. *Why am I sleeping on my stomach?* she thought. *I never sleep on my stomach.* A chill filled her and made her shudder as she slowly regained consciousness. The pain in her joints and her head made her wish she was unconscious again. Her eyelids felt like lead weights, but she managed to open one a little. To her surprise, she was laying on a floor. In the dim lighting, she saw something scurry across the floor on the other side of the room. Her head jerked up when she thought it was a large spider, but the movement made her dizzy, so she closed her eyes and put her head down again.

Where am I, she wondered. She moved her legs and hit something. Opening her eyes just enough to see, she found the leg of a desk inches from her face. *I must be in my office,* she thought and closed her eyes again.

Thick dust on the floor stirred with her breath and entered her nose. She sneezed, causing dust to fly into the air over her face. When she tried to wipe the dust away, she discovered that her hands were tied behind her back. She rolled on her side as much as she could to get out of the dust. She sneezed again. Still groggy from the chloroform, she lay still, trying to remember why she was there and why she felt compelled to be quiet.

There's not this much dust in my office. I must be upstairs in the museum.

Gradually, the horrors of the night came flooding back. Mr. Woodson, Leon, their threats, her kidnapping. Was it still nighttime? How long had she been here? Was it an hour, two, or had it been days?

Get out! Get out! screamed her inner voice. *They may come for you. Get out!*

She struggled in vain against her bonds until her wrists were badly bruised and she was exhausted. Tears filled her eyes and dripped off her face into the dust on the floor. As panic threatened to overcome her, she tried to calm herself so she could formulate a plan for getting out of this situation.

Her eyes were adjusting to the dim lighting. The desk she'd kicked was in a small office, but she didn't recognize the setting. It didn't matter. She needed to get out of here. The sudden kick of adrenaline empowered her and she struggled to sit up. The desire to lie down and sleep was almost overwhelming, but a gnawing fear kept her upright. Getting her knees under her, she sat on the dirty floor, too dizzy to stand. Slowly, she made it to her feet and leaned against the desk, her knees wobbling slightly. Gradually, her mind cleared and her nerves steadied.

She remembered seeing Bonnie lying in a heap on the floor. *Where is she now? Is she all right? Is she here or back in the library?*

"Bonnie?" Charlea whispered into the emptiness. She looked around, but saw no one else in the small space.

Across from the desk was a door that led to…where? Away from here, but would it open up on Mr. Woodson and Leon? She had to take the chance. *Lord, help me get out of this and I won't play Richard's game ever again. And please let Bonnie be okay wherever she is.* Charlea slowly walked to the door and leaned against it. Backing her hands to the knob, she turned it and heard the push-in lock come out with a click. She paused a moment to see if the soft sound alerted her adversaries. Hearing nothing, she turned the knob and opened the door. A slight smile stirred across her face. Only Leon would lock her in a room that unlocked from inside. He was all brute with no brains.

She peered out into what appeared to be a warehouse. The only warehouses around the town were beside the train tracks, away from the residential and business areas of town. She was being held in a place that was relatively isolated, the only witnesses to a crime being the rats and vagabonds who happened to be wandering by.

No one knew where she was—except maybe Bonnie, and Bonnie had helped put her in this predicament. She was on her own to find a way out. The first order of business was to free her hands. Her knife was tucked away in her bra—at least they hadn't thought to search there!—but with her hands tied behind her, she could not reach it. She had to find something else sharp to cut the ropes.

Large wooden crates surrounded her and kept her from seeing whatever was beyond them. She heard movement nearby, but it didn't seem to be footsteps. Spiders! Or rats! Fear intensified her struggles as she realized it might be rats moving around the crates.

She hated rats almost as much as spiders. They were probably everywhere. Once again, panic overtook her.

Her steps were wobbly and she almost fell. Leaning against a crate, she let the room quit spinning before trying a few more steps. She staggered along the row of crates, looking for anything that would cut ropes. Gradually her steps became steadier and the fog dissipated in her head. Occasionally, she paused to listen for Leon or Mr. Woodson. They were facing charges of assault and battery, not to mention life in prison for kidnapping and extortion. Mr. Woodson would stop at nothing to get his hands on as much money as he dared ask for. He must be in real trouble with whomever he owed gambling money to go to such lengths to repay them. Was he capable of murder? Charlea pushed it out of her mind so she could focus her attention on getting out. They would look for her as soon as they discovered she'd escaped. Time was short.

Charlea peered around the corners of the crates and strained to hear every sound in the building. She crept along the line of crates, staying in the shadows to hide. Pausing, she heard an unusual sound coming from the other side of a line of crates. The sounds were of someone struggling. She didn't know whether to find out what the noise was or to go the other direction. With her limited options, she decided to find out if the sound came from friend or foe. If it was a friend, then she could get help to get out of here and call the police. If the sounds came from Leon or Mr. Woodson, she would get out of there as quickly and quietly as possible. She had to take the risk.

Moving silently, she crept closer to the sound until they were directly on the other side of the crates. She heard a man's groans as he struggled against something. The person seemed to be stationary and none of the sounds were conversational. If it were Leon or Mr. Woodson, surely they would be free to move around and speak as they wanted.

Her heart pounded in her ears, blocking out other sounds. Charlea slowly peeked around a corner of the crate, then drew in her breath quickly. A man was there, with his hands bound behind him around a pole that held up a staircase leading to a second level of the warehouse. The sounds she heard were his struggles to free himself. His shirt was torn and sweaty and his hair hung into his eyes. When he cursed, the voice was familiar. As he struggled to break free of his bonds, his face came into view. It was Roland!

What was he doing here? Mr. Woodson's must have called them about the gemstones. He must have tried to contact Richard as well, but Richard was away. Would he be contented with only the gemstones? Probably not. He wanted Richard's money too. His greed was the driving force pushing him to get all that he could possibly get. That fact made him more dangerous.

Charlea slowly stepped around the corner of the crate, but stayed in the shadows, surveying the area. If Roland was here, where was David? Roland seemed to be alone, but it could be a trap. He would warn her if it was. No matter. He was a welcome sight, although he was in the same predicament she was in. Seeing no one else around, Charlea stepped out so he could see her. His relief was evidenced by his broad grin. She ran up to him and leaned against him in an armless hug.

"Charlea! You're here! Are you okay? Did they hurt you?" A look of horror crossed his face. "You're covered with dirt! They didn't..." He paused, unable to bring himself to say it.

Charlea shook her head. "No, I am—unmolested, if that's what you're thinking." His statement brought back the memory of Mr. Woodson running his hands across her body looking for weapons.

"I'll kill them if they touched you!"

She shushed Roland and whispered, "Keep your voice down! I don't want them to know I'm awake." She looked around nervously, listening for the sound of approaching steps. Hearing nothing, she asked, "What's going on? Where are we? And why are you here? Where's David? Mr. Woodson told me he was going to let you two go."

"We're at a warehouse that Woodson owns. The area is deserted so we'll have trouble getting help from close by." He shook his head and sighed. "He called us and told us he'd trade you for the stones. When we came to make the trade, I came in first to see if I could negotiate a deal for you. David was supposed to look for you while I kept them occupied. I guess he didn't find you. Woodson was furious because David and I didn't come together. We must have messed up his plans." He was suddenly angry. "How did they get you? We left you safe in your apartment. What happened?"

"Bonnie helped them lure me to the library under false pretenses. Mr. Woodson and Leon were there. They knocked me out with chloroform and I woke up here a little while ago."

"Bonnie helped them? I thought she was your friend?"

"He used her against me and then hurt her when she tried to leave. She was unconscious the last time I saw her in my office. Have you seen her tonight?" Tears burned her eyes when Roland shook his head. She turned to the side so he couldn't see her face.

Roland gasped. "Is that blood? Did that brute cut you? I'll kill him!" Roland struggled harder against his bonds.

"Save your strength. Yes, he cut me, but we'll deal with him later. Where's David now? Is he bringing the police?"

"I'm not sure. He was supposed to get you out. I haven't seen him since I left him outside."

"Didn't one of you call the police?"

"Yes, right after Woodson called us. But they acted like they didn't believe us. They wanted us to come to the station for questioning. Woodson only gave us one hour to give them the stones or he would hurt you. That didn't leave time for questioning so we came here. We had to save you."

"You don't think David would try a rescue by himself, do you? Surely when he couldn't find me, he would leave to call the police again." Charlea looked at Roland, seeking reassurance that this situation would end peacefully. Mr. Woodson had told her that he had nothing to lose. He didn't. And he would do anything to get what he wanted.

"I hope he did," Roland replied. That wasn't the answer Charlea wanted to hear. "In the meantime, we need to find a way out of here. These ropes are so tight that my hands are numb and I can't feel very much. Can you try to untie the knot?"

She walked behind him to see how tightly he was tied. His hands were starting to swell and the ropes were cutting into his wrists. Turning so she could feel the ropes with her fingers, she did her best to loosen the knots. In the dark and with her own bonds restricting her wrists, she had no success.

"It's no use. I can't do it."

"We'll have to find something to cut with. Lucky for us you can walk around."

"I've been looking for something sharp, but I haven't found anything yet. But we may have another option."

"What is it?"

Charlea was afraid to answer him. Her method involved uncomfortably close contact with Roland. He was tied at the wrists, but had some movement in his hands and fingers. He could reach her knife. Without other alternatives, it was their fastest means of escape. Maybe even their only hope.

"Roland, I have an idea, but I'm not comfortable with it."

"Comfort is not a high priority right now. I'll try anything."

"I'm sure you will." Charlea cleared her throat and shuffled her feet. "I have a knife."

"Get it out!"

"It's not that easy. I can't reach it. You see," Charlea looked away, "it's in my bra. Looking at him sideways, she expected to see him smiling. He was.

"Wow, Charlea," he said, "you're full of surprises."

Wanting to stay on track with the issue, she ignored his remark and continued, "If I stand behind you, maybe you can use your hands to—to retrieve it." She was glad it was dark, because she didn't want him to see her blushing.

There was a flicker of amusement across his face, but he quickly grew serious. "I understand why you're uncomfortable. But time is short, and we've got to get out of here before they come looking for us."

"You're right." She looked down at her blouse. "You might want to undo the top button or two to get more room to—uh, work. It's on the left side."

"Your left. That's my right, isn't it? No, it's not. You'll be facing the same way I am. The left. Got it."

Charlea moved around behind Roland and knelt down by his hands. She drew a deep breath and stuck her chest out. The lack of circulation made his hands cold, so cold that she could feel them before they touched her. Roland slid his fingers down her blouse until he found a button and fumbled with it until it popped off. His cold hands touched her warm chest inside her blouse and moved down until he reached the next button that he managed to loosen. Finally, he found the top of her bra. She felt the knife move as his fingers touched it.

Charlea asked quietly, "Can you feel it?"

"Yes, but my fingers are stiff and getting numb. I'm trying to get a hold of it." After a minute, his fingers gripped the knife as he moved it.

"Please don't drop it."

He paused to get a better grip on the knife before he pulled it completely out. She pulled away from his hands. Her heart was pounding, whether from fear or being touched by Roland, she couldn't tell. She tried to push that aside to focus on the task at hand.

"I'm not sure I can open it," he said as he fumbled with it.

"It's a switchblade," she said, trying hard to catch her breath that he'd taken away. "Can you feel along the side of it for the release button?" After a few moments, she heard the blade spring open.

"Hold it still," Charlea told him as she turned her back to him. Gingerly feeling for the blade with her hands, she moved her ropes back and forth against the blade. The ropes began to loosen and, with one last swipe, they fell from her wrists. She was free! Her shoulders hurt to pull her arms around to the front. She rubbed them for a moment and then took the knife from Roland's hands.

"Get me out of this," Roland said impatiently. He was looking over his shoulder to see what she was doing. Charlea held the knife to cut his bonds when a thought arose in her mind. Shaking her head, she made a move to cut them, but hesitated. Her pounding heart wouldn't let the thought leave her head.

"What are you waiting for?" Roland was growing more impatient. "Cut me loose!"

Charlea shushed him again and stared at the fine features of his profile. He was very handsome in the dim light. The impulse was strong and she had no strength to resist it.

Walking around to face him, she said, "Forgive me." She pressed her body against his and kissed him. He did not resist her, but responded to her eagerly. He knew how to kiss and kiss well. Overwhelming emotions took her back to the days when she and Mark had kissed that way. Reluctantly, she pulled away from him, breathless.

"Have mercy," she muttered, still trying to catch her breath. She walked behind him to cut the ropes that tied him to the pole. He took the ropes off his wrists and flexed his fingers to get the feeling back.

Coming back to her senses, reality hit her hard. They were in danger and had to leave as quickly as possible. She moved toward the shadows while she stuffed her knife back into its hiding place. Her heart started racing again as she remembered his touch.

Roland caught up with her as she reached the shadow of the crates. He grabbed her around the waist and pushed her up against them. The darkness hid his face, but she could feel his breath against her cheek.

"No quarter, darling," he whispered in her ear. He pinned her against the crates. He kissed her hard as she accepted his caresses and embraced him tightly.

The sound of a slamming door reverberated through the warehouse. The pair pulled apart and looked around quickly.

"We've got to get out of here!" they said simultaneously. Grabbing her hand, Roland started through the darkness. Tall piles of wooden crates lined the walls two or three rows deep. Occasional aisles allowed access between the crates, creating a maze in the warehouse. A thin layer of dirt covered the floor, the crates, everything in sight.

They walked quickly along the wall, searching for an exit. They kept on constant vigilance for Mr. Woodson or Leon. On the far end of the building, they found a door, but their hopes were dashed when they saw the padlock. Reluctantly, they made their way further along until they ran out of crates to hide behind.

Roland suggested that they climb to the top of the crates and get a look around. They made their way to the top and found a vantage point that overlooked the large warehouse. The center area was empty except for several vehicles parked there. Charlea recognized Mr. Woodson's huge Pontiac, which indicated that he was still in the building. On the far end of the warehouse was a glassed-in office. Light shone through the large window, illuminating the center area of the warehouse. They heard voices coming from that direction and occasionally saw Leon pace by the window, talking to someone they could not see.

Charlea looked for other doors that might allow them to escape, but could see none on their side of the building, save the large overhead doors on the end of the warehouse. They couldn't open those doors without drawing attention to it and bringing Leon and Mr. Woodson down on them. The center was too well lit for them to cross it without being seen. Unless they found an open window, no escape route could be seen.

Charlea's head hung as she realized the hopelessness of their situation. Roland put his arm around her to comfort her. He pulled her away from the top to a cubbyhole where several crates were missing. The perfect hiding place. A dark tarpaulin was there which he pulled back and motioned for her to get under. She sat down and he pulled the tarp over them, hiding them from searching eyes.

Roland put his arm around her and pulled her close, picking up on her discouragement. "Charlea, it'll be okay. We'll wait until daylight and find another way out. They won't find us here. Maybe they'll even think we left the building. Or maybe David will bring the police. It's just a matter of time. I won't let anything happen to you. I promise."

Charlea shook her head and wrung her hands. "You shouldn't be here. I shouldn't be here. This wasn't supposed to happen. Everything is all my fault. I've put you in danger. I'm so sorry. I should have never let this go on this long. If anything happens to you or David, I'll never forgive myself."

"What are you talking about?"

"I'm sorry. I'm babbling." She silently chided herself for saying too much. Now was not time for confessions. She hated feeling out of control and this situation was completely out of her control. Leaning her head against Roland, she began to softly cry. Fear and regret had overtaken her and she couldn't help it.

Roland held her close, gently rocking her back and forth. He dug a handkerchief out of his pocket and handed it to her. She dried her eyes, then put her arms tightly around him. She was comforted to feel him so near. They clung together, saying nothing for a long time.

"Roland, you're not going to tell David about what happened back there, are you?" she asked, feeling guilty about losing control of herself.

"Are you nuts? He'd kill me! Not literally, but he'd be so jealous that I'm not sure what he'd do to me. No, that's just between us."

"Thank you. I'm fond of you. I don't want to hurt your feelings, but…"

"You don't have to say it. I know you like David. He's very fond of you. I don't know…we're stuck here…bad people are looking for us…we lost control. I won't apologize for it. You're a sexy lady."

Charlea chuckled. "I don't believe you. But to tell the truth, and I'm ashamed to say it, I wanted to kiss you since the day I met you."

"You didn't have to wait until I was tied to a pole to do it."

"I saw the opportunity and took it. I apologize for taking advantage of you like that."

He pushed strands of hair away from her face. "Please don't apologize. That makes me feel used. I'm glad you kissed me. I've wanted to kiss you too, since that first day. Now that David has your affections, I didn't think I'd get the chance."

At that point, they heard a door close and footsteps going somewhere. The footsteps stopped, then sped up. Another door slammed. Footsteps sounded everywhere. Apparently a search was on.

Charlea trembled. The sounds meant that Mr. Woodson and Leon knew they had freed themselves. If they found them, they would be very disagreeable, if not cruel. Roland assured her again that their hiding place would conceal them until help came. They listened closely, straining to hear any movement or sound coming closer but they heard none.

"I'm scared, Roland." Charlea snuggled closer to him, drawing strength from his presence. He kept his hand on her face, shielding her from whatever might come their way. She looked up at him, looking for reassurance. He nodded at her and hugged her, putting his face against hers. His skin was soft against her cheek. So were his lips. He kissed her again and again, until he found her lips. Charlea softly gasped for breath as he kissed her neck. Time stood still as she forgot the danger and melted into his embrace.

Chapter 26

BANG!

Charlea and Roland jerked and lay still, straining to hear any other sounds. Neither of them knew how much time had passed since they had crawled into their hiding place. Roland pushed back the edge of the tarpaulin enough to peer out. Darkness still filled the warehouse. The light in the office cast shadows about them. Seeing no one, Roland pulled the edge of the tarpaulin back over them both. Charlea held on to him, letting him make the decision on whether to run or stay. He didn't move. They must be staying.

"Charlea!" Mr. Woodson's voice rang throughout the building. "I know you're in here. I have your boyfriend, and the next shot will be for him if you don't come out right now." The tone of voice told them that he meant what he said.

Charlea and Roland froze. He had David! Charlea's heart sank as she realized that he had not gone for help. No one was coming to save them. She had not told anyone that she was leaving her apartment, so no one knew that she was in this mess. Roland flung back the tarpaulin and started to get up. Charlea grabbed him and pulled him back.

"They've got David. I have to go help him!" Roland lunged for the edge of the crates, but Charlea held him back again.

"Wait! We've got to think this thing through." Charlea held him tighter as he began to pry her fingers away from his arm. "Maybe they don't know that you're free or that we're together. Let me go out and I'll stall them. You find a way out of the building and go for help."

Roland pulled her hand away from his arm and jumped down to the next level of crates. "That's my brother out there! I can't leave him. That crazy guy's got a gun!"

"I know, Roland. It's my gun." Charlea buried her face in her hands, ashamed that her weapon was now being used to hold them hostage. "He took it from me when he captured me at the library. Please, go get help." Charlea grabbed Roland by the arm and told him firmly, "You can help David more by getting help. I won't let them hurt him. Trust me. I love him." Charlea drew a breath in quickly. She hadn't intended to say that and hoped that Roland was too preoccupied to notice.

"You love him?" Roland was looking at her. "Do you mean friend love or true love?"

"Can we talk about this later? We need to get moving." She let go of him and climbed down alongside Roland. They ran to the end of the crates where Roland peered around the end. He stepped back.

"I don't know about this. David would skin me alive if something happened to you."

BANG!

Charlea and Roland recoiled in horror. They stared at each other for a split second with the same question: Had Mr. Woodson shot David?

"Wait!" Charlea yelled at the top of her lungs. "I'm coming! I'm having trouble finding my way through the crates." She turned Roland around and shoved him. "Go!" He stumbled but headed toward the door they'd found earlier.

Mr. Woodson's mounting anger was evident as his voice echoed through the warehouse. "I'm through waiting! We know you're with your other boyfriend. I want both of you out here now! Or this guy is done for. No more games!"

Charlea's heart sunk. Roland couldn't go for help now without endangering David. Roland ran back toward her, and when their eyes met, it was evident that he knew it too. They would have to confront Mr. Woodson.

Charlea grabbed Roland as he walked past her to go out to Mr. Woodson. "Roland, before we go, I have to tell you something. It's my fault that you and David are in danger. I haven't been totally honest with you. I'm sorry…I should have told you…" Charlea was stammering but continued, "There's not time to explain it all. Whatever Mr. Woodson says, whatever threats he makes, I'll take care of it. Please, trust me."

Roland, obviously preoccupied with helping David, suddenly jerked as what she had said sunk in. He rounded on her. "What are you saying?"

"Follow my lead." Charlea straightened her blouse, making sure the remaining buttons were buttoned. She ran her fingers through her hair, trying to get it untangled.

"You look fine. We're not going to a party," Roland said angrily, grabbing her arm to stop her preening. "What do you mean, you haven't been honest with us?"

"You have to trust me. I love you and your brother and I will do all in my power to keep you safe." Turning away from Roland, she yelled out, "Okay, you win. We're coming out!" She turned back to Roland wanting to say more, but she could not find the words.

Charlea made her way toward the center of the building, without looking to see if Roland was behind her. Rounding the corner of the last crate, she walked out into the open. At the other end of the open space, she saw three men standing under the lighted section towards one end of the warehouse. The light made her squint until her eyes adjusted. She stood fixed to the spot, trying to decide what to do next.

"Come here, Charlea. And you too, pretty boy." Mr. Woodson had the gun pointed at David.

Charlea took a deep breath and moved forward. She felt Roland right behind her and he whispered to her, "How many bullets in your gun?"

"Six. Why?" she asked without turning around.

"I have an idea," he whispered. Charlea didn't know what he meant by that, but she trusted him enough to do as he asked. As they got closer to the trio, they could make out their features. She gasped when she realized that David had been roughed up some. He was holding his ribs, and it looked like he would have a black eye tomorrow, if they lived that long. Roland pushed past her and rushed to his brother's aid. The gun pointed at her while Leon had his knife pointed at David's ribs. She stopped short to face Mr. Woodson and Leon.

"You've got the jewels to pay off your gambling debts," she growled at them. "Take them and go."

Mr. Woodson laughed. "I'm not a fool, Charlea. I can't let you walk out of here. Why didn't you tell me your brother was gone on a business trip?"

"You didn't ask. Nor did you give me a chance to say it."

"So where is he?"

"How should I know? I don't keep tabs on his whereabouts. Where is Bonnie?"

"She's in a safe place nearby."

"Where? Tell me."

Mr. Woodson waved his arm behind him in a general direction. "Nearby. My biggest problem is your brother. You better hope he returns soon. Otherwise you three will be coming with me."

"You told me the guys would be free to go. You can't go back on your word."

"I guess you can't trust a crook, Charlea." He laughed again.

"How much money do you want to let Bonnie and them go? I can get it and you know it. Blackmail is a lesser crime than murder. You won't go to the electric chair when they catch you." She smirked at him as he continued to glare at her, but he seemed to be contemplating her offer, so she added. "Plus it means we all get out of here relatively unharmed. It's the easiest way for all of us to get what we want."

"It would take a lot of money. I'd need enough to start over somewhere else." He paused, but added, "And Leon too." He lowered his arm holding the gun a little. Charlea hoped that David and Roland wouldn't take that as a sign to attack. She was getting somewhere and didn't need them to mess it up. She knew Mr. Woodson could be bought, so she decided to sweeten the pot.

"Would a hundred thousand be enough?"

"Dollars?" Roland seemed astonished. "Where are you going to get that kind of money?" he whispered loudly.

Charlea wished Roland would shut up. He always talked too much and at the wrong times. Charlea shot him a look to tell him to be quiet. David got the hint and elbowed Roland.

Leon cackled. "What are you, a couple of morons? Don't you know she's one of the richest women in the country? She's got money to burn!" The moment she dreaded now faced her. She had no choice, but to meet it head on. Looking at David and Roland, she could see that they were dumbfounded.

"Richest woman in the country?" David said. He was staring at Charlea with his good eye. His surprise was obvious on his face. "I thought you were a librarian?"

Both Leon and Mr. Woodson laughed now. They were delighted to thoroughly unarm Charlea. Leon continued, "And that guy that gave you that map? He's her brother. Her very rich brother. He planted those stones so you guys would spend time with his sister. Seems she can't get dates by herself, so her brother has to buy them for her."

Leon guffawed and joined in. "And you dopes fell for it! Like a couple of gigolos, here you come chasing a treasure! Fighting over the old maid librarian who knew where the stones were all the time."

The shame of the disclosure nearly knocked Charlea to her knees. The gasps of disbelief from David and Roland broke her heart.

"Charlea? Is it true?" David barely whispered the words.

She covered her face with her hands, too humiliated to look at them. "I knew it was one of Richard's games when I saw the handwriting on the envelope. I should have stopped it then. I'm so sorry." Her voice cracked with remorse.

Desperate to redeem herself in their eyes, she entwined her hands as a sinner begging for forgiveness. She looked at Roland and David who appeared to have been sucker-punched by reality. She pled with them, "But this was my brother's idea, not mine. I didn't know he'd hidden the stones and I certainly didn't know where they were. You've got to believe me!"

David was shaking his head in disbelief. "You knew, but you led us on? Why didn't you say something?"

"I didn't know how to tell you. I was afraid of what you would do."

"Afraid? You knew that it was getting dangerous, but you gave us no warning. What were you thinking?" David stood looking at her, fists clinched and the veins on his neck protruding with anger. Roland appeared as angry as David, but for once, he let his brother do the speaking.

Nothing she could say would justify her dishonesty. They would never forgive her for deceiving them. So that was it. The end of her hope for love. Anger welled up in her. She'd had all she could take. She let out a guttural scream, which caught the men off guard. She charged Leon and punched him in the gut as hard as she could. The blow knocked him backwards a step and left him gasping for air. She turned to attack Mr. Woodson, but he had moved away from them. Leon, finally catching his breath, came after her with the knife.

Coming to their senses, Roland intercepted Leon before he got to Charlea and landed a punch across his jaw. The force of the punch knocked the knife out of Leon's hand and it clattered across the floor. David grabbed Charlea and pulled her aside. Roland dove for the knife.

Mr. Woodson raised the pistol and aimed it at Roland. A shot rang out, but Roland moved just as Mr. Woodson pulled the trigger. The bullet passed harmlessly over him. The loud noise achieved one purpose: they all stopped for a moment. David hung on to Charlea while Roland joined them.

Roland whispered in Charlea's ear, "That's three."

She was relieved to find that he was still speaking to her.

Leon jumped to his feet, grabbed the knife, and waved it in their direction, daring one of them to jump him again. Mr. Woodson had a wild look in his eyes. Charlea knew she needed to calm everyone down or someone was going to get hurt. She turned to look at Roland and David and silently tried to convey to them to stay quiet for now. They seemed to get the message.

Letting go of David and turning back to Mr. Woodson, she asked, "I'm sorry I lost control. Shall we get back to the negotiations? How much was it that you said you needed?"

"I didn't say," he growled at her. The hatred he felt for her was almost tangible around them. "You can bet the price has just gone up. I should kill you all now."

"That wouldn't be too smart," Charlea said calmly. "I'm your paycheck. Without me, you get nothing. You hurt David, Roland, or Bonnie, you might as well kill me because you'll get nothing. Let them all go and I will guarantee your money. I'm guessing that the stones won't pay off your debts and Leon too. You're desperate for more. Why else would you risk kidnapping and extortion charges?" She paused long enough to let what she'd said sink in. "I will pay the ransom for Bonnie, Roland, and David if you let them go now. Then I'll pay the ransom for myself. You get what you want and we go our way."

"You'll turn me in to the police."

"I think it's a given that you'll have to leave the country," Charlea said impatiently. "Disappear to some other place. South America interest you? Buy yourself a hacienda outside of Rio? Oh, and what about your wife?"

Mr. Woodson moaned. "I don't want to take my wife. I hate her. You're right, I need enough money to leave the country and live comfortably somewhere else."

"What about Leon? Will you pay him off or will you leave him to take the blame?" Charlea asked him, jumping on the chance to drive a wedge between them. Mr. Woodson looked at Leon and grunted, implying Leon was not a priority in his plans.

A look of fear came across Leon's face. "You can't leave me here. Not after all I've done for you!" he shouted at Mr. Woodson. "You owe me!"

"Settle down, Leon," Charlea told him. "Of course he won't leave you. You know too much. You could implicate him in a number of crimes so it's in his best interest to take good care of you. Or get rid of you. He can't leave loose ends around. That's why he had to deal with Bonnie. You should watch your back. You're money out of his pocket." Looking over at Mr. Woodson, she felt satisfaction in irritating him this way. "So how much for my two guys and Bonnie?"

"They'll go to the police, so I'm not letting them go."

"Let them go and then Leon, you, and I will go to another location—they won't know where—until I can arrange funds and transportation for you. Then you can go your merry way as a rich man, and I'll go back to my library. Our paths will never, and I mean never, cross again." She paused, hoping for an agreement.

"Not meaning to interrupt," David interjected, stepping forward. "Well, maybe I do. I'm not leaving here without Charlea."

"David, shut up," Charlea barked at him. Then she whispered under her breath, "I know what I'm doing. Stay out of it."

"I'm not leaving either," Roland added.

"Shut up both of you! You'll do as I say or, or...." Charlea couldn't think of anything she could do to force them to go. She pointed at them and then formed a fist. "You shouldn't be here, and it's my fault you are. So you will go if I say you do."

"No!" David said, his anger still evident in his tone of voice. "We won't leave you here with this scum." He swept his arm in the direction of Mr. Woodson and Leon.

"Who you calling scum!" Leon started toward David, waving his knife in a wide arc. Mr. Woodson reached out and grabbed his arm by the elbow. He pulled Leon back and told him to remain there.

Charlea was shaking her head and threw up her hands in disgust. She gave David a little shove and said, "You are so stubborn! You'll go if I tell you to! I can handle this, but I want you guys out of my way."

"Go, Roland." David pushed his brother toward the door.

Roland turned around and pushed David back. "I'm not leaving here without either one of you." The two men faced off, poised to exchange blows. Charlea came up behind David and grabbed his arm. "Stop it, please," she pleaded. "It's my fault you're here. Both of you—go!" He jerked his arm away from her and pushed her away. Charlea stumbled backwards.

David let go of Roland, then turned and faced her. "I thought you were different than the rest. But you're as shallow and deceitful as the rest of them. No, no…you're more deceitful than anyone I know! I hate you!" He turned away from her, leaving her stunned with his words.

Roland grabbed his arm and spun him around. "Don't talk to her like that! She doesn't deserve it." He pushed David. David pushed him back. The two of them locked in combat, wrestling and throwing punches, although not landing many. They tripped and fell to the ground. They rolled across the warehouse floor while Charlea tried to pull them apart.

"Stop it!" She grabbed David's arm as he flung it toward Roland, but he pulled it out of her grasp. Somewhere in the melee, she tripped and fell on top of them. Instead of stopping to help her up, they pulled her into their tangle of arms and legs. They rolled away from Mr. Woodson and Leon who looked on with great amusement.

After rolling into the center of the warehouse, Charlea found herself under the two guys. Roland whispered in her ear, "David called the police. Stall until they get here." He threw a punch at David and missed.

Relief swept over her as she realized that this was a game. At least she hoped it was a game. Roland tried to pin David down, but Charlea was between them, still trying to pry them apart. Somehow they all rolled until she was again underneath both of them and was having a hard time catching her breath. Thrashing around on the floor, she made her way out from under the pile, gasping for air, but was pulled back in before she could make her escape.

"Ow!" she yelled as her ankle was twisted in the wrong direction. She felt someone's hand on her backside.

"No, you don't!" she heard David say right before the hand was pulled away. Someone pulled her hair, but since she couldn't tell who, she grabbed a handful of Roland's hair and pulled back. Hands seemed to be touching her everywhere. She fought the urge to laugh out loud because she would really be enjoying this if it weren't for the situation they were in.

BANG!

Having had enough entertainment, Mr. Woodson fired the gun into the air. The tangled bodies on the floor ceased to writhe as the sound echoed through the building. Roland whispered to David and Charlea, "I think we've pushed it far enough." Untangling themselves, the trio stood up. They were totally disheveled, dirty and out of breath. They turned to face Mr. Woodson and Leon.

"Enough of the childish behavior." Mr. Woodson waved the gun toward them. "Charlea, I'll take $100,000 for each of the guys and they can go. You, I will hold until your brother returns from wherever he is."

"No!" Roland and David said simultaneously.

Charlea took a step toward Mr. Woodson. "Agreed," she said somberly. Turning to her two friends, she added, "You will do as he says without hesitation or question." She lowered her voice and added, "I got you into this mess, and I'll do whatever it takes to get you out of it."

"No!" David adamantly said to Charlea. "We are not leaving here without you." He emphasized each word by pointing at her as he said them.

Charlea pushed his finger away. "It's not an option," Charlea said calmly. "You will go. I will stay. I will contact my brother tonight or tomorrow and the arrangements will be made. I'll be home by tomorrow night. Now go, while you can."

Charlea turned away from David and Roland and faced Mr. Woodson to make sure he had no objections to her instructions. Inside, she was full of fear and dread of being left alone with these two monsters. Somehow she found the courage to stand up straight, giving the impression of confidence. As soon as David and Roland were out of the building, she would call Richard and make arrangements for the money. Mr. Woodson and Leon would be on their way to who-cares-where, and she would be free again. The nightmare would at last be over.

David and Roland seemed confused and unsure of what to do. Shuffling around, they looked at each other as if communicating telepathically. Roland turned to go, pulling on David's arm as he did so. David was still glaring at the other two men.

"You harm one hair on her head," he said with gritted teeth, "and I will personally hunt you down and take it out of your hide. Understand me?" Roland pulled David along as they headed toward the door.

"So will I," a voice said from the shadows. The sound startled the group. Charlea felt a huge wave of relief because it was Richard's voice. Pat must be here as well. Mr. Woodson and Leon spun around to see who was addressing them. She saw Richard coming out of the shadows with his gun pointed at Mr. Woodson.

"I will handle this, Richard," said the sheriff as he stepped out of the shadows as well. "This is my jurisdiction, not yours." He stepped toward the two astonished men with his gun drawn. "Woodson, drop the gun. Leon, drop the knife. It's all over."

Leon immediately lost all his allegiance to Mr. Woodson. He threw down his knife and turned to point at Mr. Woodson. "He made me do it. I didn't want to, but he made me. He's been threatening me and I was afraid he'd kill me." He genuinely seemed afraid of Woodson, who was glaring at him with hatred the like of which Charlea had never seen before.

"Leon, you lying coward!" Mr. Woodson pointed the gun at Leon. He probably would have fired if the sheriff hadn't told him to put his gun down again. Instead, he pulled his hand back and hit Leon across the face with the butt of the pistol. Leon went down to the floor, bleeding from his mouth as he fell. Mr. Woodson stood over him like a conqueror and turned to look at Charlea.

"Last warning, Woodson! Put the gun down!" The sheriff was edging closer.

In the long second that Mr. Woodson looked at her, she saw pure hatred in his eyes. He began to shake and sweat broke out on his forehead. Charlea knew what he had in mind and she backed away one step. Quickly raising the gun, he pointed it at her.

BANG! BANG!

Gunfire erupted from many directions.

Charlea felt like someone had hit her torso with a baseball bat. Her legs lost their strength and she fell. From out of nowhere, David caught her and cradled her gently into his arms. As the taste of blood entered her mouth, she involuntarily moaned with the intense pain that engulfed her. She moved her hands over her stomach and felt her wet, sticky clothes. Her warm blood ran around her body, soaking her clothes and dripping on the floor. She felt strangely calm as she looked at David. Roland was sitting beside her, holding her hand. How handsome they were, even with their faces distorted in dirt, bruises, fear, and concern.

She was at peace, surrounded by love. It didn't matter that she hadn't known them long. She truly loved them. She loved Roland for his impulsiveness and the way he made her feel. She loved David just as she had loved Mark, for making her feel complete. She wanted to spend the rest of her life with him and she was getting her wish. He was holding her as she died. She knew it was the end and regretted not having more time. She was growing faint.

Her eyes were staring at David, but not really seeing him. "David, are you there?" she said softly.

"Darling, I'm here. Don't talk. Save your strength." Even through the growing darkness, she heard his sweet voice.

"Forgive me for what I've done. I love you, David." Her voice trailed off.

"I love you too, Charlea." David's voice broke as he tried to comfort her. "Can you hear me? I love you. I've been looking for you for so long. Don't leave me!" She felt a teardrop on her face.

"I'm sorry—" She tried to speak more, but it took too much effort. His strong arms held her close to his chest as he rocked her back and forth. He had tears in his eyes and was talking to her, but she couldn't understand him. Richard was beside Roland. Fear and concern covered their faces.

There was confusion all around, people talking, yelling, and arguing. She was bothered to hear it, but she had no strength to tell them to stop. She dimly saw familiar faces and heard familiar voices: David, Roland, Richard, Mrs. Butterfield, Mr. Wilkerson, Bonnie. All the important people in her life were around her. She wondered if that vision was her life flashing before her eyes before she died.

She felt satisfied to know that she had many friends and had influenced many more.

Gradually she could no longer feel her body, but she was glad of that. Too much pain was there, and she was glad to be away from it. She entered a strange place that distorted everything. Blurred faces and strange sounds came through a tunnel, reaching her from a long distance. She felt disconnected from her body, observing it from afar, as through a murky glass.

Her thoughts turned to Mark. She was happy that she might see him again and talk to him for a little while. He always had good advice for her. She had so much to tell him.

The sounds and the faces around her were fading into the distance. She seemed to be going somewhere, but she didn't understand where. Turning away from the noise, she looked toward a bright light that shone from nowhere, yet was all around her. She felt very light and there was no more noise or pain. The place was peaceful, like nothing she had ever known before. She smiled and walked away from all that had been familiar toward something that drew her near.

Chapter 27

How does one describe the absence of time? Its ever-present effects are felt in one's body and one's perception of what is going on around them. The thing that always hung so heavily on Charlea's mind was not here, making her light and utterly free from all care.

Charlea felt happy. All around her was peace, like a soft warm quilt enveloping her in its embrace. Gone was the pain she had been feeling. Gone was the smell of blood and the shouting and screaming. Worries and fears were gone. There was only peace. Peace and serenity.

She looked all around her, but saw nothing to indicate where she was or which direction to go. She picked a direction and floated along, a delightful sensation to her. Something drew her along, even though she could see nothing. She couldn't tell if she was getting anywhere since there was no change in her surroundings, but there was no hurry.

She began to make out a figure in the mist, some distance away. The sight was fuzzy at first, but slowly became clearer. The figure was familiar. One she had not seen for a long time. Quickening her pace, she moved along toward him. Drawing nearer, she could see Mark smiling at her. He held out his arms to her and she floated into them. For the first time in what seemed like an eternity, she embraced her husband. Home at last.

She had no idea how long they held each other. The question didn't matter because time didn't matter. This was her first taste of eternity. She didn't have to leave this place or Mark again. She stepped back from him so she could look at his face. He looked just like the last time she had seen him, young and vibrant. Nothing had changed about him and time had not altered him in any way. She thought about how she must look to him. She surely seemed a lot older to him than the last time he had seen her. But he gave no sign that he saw the lines on her face or her drooping figure. He looked at her with eyes full of love. No words were needed. The feelings they felt for each other was enough and it passed between them in an unseen river.

Mark gently touched her face and kissed her on the cheek. He was obviously glad to see Charlea, but he had not spoken to her.

Charlea wondered if he could. Perhaps in this place, no words were needed, but she could find no reason to test her theory. Pure contentment in his presence was enough.

Mark took her hand and led her away from that spot. Each place they went looked the same as where they had been. Charlea couldn't tell if they were walking in circles or over a great distance. It didn't matter. There was nothing to see but each other. No one and nothing else mattered except for the two of them.

"I've been watching over you, Charlea."

Charlea was startled to hear the sound of his voice, a sound more beautiful than any she'd ever heard. She said nothing, hoping he would continue so she could hear it again.

He stared at her, smiling. "I heard every word you spoke to my picture. I'm sorry I couldn't answer you. I would have done anything to come back, even for only a few minutes, to tell you that everything was going to be all right."

Charlea wasn't surprised to hear he'd been with her. She had always thought that he was there with her. Now she was here with him. She could get answers to the most agonizing questions plaguing her.

"How did you die? Did you suffer for long? I want to know what happened to you."

"I didn't suffer at all. One moment I was flying and the next I was here. From listening to you, I must have been declared MIA. The plane must have crashed and my body burned."

"They never found you. I spent years wondering if you were coming home. I had nothing left but your picture. It felt natural to talk to you through the picture."

"Darling," Mark spoke tenderly, pulling her closer to him. He kissed her hands. "I need you to let me go."

"No!" For the first time since she came to this peaceful place, she felt a twinge of fear. Fear did not belong here so it was an uncomfortable feeling. "I just got you back. I won't leave you again. Do you know the anguish I felt when you never came home? Waiting and wondering if you'd ever return? I won't go through that again!" She found herself shouting at him.

He looked at her sadly. "Yes, I saw your grief. I agonized seeing you in such pain. I felt cheated at not getting to spend more time with you. But for reasons you cannot understand, it was my time to go. You had to stay behind. Charlea, I have missed having you with me, but here," Mark waved his hand around him, "I am happy. I can be with you when you need me to be. I will always be with you because I love you. I will always love you. You are not alone." Mark hesitated for a moment. "Do you still love me, Charlea?"

Charlea was taken aback by his question. "How could you even ask me that question? I love you so much that I'll give up everything to stay here with you. I'll always love you. I will be here with you forever and you'll never be alone again."

Mark smiled at her. "But I am not alone."

She looked around for the others that Mark had spoken of, but could not see or sense anyone else. To her, the place was deserted except for the two of them.

As if sensing her question, he continued. "Yes, there are others here as well. Waiting for those they love. We hear you when you call, but we cannot come to you. You have to come to us. But Charlea, you aren't supposed to stay here. You have to go back."

"No!" Charlea felt afraid. "Aren't I dead?" She searched Mark's face for an answer, but found none. She turned away from him, talking to herself, trying to reason things out. "If I were dead, he wouldn't be sending me back. But if I were still alive, then what am I doing here? Isn't this heaven?" Charlea turned back to Mark. "I want to stay. I have no reason to go back."

"Yes, you do," he told her. "I don't know why, but it's not your time yet. You have to go back."

"Don't I have a choice in this?"

"No."

Charlea felt her heart begin to break. If this was a place with no pain or heartache, why was her heart hurting? If there were no tears here, why did she feel like crying?

"Mark, I'm losing you again. Don't make me—"

"You never lost me." Mark touched her face and brought her back to him. "I come to you when you ask me to. My spirit is there with you when you talk to my picture. I've been with you when you were scared, when you were lonely, when you needed someone to listen. When you are contented and happy, you don't need me, so I wait here until you call."

"So is your purpose now to watch over me?"

Mark shook his head. "Not really. I'm just here because it's where I'm supposed to be."

"Does it seem like a long time since you came here?"

"No. It seems like only a moment."

Charlea didn't understand, but didn't question him further. She felt confused about many things, but didn't know what questions to ask. This was all beyond her comprehension in many ways. She felt very tired all of a sudden.

Mark's eyes never left her face, as if to etch its image in his mind once again. He hesitated to speak, but finally found the words. "It's almost time for you to go back."

"What do I do when I get there? Things are in a mess. I don't know what to do."

Mark smiled at her again. "You've got Richard. And now Roland and David." Charlea jerked her head towards him, startled again that he knew about them. "Yes, I know you have feelings for them."

"And that doesn't make you jealous or anything?"

"Charlea, you vowed that you would be faithful to me until death parted us. Well, darling, death parted us. You fulfilled your vow to me. You are free to love again. Without guilt."

Charlea shook her head. "I can't. I feel like I'm betraying you."

"But you're not." He took her by the shoulders. "You have to move on. You're too special of a woman to waste your life away. You have too much love inside you to keep it there." He paused to let his words sink in. "Roland and David are waiting for you."

"They may never forgive me for what I've done. What should I do?"

"Follow your heart, Charlea."

"My heart doesn't know what to do either."

"It will come to you. Give it time." He paused for a moment. "Charlea, don't despair over getting old. Aging. That's what you're supposed to do. Let your heart be young, even if your body is not. When you get here, then it's time to be forever young."

Charlea put her arms around Mark and tried to hold on with all her strength. She loved having him listen to her problems and offer words of advice. He always knew what to do and knew how to reassure her. His encouragement was one of the things she missed most about him.

"Charlea, it's time."

"Not yet. Please! Just a little longer."

"It's out of our control."

"I love you, Mark. I always will."

"I know. I will always love you too. You're right, Charlea, love never dies. Love goes with you wherever you are. That's why it's so powerful. I'll always be there when you need me." Mark kissed her on the forehead. "See you later."

Charlea looked at him, desperately trying to make a memory of him in this timeless place. She clung tightly to him, but her arms were becoming empty. He was growing dimmer and the light was fading. The white light dimmed until only darkness came again.

Chapter 28

Richard and Pat walked across the green, clipped lawn, dodging the simple white headstones as they made their way through the cemetery. Richard carried flowers as he made his way between a tall tombstone topped with an angel and a smaller one displaying only a cross. Seeing the large tombstone with the name Ludlow on it, he stepped beside it to lay the flowers on the ground.

"Ready to go?" Richard asked, looking down at Charlea as she sat silently staring at Mark's headstone. She made no move to get up.

Richard had come to the hospital earlier in the morning to take her home, but she had insisted that he bring her to the cemetery first. Before she had left the hospital, she'd insisted that a plot be purchased and a headstone erected for him. He deserved a memorial so people would know that he lived and died in defense of his country. They carried her to the gravesite where she asked them to leave her alone while she spoke to Mark. Richard and Pat made a circle around the cemetery, all the while keeping an eye on her to make sure she was all right.

Richard shook his head as he bent down to pick her up. "I can't believe I let you talk me into bringing you here. You barely have the strength to sit. I need to take you home." He and Pat took her by the arms to help her up. Offering no resistance, she got to her feet. Her legs were shaky and weak, forcing her to lean heavily on the two men.

Weaving their way among the headstones and flower arrangements, the three of them reached Richard's car. All her strength was gone as they helped her into the backseat of the car. Richard closed the door and hurried to the other side while Pat got in the driver's seat.

The warm sunlight felt good to her as she leaned against the door. She regretted being hospitalized for so many weeks, missing out on the best part of summer. She always loved summer, when everything was green and flowers bloomed in bright colors. This year, she had watched the summer days pass by her hospital room's window. For most of the summer, she had been bedridden, healing from the terrible wounds that Mr. Woodson had inflicted on her. Still recovering, she tired easily, requiring her to rest often and long. The doctors told her that in time she would regain her strength. Until then, Richard would care for her at his home in Dallas.

They all sat silently as they wound their way down the streets. She was glad that she had stopped to see Mark. The burden she had carried for years was gone, and she felt relaxed and at peace, ready to start life again after being in the hospital for so long.

"Thanks, Richard," Charlea said, breaking the silence, "for stopping by the cemetery. I had to tell Mark goodbye. I'm moving on because that's the way he wants it." She heard Richard draw a breath in surprise, and she laughed at hearing the sound. "Yes, it's true. I'm finally letting go, like you've hounded me to do for so long. You are getting your way for once.

"I'm happy to hear you say that. You've grieved long enough. This little episode," he almost choked on the words as he said them, "helped you find yourself again." He chuckled lightly. "You picked a hard way to learn that lesson."

"I have no regrets. Mark and I had a long talk. He told me it was time." She cast a sideways glance at him. He was looking at her puzzled. She hadn't told anyone about seeing Mark and their conversation.

"He what? What do you mean you had a long talk?"

Wishing to change the subject from herself, Charlea asked, "I've been meaning to ask you, how did you find out about the Williams brothers dying in a car accident? I mean, you tied that story to the house in a neat bundle."

Pat spoke from the driver's seat. "I found the story about their accident while researching issues with the property before we bought it. Robert was a veteran who fought in Europe, like me. I saw several soldiers make off with the spoils of war, so it was easy to make him seem one of them. You worked in the old hospital, so we figured you'd know about Dr. Williams and the whole story fell into place. I hid the gems in the house a couple of weeks before Mr. Collins and Mr. Parker showed up in the library."

"Aren't you the clever one, coming up with all that." Charlea shook her head. "My heart still hurts for Dr. Williams and his wife, losing their sons like that."

Silence filled the car until Charlea asked, "Have you heard more about when Leon's trial is scheduled? Bonnie was cleared of charges, right?"

"Charlea, why can't you leave the legal stuff to me? Relax, will you! I'm taking care of it."

"I'm curious, that's all." She saw Pat looking at Richard in the rearview mirror. A look passed between them that hinted that they knew something and they were keeping it from her. She decided to press the issue. "I want to make sure Bonnie is fine. And I assume I will have to testify at Leon's trial in some capacity, and I'd like to know when."

Richard looked out the car window for a moment. "All charges against Bonnie were dropped. She was a Woodson's puppet and didn't knowingly assist him in his criminal actions. For her, things are as back to normal as they can be. Because of the skull fracture inflicted by Leon, she may never regain the hearing in her right ear. She's doing really well for what she's been through. I bought her a new car and set up a small annuity for her."

A smile spread across Charlea's face. "Thank you, Richard. She deserves it, after all Leon did to her."

Richard continued. "Leon's lawyer has asked for a change in venue because he says he can't get a fair jury trial there."

"He would be convicted. He never had too many friends there and probably has less now."

"He hurt you. He deserves to be hung," Richard replied bitterly. "He should have died at the warehouse like Woodson."

"Seems inhuman to say it, but I can't argue with you." Charlea felt bitter as well, recalling the awful things Leon had put her through. Rubbing the scar on her neck where he had cut her that night, she dreaded the idea of testifying against him at his trial. She barely lived through that terrifying night and didn't want to relive it, even on the witness stand.

She had a worried look on her face so Richard reassured her, "They're still working on a plea bargain. Let's keep our fingers crossed that they reach a settlement of some sort. That would relieve you of having to testify."

"If they don't and it goes to trial, will they bring David and Roland in testify against him as well? And will it come up on how they came to be there?"

Again Pat and Richard exchanged unspoken thoughts in the rearview mirror again. Charlea knew they were hiding information from her. Richard cleared his throat. "I'm taking care of everything. Can't you leave it at that? I promise to let you know as soon as I know anything. Trust me, please." His eyes pleaded with her to let the matter drop.

She was too tired to argue with them about what they were hiding. Every time she mentioned David or Roland, Richard immediately changed the subject or brushed her off. Not getting answers from him infuriated her. Not to be put off long, she'd pry for more information later.

Pulling through a gated entrance into the circle driveway of a large manor, Pat drove the car along the manicured lawns and rose gardens. As they stopped outside a massive double door of a large portico, Maggie, the white-haired motherly housekeeper, came rushing out. Richard carried Charlea into the front study that had been converted into a bedroom for her. A large room, full of bookcases, it held their father's extensive collection of books. This place was perfect for her recovery.

Richard and Maggie helped her into the bed set up for her. Richard sent the others away and took off the shoes Charlea was too exhausted to kick off. He covered Charlea with a blanket and tucked it around her, then sat in a chair beside her and rubbed his forehead. The lines on his face showed the exhaustion and stress from the past ten weeks when he thought he would lose his only sister. He reached for her hand and held it tight.

Richard let out a long sigh. "I almost lost you, Charlea, and all over a foolish adventure I sent your way. It's my fault this happened to you. I wanted you to have some fun and it got out of hand. I should have come earlier. I might have stopped it and—" A man of power weakened by his love for his sister, he sobbed. "I'm so sorry."

"Richard, stop blaming yourself," Charlea told him firmly. She sat up and put her hand on his shoulder. "You did not do this to me. Mr. Woodson did it. The horrible event is behind us now. I will regain my strength in time and things will return to normal."

Her words did little to comfort him. "You're my sister and I almost killed you."

"Stop it! I never want to hear you say that again." She shook him as hard as her feeble strength would allow. "Never again and I mean it!" Then she hugged him as he leaned forward to wipe his face with the edge of her sheet. "You're exhausted. Get some rest so you'll feel better. Maggie will take care of my every need." He made no move to leave, so she added, "Do it for me."

"You're right," he conceded as he sat drooped on her bed. "I am tired in every fiber of my body. I haven't had a full night sleep since before that night."

"Let Pat and the people at the office run the company for a little while longer. They've done a great job while you were at the hospital with me. If you rest, you'll function better when you get back to work."

Richard agreed with her suggestion and got up to leave. As he reached the door, he turned back to ask, "Is there anything I can get for you before I take a nap?"

"Tell Maggie to check on me in a little bit. I'm hungry and a snack would taste good."

Richard smiled at her. "Hunger is a good sign. It means you're getting better." She smiled back at him, glad to see his spirits lifted some.

"And I would like a phone. I need to call about the library and I want to call David's office. I owe him and Roland an apology."

"No!" Richard's peaceful face took on a tinge of red and the veins stood out on his face. "I won't allow it!"

"Won't allow it? What is this? A prison?" Charlea matched his anger.

"My house, my rules. No contact with Mr. Parker or Mr. Collins while you're here. I'm still getting those affairs settled and I don't need your meddling. Wait for a while."

"But I need to apologize! I must apologize! I cannot rest until they know how sorry I am for putting them in a dangerous position." Charlea's tension faded into sorrow. "Please!"

Richard stiffened. He seemed reluctant to answer. "I'm sorry, but you have to leave them out of it. I know this hurts you, but think of it from their side. What if the story got out? Their reputations would be ruined. They might lose their jobs. Who knows what else.

I'm sorry you got so attached to them, but drop it and concentrate on getting well and putting your own life back together."

Seeing tears in Charlea's eyes, he continued, "At least don't contact them yet. Maybe in time."

"They risked their lives for me. I must see them one more time. I love them."

Richard shook his head as he walked to the door and ran his fingers through his thinning hair. "I can't understand how easily you give your heart to the most inappropriate men. No contact with them until I get things straightened out. End of discussion."

"But—"

"No, Charlea. Now, if you don't need anything else, I'll send Maggie in, and I'll go rest." Richard left the room and shut the door.

Charlea grasped the corner of the pillow and slammed it against the bed. Richard never understood her, but she wouldn't allow him to stand in her way. She'd find some way to call David.

A soft knock at the door brought her out of her thoughts. "Mr. Richard said you were hungry." Maggie came into the room. "I'm so happy about that. The food will give you strength to mend. Are you hungry for something special? I'll make you anything you want." Maggie was a kind, thoughtful woman who had worked for them for many years and was considered part of the family. Maggie always made a fuss when Charlea visited Richard.

Charlea smiled at Maggie who was busy tucking her in again. "A grilled cheese sandwich, please. For some reason, that appeals to me."

"I'll be back in a few minutes with your order. By the way, I saved all the cards and letters you got from Mrs. Butterfield and others while you were in the hospital. You can read them tomorrow. You have lots of friends." Maggie fluffed the pillows and made sure Charlea was comfortable before scurrying off to the kitchen to make the sandwich. In a short time, she was back with a warm sandwich and a glass of ice tea on a tray. Sitting in the chair beside the bed, she watched as Charlea quickly ate the sandwich.

"Would you stay and visit with me for a little bit?" Charlea asked as Maggie took the tray from her. "You always know the latest gossip about everyone, and it's been a long time since I've heard any."

"Oh, Miss Charlea," Maggie said as she put the tray on a table near the door, "You know I don't gossip." She settled in the chair again and brushed a few stray bread crumbs off the sheet. "What did you have in mind?"

"Can you bring me a phone?"

Maggie cocked her head. "Now Charlea, you know I can't do that. Richard would scold me too harshly and I'm too old for that. Is there anything else?"

Charlea shook her head. "I'll get some rest. Thanks, Maggie."

"I'll check back in on you in a bit. So good to have you home again." Maggie patted her hand and left.

Charlea knew she couldn't push Maggie for a phone. Too restless to sleep, she pushed back the covers and got out of bed. Her wobbly legs carried her to the window to watch the last rays of the day shining on the trees across the yard. How often she had gone out there as a girl and climbed those trees to get away from her awful music teacher. When she was a teenager, she had taken her books out there to read when her mother criticized her too much. Her father bought her a comfortable lawn chair to read in and sometimes joined her out there under the trees—a happy golden time in her life that still warmed her heart. How long ago those days seemed to her. She longed for a time when there were no worries or burdens like she carried now. The serenity and peace of the past accentuated what lay ahead for her. Facing further recovery from her wounds and testifying at Leon's trial, the future looked bleak, especially without David and Roland. Her heart felt heavy.

Turning away from the window, Charlea went to the bookcase. This library was where she first learned of the magic that books held. They took her on adventures to faraway places, introduced her to amazing people, and comforted her when she was blue.

She needed an escape from her present troubles. Running her hand along the book spines, she read the familiar titles while looking for one in particular. Finding what she wanted, she pulled the book out of its place and took it back to the bed. The short time on her feet left her very tired. She curled up and opened the book *Treasure Island*. She couldn't do anything about it now, but as soon as she got home, she'd call David's office and apologize to him. She only hoped that he'd forgive her.

Chapter 29

A few weeks later, Richard reluctantly took Charlea home to her apartment where he left her in the capable hands of her friends who provided her with food and checked on her daily. Charlea put Mark's picture in the closet, wrapped in a pillowcase. Much to her surprise, she found it liberating and discovered renewed strength to guide her own life the way she wanted it. Knowing that Mark was watching over her eased her loneliness and gave her new confidence.

Charlea's physical ordeal was mostly over, but her social ordeal was just beginning. People who used to be friendly to her now seemed stand-offish or afraid to speak to her. The local paper had credited her with finding proof of Mr. Woodson's criminal activities and hailed her as a courageous heroine. The stares from some of the townsfolks bothered her. She wanted things to go back to the way they used to be.

One Sunday afternoon, Charlea was reading a book in her apartment when there was a soft knock at the door. Mrs. Butterfield stuck her head in.

"Someone is here to see you. Are you feeling up to having a visitor?" she asked.

"Of course," Charlea replied, putting her book down. "Who is it?"

Mrs. Butterfield swung the door wider to reveal Bonnie standing in the hallway. She timidly looked at Charlea, then looked at the floor.

"Bonnie!" Charlea said, rushing to her friend to embrace her. "I'm so glad to see you. Come in!"

"I have things I need to look after, if you two will excuse me." Mrs. Butterfield closed the door on the slightly uncomfortable room.

Bonnie adjusted the wax paper around a plate. She looked around the apartment. "I brought you David's phone number in case you didn't have it. And brownies. I know they're your favorite."

"Thanks, Bonnie," Charlea said. "That was very thoughtful of you. I'll make us some coffee."

"Please don't bother. I can't stay long."

"Come sit down."

Bonnie sat next to Charlea on the sofa. She slid the plate of brownies across the coffee table.

Charlea took the first stab at breaking the ice. "How are you doing? Are you well?"

"I have headaches pretty often, and I can't hear out of my ear. I wanted to thank you for the car and for the monthly payment. It really helps us out."

"I'm so happy to do it. It's so little after all you've been through. I'm so sorry, Bonnie, about everything. I handled it all very badly and you suffered because of it." Charlea began to cry.

Bonnie took a tissue out of her purse and wiped her eyes. "I don't understand why you didn't tell me about yourself. It's like I don't even know who you are. I thought you were just a regular person. What other secrets are you hiding from me?"

"I am a regular person trying to live a normal life. Yes, my family has lots of money, but it's money my father and grandfather earned. It's not *my* money. I wanted to make it on my own and live the way I wanted to. I married Mark who died in Korea and here I am. That's all there is to it."

"And that's everything?" Bonnie fumbled with a tissue in her hand.

"Yes, you know it all now." Charlea had to bite her tongue. Another lie had slipped out. *Lord, forgive me again.* Bonnie didn't know about the gems Richard planted to lure David and Roland to town. She had to guard that secret closely.

"I'm so sorry for my part in all of this," Bonnie said as she cried softly in the tissue. "Mr. Woodson convinced me that you were taking money from the library. And…"

Charlea held up her hand. "He was a well-polished deceiver, Bonnie. A lot of people were fooled by him. But he's gone now and we don't have to ever deal with him again. I don't even want to hear his name again."

"Me either," Bonnie said wiping her eyes.

Bonnie and Charlea hugged each other while the tears flowed, each woman emptying her anguish and ridding herself of guilt. After a good cry, Charlea forbade Bonnie to speak of it again.

After Bonnie left, Charlea stared at the phone wanting to pick it up and call David's office. For weeks, she'd been waiting for the opportunity to call him. She needed to hear his comforting voice. She slowly dialed the number, but hung up before it could ring. What if he hated her? What if he could never forgive her? Risking possible rejection overwhelmed her desire to talk to him. Maybe it was best not to know.

She grabbed a brownie and leaned back on the sofa. What was she afraid of? David would either say he forgives her or he'd tell her to get lost. She had to know which it would be. She picked up the phone receiver and dialed.

Chapter 30

"Dallas Utilities Company, how may I direct your call?"

Charlea's heart felt like it would pound out of her chest. She hoped the lady on the other end of the line couldn't hear it. "I'd like to speak with David Collins please."

"I will transfer you to his secretary. Please hold."

Charlea was surprised that David had a secretary. He must be higher up in the company than she previously thought. She waited for a few moments when another woman answered the phone.

"Mr. Collins' office. How may I help you?"

"Hello. I need to speak with Mr. Collins if he is available. My name is Charlea Ludlow."

A long pause carried over the phone line. "I'm sorry but Mr. Collins is in a series of meetings. He won't be available today or tomorrow."

"Could you have him call me at his earliest convenience?"

"I will let him know you called. Good-bye."

The click on the line resounded in Charlea's ear like a door clanging shut behind her. She'd found David, but she couldn't reach him. Or he didn't want her to reach him. Maybe he'd instructed his secretary to dead-end her calls. Would the secretary even give her message to him? Would he ever know that she was trying to reach him?

Charlea hung up the phone and let out a whispered scream as she realized her efforts to reach David might not succeed. A knot of desperation twisted tight in her chest. She had to see him whether he wanted to see her or not.

After two days on a roller coaster of anxiety and hope, Charlea reached the end at the sea of desperation. David was not going to call. Whether the secretary didn't pass along her message or David refused to call, she couldn't tell. After crying for a spell, she wiped her eyes and devised a plan.

For the next week, Charlea called David's office each day, asking to speak with him to set up a meeting. Each call was met with the same message from the secretary: David was tied up in meetings and was not available. No matter. She called again the next day. If he wouldn't return her call, David would at least know she was determined to see him.

Richard called her often to ask about her health. Charlea always asked him about David and Roland, but he always said he didn't know anything. He repeatedly reminded her that if they wanted to see her, they knew where she lived. He urged her to forget about them. Their calls would end in an argument.

"Hello, Charlea." Pat stood in the doorway of her apartment. "I've been wondering about how you're doing. You look good!"

Charlea motioned Pat to come in. "I'm feeling better every day. What brings you here? Did Richard send you to check on me? You usually don't show up here without some ulterior motive."

Charlea sat on the sofa and pointed to an arm chair for Pat. He pulled out a folded set of papers from his coat pocket and laid them and his fedora on the table by Charlea. He also pulled a pen out of his jacket pocket and offered it to her. "You need to sign these papers to make the donation to the museum. As you requested, the gift will be anonymous so no one will know it came from you. I'll take them back and a check will be sent next week."

Charlea leaned over the coffee table as she read through the papers. Satisfied, she signed them and handed them back to Pat. "Tell him thanks for taking care of this for me."

Pat returned the papers and pen to his suit pocket. "There's also another matter I'm to discuss with you. We know that you've tried to contact Mr. Collins. Have you talked to him?"

"Why do you ask? And how do you know of my phone calls? You tell Richard I don't like being spied on!"

"Richard is interested in your welfare. You're his sister and he cares about you."

"He doesn't care enough to help me! He wants to run my life the way he thinks it ought to be. I'm tired of it!" Charlea growled in frustration. "I will find David, even if I have to go wait in his lobby for a week. Sooner or later, I will find him to apologize. If I had any idea where Roland is, I'd find him first. But I will find them with or without Richard's blessing or help."

"Charlea, you're not aware of all of the details. Mr. Collins and Richard came to an agreement. He's out of the picture. Leave him alone."

Charlea's mouth fell open, then slapped her forehead. No wonder David never called back. "I should have guessed. Richard would make sure he couldn't be sued or drug through the newspapers with what he did. He had to cover his tracks."

"He's also protecting you and your interests."

"Just so I don't become an embarrassment to him. And he can keep all his precious money."

"It's your money too."

"So it is. I think I will start using my part of it. You go tell Richard that I will be calling him about meeting with David. And tell him to find Roland so he can be there too."

"Charlea—"

"Tell him! I'm done playing games. He can't control me anymore."

Pat stood to leave and put his hat on. "He won't be happy."

"Good. He can join me in the mire of unhappiness."

Charlea went to the library long enough to give her two weeks' notice. Bonnie ran the place now and was happy there. The City Council was surprised by a large anonymous donation for the completion of the museum. Mr. Calhoun was hired to get it organized and opened for the public. Everything was in order. Her purpose there was fulfilled.

The lingering memories of the terror that took place in the library haunted her while she cleaned out her office. The charm of the library that she loved so much was gone. The stares from library patrons made her uncomfortable. Only one chore remained before she left.

"Mr. Calhoun, here's the key to the administrator's office upstairs. I hope you can make it a showplace for the museum." With that, Charlea picked up her box full of personal items and happier memories and left the library for good. A more difficult task lay ahead: she had to tell Mrs. Butterfield she was leaving.

Chapter 31

"Dearie," Mrs. Butterfield said, "I can hardly bear the thought of you leaving my building. How will I get along without you?" She brushed a tear away with her napkin. "Are you sure there's nothing I can do to persuade you to stay?"

Charlea and Mrs. Butterfield were at a restaurant for lunch, honoring—or mourning—Charlea's upcoming move to Houston. At least that's where she'd told Mrs. Butterfield she was going so the old woman wouldn't worry. She'd likely end up on the other side of the planet, putting as much space between her and the library as she could.

The window by their booth was filled with the blue skies of early summer and with promises of delightful days ahead. Charlea looked out and let out a sigh. "I'm sorry, but no. I'm determined to find a new position somewhere out in that great big world. Oh by the way," Charlea pulled out a paper sack and pushed it toward the older woman, "here's a replacement for that book David borrowed from the library. He never returned it."

Mrs. Butterfield chuckled. "Making good on his debt, are you? I will miss you, sugar. I guess I can understand why you want to go," the older woman said. "After what you went through, I know there are a lot of bad memories for you. But that's not all, is it? Why don't you tell me what else is bothering you."

Charlea continued to push her salad around her plate, but not eating it. "First, I'm going to Dallas. I need to see them. To apologize. To set things right. To leave peace between us. They may hate me, but I'm going to have my say. Then I'll say goodbye."

"I doubt they hate you."

"They should. I deserve it. Richard said I was nothing but trouble to them."

"Trouble! That's a lie!"

Charlea was surprised at the older woman's outburst. How would she know it was a lie?

Mrs. Butterfield seemed embarrassed. She wiped her mouth with her napkin and pushed her plate away from her. "Sorry, dear, I didn't mean to call your brother a liar, but are you sure he's telling you the truth?"

"Why would he lie to me?"

"Because he…never mind." Mrs. Butterfield shrugged and looked away. She quickly finished her iced tea. "I have to get back to work." She grabbed the check as she got up to go.

As Charlea left the restaurant, she wondered what Mrs. Butterfield was implying.

Charlea was taping shut the last of the boxes in the kitchen when her phone rang, causing her to jump. For a split second, she imagined that was David calling her back.

"Hello?" She hoped for a miracle, the sound of David's voice.

"Hey, sis!"

Charlea let out a sigh of disappointment. "Oh, it's you."

"Not an especially warm greeting for your favorite brother. What's wrong?"

"Nothing. I'm packing up my life and taking it to Houston for a while. But before all of that, I will be in Dallas looking for David and Roland. You have that meeting set up yet? Surely Pat told you about my request."

He paused, as if carefully choosing his next words. "Charlea, why can't you forget about those men?"

Suddenly, frustration and grief bubbled out of Charlea and she was instantly infuriated. "Richard, quit telling me to forget the people I love! You pushed me for years to forget about Mark. Before we got married, you told me to leave him and forget about him. After he died, you told me to move on and forget him. He was my husband! I loved him! I will never forget him!" She could feel her anger rising higher. "Then I met David and Roland and I fell in love with them. Now you're pushing me again to forget. I've had it! I don't need you telling me to forget!"

She laughed on the verge of hysterics, but tried to maintain some semblance of control. She took a deep ragged breath.

"Those men risked their lives for me, and I will not accept that they walked away without a word to me. I don't know everything that happened that night, but I know David stayed with me. He held me in his arms while I was bleeding. He told me that he loved me. I remember that very clearly. I have to talk to him one more time, to apologize for all that you and I put them through. Yes, we both put them into a dangerous situation. We should both apologize to them." Charlea's voice broke through her desperate pleas so she paused to get a grip on herself before continuing. "Then, and only then, will I consider forgetting them and moving on." Too late. She lost control and began to softly cry.

Richard did not respond as she fought to regain control of herself.

Charlea wondered why he didn't offer words of comfort to her. Maybe he knew he was losing control of her and the situation. He wouldn't like that. He liked to control everything.

"Richard, did you pay them off to leave me alone?"

"No. We have an agreement that works in the best interests of us all."

"Not in my best interest!"

Silence. She knew the answer.

"What did you do? Did you tell them I didn't want to see them?"

"Charlea, it's better this way."

"No, it's not! What were the terms of this agreement?" Charlea said, feeling desperate at this point. "Either tell me now or I will come there and choke it out of you!"

Silence. Charlea bided her time, waiting for an answer. She knew Richard was struggling to find an answer that wouldn't reveal too much. She continued to wait, which gave her time to calm herself.

He answered her in a voice that signaled defeat. "We agreed that it was best for them not to contact you. Complications could arise if they did."

"What kind of complications?"

Richard grew angry with her persistence. "Complications that might result in problems at work or finding other work. Maybe you don't realize how much influence I have in this town. Nothing is going to smear our good name!"

"You threatened them? How dare you, you pompous good-for-nothing! You've smeared our name with your arrogance." She came very close to hanging up on him, but something within her made her wait for an answer. He gave none.

"I've trusted you for too long," she replied firmly, finally taking control. "But no more. I'll tell you what you're going to do. First, you'll contact David and Roland and set up a meeting with them for tomorrow afternoon. Tomorrow, Richard! You and I will have a little conference with them and set the record straight. Next, you are going to transfer my trust fund to me, granting me sole ownership of it. Richard," she paused for effect, "none of this is negotiable. You will follow my instructions or I will take you to court over it. That ought to do wonders for your good name."

"It's your name as well."

"I'll shed it if I have to."

Richard paused for a while. "Are you sure you know what you're doing? Those two men..."

"They have names, Richard, please use them," Charlea shouted at him.

"Mr. Parker and Mr. Collins," he almost choked on the words, "were pretty mad about everything. Are you prepared to face that?"

"I can deal with how they feel about me. The main thing is I will apologize for my part in it."

Charlea knew Richard was mulling the whole thing over in his mind, but she didn't care. She had waited long enough and was at last taking full control of her life, with or without Richard's blessing.

"I'll make the arrangements." Richard seemed defeated.

"Thank you very much," Charlea said triumphantly. "I will meet you in your office tomorrow around 2 o'clock. Don't bother fixing the guest room at the house for me. I will be staying at a hotel. I don't want to be near you right now."

Richard hated losing control, and he especially hated being told what to do. "What I did, I thought best for you. I thought they would harm you. I had to protect you from them! I'm the only family you have. I'm your brother!"

"Richard, you are a fabulous businessman, and you're really good at it. But as a brother, you're really lousy. I've been living with this broken heart all this time. You let me think that they abandoned me. Do you know how many tears I have cried over this? Of course you don't. You're too busy thinking only of yourself." Charlea waited a moment, trying to find words to express herself further.

Finding none, she simply said, "See you tomorrow afternoon." She hung up.

As she finished packing, her mind roiled, full of questions. Would they give her and Richard a chance to explain? Would they even see her at all? She tried to think of every possible scenario and how to handle it, what to say, what to do.

She tried to prepare herself for the worst case scenario, if David and Roland wouldn't see her. To prepare for the worst was better than being unprepared, she told herself. No, she thought, no other way was possible. They had to see her. She would insist upon it. If they rejected her apology, then at least she had tried to make amends. Surely comfort would come from that.

Her anger with Richard had not subsided, but she had to calm herself down. No purpose would be achieved by antagonizing him. She needed him in a cooperative mood for their meeting. The truth, whatever that was, had to be told. She didn't even know what the whole truth was herself after Richard's revelation last night. What else might he have kept from her?

After an endless night of little sleep, Charlea packed her car. The movers would come later in the day to take her belongings away for storage. She met with Mrs. Butterfield to turn in her keys and say a heart-wrenching good-bye. The elder woman cried out of sadness at Charlea leaving, but seemed to cry with happiness because she was going to see David and Roland.

"So your brother confessed," the elder woman said as she wiped her tears. "I knew something didn't seem to be right about how things turned out. They will be so happy to see you again and you can—" Mrs. Butterfield stopped and her face blushed.

Charlea tilted her head and looked at the wrinkled face closer. "I can what? Do you know something I don't?"

Mrs. Butterfield giggled and said, "Don't be silly. How would I know anything? Everything will turn out just fine, you'll see." Charlea thought that was odd coming from her, but with so much on her mind, she dismissed her friend's comment. With a last heartfelt hug, Charlea hurried out the door without looking back. The car started with a roar and off she headed toward the unknown.

Chapter 32

Richard's secretary greeted Charlea warmly and informed her that Richard had cleared his calendar for her and told her to go right in. His spacious office sported a large polished, wood desk, complete with the latest dictating gadgets and multi-button phone. The extra-long conference table was surrounded by well cushioned chairs, ready for the next high-level meeting. The deep carpeted floor gave the room an elegant feel. Looking out and down at the city of Dallas gave the whole room a sense of power.

Richard was staring out the window with his back to her. He didn't turn around when she shut the door. Neither of them knew what to say, knowing the next few words would be critical for their future relationship. Even in the silence, they seemed to communicate telepathically. Both of them knew that they wanted things to be fixed between them.

Drawing a long breath, Richard turned toward her, but didn't make eye contact. "The papers granting you full control of your trust fund are there on my desk. You'll want to look them over. I advised my lawyer to file the papers immediately after you sign them." He paused for a moment as she walked to the desk to pick up the papers. While she looked through them, he added, "You should have your lawyer look them over as well."

"Thank you, Richard. I appreciate your expediency in this matter." Her voice sounded shaky and the papers trembled as she looked at each page. She put them back on his desk. "I'll look at them later. We have other things to discuss first. Do you have a meeting set up for later this afternoon?" She didn't mention David or Roland's name purposely in an effort to keep this meeting on as positive a note as she could.

"Yes, at 4 o'clock at Mr. Collins' office."

Charlea smiled slightly. David was smart, getting them to meet him on his home turf. That way he would have the upper hand for this delicate meeting. Sitting across a conference table from him would be—but did he know—

As if reading her mind, Richard said, "Yes, they know you will be there. They were reluctant to meet with us, but I was able to persuade them otherwise. I detected some hostility. You need to know that so that your hopes are not too high."

Fighting back bitter disappointment, Charlea walked to the window and looked out at the bright sunny day. Below her, people were walking, cars going places, and birds flying everywhere. She felt like she was trapped, chained to that pole like Roland had been. She felt doomed. Richard put a hand on her shoulder. Surprisingly, the gesture was comforting to her and her anger with him cooled a little.

"Charlea," he began softly, "I had no idea, no real idea how attached you were to these men. I mean, they're strangers to you...and I'm your brother. You seem willing to cut ties with me for the sake of being with them. I don't understand that."

"Why did you set up the hunt for the gems, Richard? Why did you pick them to come meet me?"

Richard stepped away from her. "I thought you needed some fun and excitement. I wanted to give you something special, something to get you out of your rut. And I thought I had sent only one man, not two. The arrangement was supposed to be a fun weekend for you."

"You got your money's worth, in more ways than one." Charlea smiled slightly at Richard, who smiled slightly back. Neither was ready to totally forgive yet.

Charlea fumbled with her purse strap and continued, "It's hard to explain what happened. When I met Roland, he took my breath away because he was so good-looking. And being a normal, red-blooded woman, I was immediately attracted to him. He's a gentleman in most ways. A little boy in others. And a little intimidating." Charlea stared off into space while his face filled her mind. "But when I met David, I felt so comfortable with him, like I'd known him for ages. We have so much in common that it feels right to be with him. He reminded me of Mark in that respect and I fell for him...hard. And yes, I think I even fell in love with him."

Charlea paced around the office, then sat in one of the conference table chairs. "When everything happened with Mr. Woodson and Leon, they were there for me. They risked everything to save me, more than once. They jumped Leon in the parking lot that first night. They defended me when Leon came to the library. They came to the warehouse to rescue me. They came for me, the small town librarian, when I was in trouble. That's the kind of men they are."

"Charlea, I—" Richard started.

Charlea held up her hand and cut him off. "They may hate me, but I have to explain things to them. They have to know that I'm sorry for what happened, that I'm sorry for deceiving them and not telling them about your game. If they don't want to forgive me, there's not much I can do about it. I'll get on with my life knowing I did my best." Charlea had her fists clinched with desperation. She turned to look at Richard, "I know you think they were after my money. But I say you're wrong. Anyone who is willing to help me in times of trouble is someone I want around me. And that includes you."

Richard stared out the window, the muscles in his jaw working while he thought about her words. Neither he nor Charlea spoke for a long time, lost in their own thoughts. Richard cleared his throat, put his hands in the pockets of his tailored slacks, and paced the floor. He seemed unsure of himself which, as Charlea observed, was out of character for him. He was usually in control of every situation and his confidence hid any uncertainty. He sat in his chair and swiveled around to look at Charlea.

"I thought I was doing what was best for you." As she drew a breath to argue with him, he imitated her gesture, holding up his hand to keep her from interrupting him. "I was afraid that they might have set you up. Yes, Charlea," he insisted as she looked at him, not believing what he was saying, "I was afraid that they were part of the conspiracy to hurt you. Afraid that they found out that you had a fortune. Afraid that they were working together with Woodson to get as much money out of you as they possibly could." He paused for a moment to let her consider the implications. "It was not out of the realm of possibility. I had Mr. Parker checked out, but I knew nothing about his brother. I didn't know for sure that he was okay." He looked at her for her concurrence, but she just stared at him in disbelief.

Barely able to speak, she squeaked, "What?"

"Think about it. The idea might have been true. Maybe they found out how much money you had and wanted more than a few jewels' worth. How was I to know for sure? You were completely blinded by them, by their charm or whatever you women see in such men. I didn't know what their motives were and had no way to find out. I had to protect you and that's what I did." He stood up again and strode around the room. "So hate me if you will, I did what I thought was best for you."

"Why didn't you ask me what I thought was best for me? Do you have so little respect for what I think?"

"I knew what your answer would be and I knew I wouldn't like it. I took charge without asking. It's what I do."

Charlea smiled to herself. Yes, that's what he always did. "Do you still think they set me up?" Charlea asked him.

"After my investigations, no, I don't. I think they were set up by Woodson, just like you were."

"So why didn't you tell me about the agreement between you and them?"

Richard shrugged his shoulders. "There was no reason to stir things up again. I still don't trust them…plus I thought you'd be over it by now. You've got to believe me! I never, ever meant to hurt you."

Charlea's head spun. She walked across the room and dropped into a chair. She had never doubted David and Roland's intentions, but after listening to Richard, she understood why he had. She finally understood why he'd taken the actions he had. He really was protecting her from people he considered dangerous.

"Why didn't you tell me all this sooner?"

"I hoped it would blow over and you'd move on. You hang on to things too long, you know that?"

Charlea laughed quietly. "I suppose I do. I hang on tight to the things I love the most."

Richard looked at his watch and announced, "We'd better get going. We don't want to be late." He took his suit coat out of his closet and put it on. He called his secretary to have her order his car around. Hanging up, he walked over to Charlea and brushed a strand of hair back out her eyes. "You look great today. If nothing else comes of this meeting, at least they'll see what a beautiful woman you are."

Charlea smiled shyly. "Thanks, Richard. For everything. I hadn't considered things from your vantage point. I understand why you did what you did. Now let's see if we can clear things up with David and Roland."

"I still don't like them."

"Give them time and you will." Excitement filled her. She was going to see David and Roland! Surely when they heard Richard's side of the story, they would understand too. She put the papers for her trust fund into her purse as they left his office.

Richard's limousine stopped in front of the utilities company downtown. Walking in the front door of the elegant building, Richard approached the receptionist desk. "We have an appointment with David Collins. We're Richard Breyerman and Charlea Ludlow."

The receptionist called someone to announce their arrival. Charlea looked around her. The elaborately decorated lobby area echoed with the sounds of telephones, typewriters, and people coming and going in all directions. The tile floors and marble accents on the walls were in the art deco style. The soft sounds of ringing phones and people in business suits going here and there gave the sense of corporate America at its best. The hustle and bustle was quite a contrast to her quiet little library. She imagined David striding through the crowd to get to his office. How dull her little town must have seemed to him!

The receptionist broke up her daydream. "The General Manager is expecting you. His office is on the tenth floor, fourth door on the right."

When elevator doors closed, Charlea asked, "So you threatened the general manager of a major utility company? You're kindred spirits, managers of people, big budgets, and projects. He wasn't after my money and you knew that!"

"Not at first. I found out later." He was pacing in the elevator.

"Nervous?" Charlea asked him.

He paused for a moment and took a deep breath. "Nervous? No. Uncomfortable? Yes. I don't want to be here, and I especially don't want this to turn confrontational. If it does, we're leaving. Nothing more can be done. And you will come with me. Understood?"

Charlea felt anger rise up in her, but she was determined. "I'll leave when I am done and not before. I haven't come this far to leave before I have my say. If you feel the need to leave, go ahead. I'll catch a cab later." Richard's sharp look at her told her that he did not approve, but she didn't care. Her resolve increased her confidence.

The elevator doors opened to reveal a large hallway with a number of offices opening off of it. The lovely décor on this floor matched the one in the lobby. Richard turned to the right, counting doors as he walked along. Charlea followed, looking all around her as they went along.

They entered the fourth door and found themselves in a lush office area. The secretary stopped her typing and greeted them warmly, then apologized because David was in a meeting that was taking longer than expected. Exasperated, Richard moved to leave, but Charlea grabbed his arm and held him back. The secretary assured them that he would not be delayed more than 30 minutes and politely asked them to wait. Inwardly smiling, Charlea knew David's ploy was to put Richard at a disadvantage.

As they sat in the cushioned chairs, Richard and Charlea accepted the secretary's offer to get them tea or coffee. A few moments later, she brought Richard a cup of coffee and a *Wall Street Journal* to peruse. To Charlea, she gave a cup of tea and a copy of the company's brochure. She wasn't really interested in reading, but she needed something to do to pass the time. Absentmindedly, she opened the brochure to look through it. Her heart skipped a beat when she saw a message written inside the front cover for her eyes only. Taking several sips of tea and trying to remain calm, she let Richard bury himself in his paper. Setting down her cup and putting the brochure in her purse, she asked the receptionist for directions to the ladies room. As she left the room, Richard looked up at her.

"I want to freshen up. I won't be long," she said as she left the reception area. He nodded and went back to his paper.

Hurrying down the hallway, Charlea turned the corner and saw *Adonis*, with his dark eyes and handsomeness beyond all others, waiting for her. He signaled for her to come quickly. Her heart jumped for joy when she could see no anger or hostility in his face.

She briefly looked behind her to make sure Richard had not followed. Not seeing him, she hurried down the hallway to the door of a storage area. There in the doorway, wearing a suit and tie, looking more handsome than she remembered, was Roland.

Suddenly she felt very nervous, not sure what to do, looking for a sign to know what he was thinking.

"Charlea!" Roland pulled her inside the small room and drew her near. She threw her arms around him, holding on for dear life. At last, she'd arrived at the place she wanted to be for so long. It seemed like a lifetime. They held each other for a long time, not saying anything. When they finally pulled apart, Roland kissed her softly on the cheek.

"Charlea, you're more beautiful than ever. You look much better than the last time I saw you."

Charlea laughed out loud. "I feel better too. I've missed you so much!" Charlea exclaimed as she hugged him again. "I was so afraid I'd never see you again!"

"We would have seen you earlier." Roland pulled away from her. "But your brother was adamant about no contact. That's all he could say. No contact, no contact." Roland seemed to grow a little angry.

"I didn't know anything about that."

"We were at the hospital with you. Richard wouldn't let us see you. We were escorted from the hospital by the police. David was livid, but there was nothing he could do. I literally had to drag him out of there so he wouldn't be arrested."

"I'm so sorry," Charlea pleaded, "I had no idea."

"How could you? You were trying to survive."

"Does David know I've been trying to call him?"

"Of course, but he couldn't respond because of Richard."

"Richard! I'm ashamed of him right now."

"There's something else you should know." Roland shuffled nervously. "David knows what happened that night, between us."

"You told him!"

"No! Well, not exactly. The police were very thorough in their questioning, and it sort of came out. I guess he overheard."

Charlea groaned. "Oh, no. What did he say?"

"Nothing to me for months. He was so mad that he kicked me out of his apartment and told me never to come back. I tried to tell him that it was an accident, but he wouldn't believe me."

Charlea shook her head. "I was terrified. I lost my head when I saw you. You comforted me when I felt hopeless. Didn't he understand that?" Anxiety filled her. "Is he angry with me? Will he ever forgive me?"

"You'll have to ask him." Roland checked his watch. "I better go." He opened the door and peeked out to make sure the coast was clear. He held the door for her as she stepped out into the hallway and made her way back to David's office. She stopped short, remembering that she had not combed her hair or reapplied her lipstick. Quickly, she pulled a lipstick out of her purse and put some on. She ran her fingers through her hair and tried to smooth it down.

When she walked in, Richard was still reading the paper. She sat in the chair, trying not to let her quickened breathing betray her rush to get back. Her tea was cold so she pushed it aside. Richard put down his paper and let out a sigh of impatience. He looked at Charlea, looked at his watch, and tapped his foot. He rarely waited on others; usually he was the one who kept others waiting. Charlea smiled to herself. Now he knew how it felt to be on the other end of things.

Shortly after Charlea returned, the secretary's phone rang and she announced that David was back in his office and ready to receive them. Leading them down a small hallway, she softly tapped on a large wooden door, then opened it to announce them. As they entered the room, they saw David sitting behind a large desk, silhouetted against the large windows behind him. He definitely had the advantage since he could see their faces while his was obscured in shadow. His large office was similar to Richard's in size and accommodations. The rich brown carpet added comfort to the executive furnishings.

On one side of the desk, Roland sat in a plush chair, looking solemn. After the secretary left, Charlea and Richard took their seats in front of the desk and waited for someone to speak. Hostility hung in the air like a thick fog, which accentuated the fact that David and Richard didn't like each other very much.

David took the lead, "So what can I do for you?" He leaned back in his large executive chair, tapping his fingertips together, clearly in control of the situation.

Richard shuffled uncomfortably in his chair. He took a breath to speak, but Charlea cut him off before he could begin. "David, thank you for seeing us on short notice. I wanted to see you to apologize for all that transpired when we were last together." The words spilled out of her before she could stop them. She'd rehearsed a better way of saying it, but her heart spoke before her brain could sort through her rehearsed script. No reason to keep any more back.

"I apologize for not telling you about who the letter came from or who planted the gems. I wasn't sure at first, but I should have shared that information when I knew it. I should have warned you before things got so out of hand. I'm truly sorry.

Charlea thought she saw a slight flicker of emotion on David's shadowed face. She fumbled with the straps on her purse, hoping he would speak.

Say something! she wanted to scream out. *Say that you understand. Say that you forgive me. Say you're glad to see me. Say anything!*

The room remained quiet.

Having said her piece, she finished with, "I tried to call you about this, but this is better because I can tell you face to face. I want you to know how deeply sorry I am…in hopes of clearing up any misunderstanding. Thank you for listening and letting me explain."

David cleared his throat and answered, "We, my brother and I, did not want to cut off contact with you. In fact, we stayed at the hospital while you were unconscious and donated blood on your behalf. We would have done more if we could. But we were forced to leave. We were told that you had regained consciousness and insisted that we be sent away."

Charlea turned to Richard who was looking at his folded hands in his lap. He made no move to explain himself to anyone.

"I was unconscious for four weeks. I had no idea you were there. I was told that you returned home after you left the warehouse that night." Turning to Richard, she said pointedly, "You lied to me about that!" Richard said nothing. "I wonder what else you've lied to me about. Did you really believe they were partners with Mr. Woodson and Leon or did you make that up too?"

The accusation elicited emotion in David for the first time. "Partners with that scum? That's preposterous! We hated him and Leon. You didn't need to be a rocket scientist to know that those two were trouble." David looked straight at Richard. "Your investigations and background checks on us should have revealed that we were no threat to you or her." David stared at Richard who kept staring at the floor.

Richard shuffled slightly and turned to face Charlea. "I've told you why I did what I did. I didn't trust either one of them, so I felt it was better if they were out of the picture. I was protecting you from being hurt any more than you were." He turned to David and finished, "I love my sister, Mr. Collins. I will take whatever action I deem necessary to protect her, especially if I think she's in danger." He paused and added sincerely, "However, I—" Richard cleared his throat and wiped imaginary lint from his slacks before going on, "I owe you and your brother an apology for putting you in danger's way. I meant for it to be a fun weekend for you, Charlea." Richard turned toward David. "But it turned out quite differently than expected. I regret that deeply."

David didn't immediately respond, but seemed to be thinking over what had been said.

Roland squirmed in his seat, but held his tongue, much to Charlea's surprise.

She took her cue from him and held her tongue as well. David and Richard would have to work the rest of this out themselves. An uncomfortable silence descended around them.

After a few minutes, David broke the silence. "On behalf of Mr. Parker and myself, I accept your apology. I also apologize for Mr. Parker's big mouth, which is really what started the problem." Roland started to protest, but David held his hand up and silenced him. "If he'd been quiet, then we could have gone on our adventure and been none the worse for wear. Most of all, Charlea, we are very glad that you survived. I think we all agree on that one point." He looked to Richard who nodded, so David told him, "I loved her too and wanted to protect her. Had I known who you were, I would have contacted you immediately. We could have done it together."

A pregnant pause filled the room. Roland fidgeted impatiently, but said nothing. David stood up and said, "If that concludes our business, I have other matters that need my attention. Thank you for coming, Mr. Breyerman. Charlea, it was nice to see you again." He held out his hand to shake their hands.

His sudden dismissal caught Richard and Charlea off guard. Richard stood up and shook his hand, mumbling a good-bye. Charlea sat fixed to the chair, unbelieving of the abrupt ending. Richard took her by the arm and led her to the door. Her mind was too stunned to think clearly. She expected more from David—anger, accusations, compassion. Anything but this curt dismissal. He was sending her away.

"Charlea," Roland called out as he followed them out the door. "It was nice to see you again." He took her hands in his and stealthily slipped a piece of paper into her hand. "Take care of yourself." He returned to David's office, pulling the door shut behind him. Charlea palmed the note and followed Richard out of the office.

Chapter 33

As the limousine moved through traffic, Charlea and Richard sat in silence a long time. Charlea was stunned by David's rejection and his coolness toward her. At the same time, she couldn't blame him for it. She would feel the same if he had deceived her like she'd deceived him. No, he wouldn't forgive her for that. Nor would he forgive her that night with his brother or for not revealing who she was to him. Three strikes. She was out.

A pothole on the city street shook her out of her thoughts. Suddenly, she remembered the piece of paper that Roland had slipped her. Quietly she opened her purse and dropped it inside as she reached for a tissue.

"Are you crying?" Richard asked as he watched her.

"No, not really," she replied as she daubed her eyes. "I'm terribly disappointed. I expected more. You warned me about that and you were right."

"I thought Mr. Collins handled the situation well and with dignity. I must say that under different circumstances, I might like the man." Neither spoke while they waited at a red light.

"So what will you do now?" he asked her. "Still going to Houston?"

Charlea sighed and looked out the window at the city passing by. "Maybe for just a week or two, but then who knows. I'd like to see more of the world before I die. I have no one to leave my trust fund to, so why not spend it myself?" She laughed in a regretful way. "I want to see the pyramids in Egypt," she said, "and explore Greece a little more. And I think I'll look for a place to live in Europe. Maybe Scotland. Or France. You're right. My life has been much too narrow and it's time to broaden it. Before I'm too old to enjoy it."

Richard stared at her, then shook his head. "Why, Charlea, you've taken me completely by surprise. What brought about this change of heart?"

"A brush with death. Nothing is here to keep me hanging around. I've said my good-bye to Mark. I've apologized to David and Roland. I've made my peace with everyone. It's time to move on. Just like you've always wanted me to."

"All I ever wanted was for you to be happy."

"And so I am." Charlea opened her purse and took out the trust fund papers. "Here. Take these back. If you don't mind, keep investing for me. You've done a good job of it all these years. I'm out of work so I need an allowance to support myself. Can you arrange that for me?" For a moment, she thought he was tearing up.

Richard took the papers from her, folded them, and put them in his coat pocket. He was too choked up to speak. He patted her hand and said, "I'll do it however you'd like. Does this mean you don't hate me anymore?"

Charlea daubed her eyes again. "I'm sorry. I never hated you. The words were said in anger. Please, no more interference in my life though. No 'gifts' of men or contrived adventures. Ever again. Let me find my own happiness in my own way and in my own time."

"I promise. I've learned my lesson."

The car stopped in front of her hotel. As Charlea reached for the door handle, Richard grabbed her arm. "Won't you consider staying at the house with us?"

Charlea shook her head. "I need to be alone right now. The meeting didn't turn out like I wanted it to, but I'm glad we did it. A huge weight has been lifted off me. I feel better than I've felt in a long, long time."

She got out of the car. Over her shoulder, she said, "Give my love to the family. I'll call you before I go overseas." She closed the door and rushed into the hotel.

Thinking of the note Roland had given her, she rushed to the elevator and pushed the button. Getting no immediate response, she pushed it again. And again. And again. At last, the doors opened and she was on her way to her room. Once inside, she dumped the contents of her purse on the bed. Frantically, she sorted through the items until she found the small folded piece of paper. Her hands were shaking as she unfolded it and read:

Charlea: Please be my guest at Leonardi's restaurant, where I work. My treat. Your reservation is for 7 pm. Come alone. Love, Roland

Oh my, she thought, *Leonardi's is one of the most glamorous restaurants in Dallas. So that was where Richard first met Roland.* She really didn't feel like going out tonight, but it might be the last time she would see him. Maybe she'd even get a good-bye kiss. Oh yes, it was worth the effort to go.

"Welcome, madam," the maître d' told her. "We have your table ready. Right this way." Charlea followed the man in the tuxedo as he threaded his way through the finely dressed customers and elaborately set tables. She looked around at the beautiful setting of soft lights, white tablecloths, candles, and greenery. The lights were dim so that faces in the room were not clear. Soft background music created a wonderful ambience.

The maître d' led her to a private booth in a corner and seated her there. "Your waiter will be with you in a moment." He handed her a menu and left. The booth afforded privacy while still providing a view of the restaurant. Undoubtedly, she was seated at the best table in the restaurant. If she weren't alone, the setting would be very romantic.

"Good evening, Charlea. May I bring you a drink?" She looked up to see Roland smiling at her. "Thanks for coming tonight. I'll be your waiter."

"Thank you for asking me to come! I'm so happy to see you again. What a nice place you work in."

"Thank you. Wait until you taste the food! May I offer you a glass of our best wine?"

"That would be nice. Thanks. But before you go, I have to ask. Why are you still working here? I thought your—" Charlea's voice dropped to a whisper"—treasure would allow you to quit."

"I'm saving the money I got from them to open my own restaurant. I'm only here until I learn the business a little better to make sure my restaurant will be a success. I'll get you that wine now." Roland left to go fill her order while she studied the menu. With so many choices, she couldn't make up her mind. She decided to let Roland order something for her. Whatever he recommended would be good.

Roland was back in no time, setting her glass of wine in front of her. "I'm sorry to inconvenience you like this, but all our tables are full and one of our best customers needs a place to sit. Would you mind sharing your table with a gentleman?" Charlea glanced around and spotted several empty tables. Confused, she looked back at Roland who stepped aside, revealing David standing behind him.

Roland whispered to her, "He's a very nice gentleman. We did a background check on him and he's clean. Charlea Ludlow, this is David Collins, a prominent businessman in town. Mr. Collins, this is Charlea Ludlow, a librarian and museum curator. I think you'll find her quite charming." He loudly whispered to David, "We checked her out, and she's clean too, although we didn't check her for weapons. But I know where she keeps her knife. I'll tell you where later, in case you're interested in looking for it." Roland laughed, Charlea blushed, and David smiled. Whether he smiled because he'd heard the story or he smiled because he was thinking of searching her, she could not tell. She was uncomfortable thinking about how much he knew about that night at the warehouse.

David held out his hand and said, "It's nice to make your acquaintance, Miss Ludlow." She reached out her hand to his, and he raised it to his lips and kissed it. A spark of electricity shot through her arm straight to her heart. He slid next to her in the booth. Roland stood over them grinning.

"Do you believe in love at first sight?" David asked her.

Charlea was thrilled with the question. "Yes, I do." She reached out and touched his arm, just to make sure she was not dreaming again. The warmth of his skin confirmed that he was real. As if experiencing the same thoughts, David ran his hands along her neck and to her face, brushing her cheek with his fingers.

"Can we get a bottle of your best wine, please, waiter?" David said. Roland continued to watch them, not reacting to David's request. David cleared his throat and said, "Three's a crowd, Roland. Don't you have work to do or something?"

"You two look so good together," he crooned. "But if you'll excuse me, I have other customers." He bowed to them and left.

"Should I search you for weapons?" David asked Charlea, with a slight smile on his face.

"I don't carry a gun any more. I had a bad experience with one. Why do you ask? Will I need it tonight?" She looked at him coyly.

David shook his head. "No, you won't. I'll make sure nothing happens to you." He reached up to Charlea's neck and ran his finger along the scar, lost in memories. She touched his arm and he grabbed her, pulling her tight against him.

"David, I'm so sorry for everything…"

"Shh!" he interrupted as he pushed her away from him slightly. "We are starting over. The past is gone and everything is new from here on."

"But I have so much I want to tell you. I've missed you so much. You were in my thoughts every day. I nearly went crazy thinking I might never see you again." She stopped long enough to draw a long breath. "I can't believe you're really here with me now. My dreams are coming true."

David let go of her and sat back against the seat. "It's been an agonizing time for me as well, Charlea. Holding you in my arms as your life drained out of you. Watching you fight for your life in the hospital. Being utterly helpless to make things better. Then Richard took you away from me. I couldn't stand being away from you. I could only watch you from a distance." David paused for a moment as he looked at Charlea slyly. "Mrs. Butterfield and I have become good friends, talking on the phone. I don't think she'll be chasing me with her bat again."

"Mrs. Butterfield?"

"Yes, I called her weekly to get a report on you, to hear what you were doing and how you were handling things. Whatever you told her, I heard about later. She called me last night to tell me you were coming today."

Charlea laughed. No wonder Mrs. Butterfield seemed so pleased that she had confronted Richard. No wonder she seemed all too eager for her to see David. Charlea had had no clue that what she had said was being relayed to David or she would have sent more messages.

"Why didn't she tell me that she was in touch with you? This mess might have been cleared up a long time ago."

David went on, "I asked her not to. Your brother made it perfectly clear that he would ruin me if I contacted you in any manner. That would have hurt my career and maybe yours, so I was stuck with hearing about you. Mrs. Butterfield told me to have patience and faith, that you would find a way to get in touch with me. It was hard. I wanted to drive down there to see you, even from a distance."

"I wished I'd known."

"David smiled. "I decided to wait a while to let emotions settle and things heal. After that, I would set up a meeting with you and Richard to discuss the situation. But even if he said no, I would have risked everything to see you. Everything would hinge on you stepping in on my behalf. I'm glad I followed Mrs. Butterfield's advice to be patient, because you beat me to it."

"I'm sorry it took me so long," Charlea said quietly. She held her head for a moment, trying to think clearly. She should have trusted David more and forced the issue with Richard. Returning to the present, she asked, "Why didn't you tell me you were the general manager of a utility company?"

David shrugged and smiled. "I wanted you to love me for who I was, and not for my money or my position. Why didn't you tell me you were a woman of substantial means?"

Charlea shrugged back at him. "Same reason." The irony of the situation provoked a laugh between them.

David grew thoughtful and looked sternly at her. "There's one other thing we need to talk about. You and Roland. I heard about what happened in the warehouse. All of it. I was really hurt to know that you and he—"

Charlea cringed as David trailed off. She couldn't look at him. The guilt wouldn't let her.

David continued. "I shouldn't be surprised. Women cannot resist him and I supposed you're no different. I've been down this road before."

Charlea knew he was referring to his last heartbreak at his wedding. His reluctance to have that piece of history repeat itself was understandable. She loved Roland, but not in the same way that she loved David. Would he understand that? How could she explain it to him? The right words eluded her.

At that moment, Roland brought their bottle of wine. "How's it going?" he asked them. They looked away and both mumbled something. "That bad, huh? Maybe this will help." He poured two glasses of wine. "Are you ready to order?"

David picked up the menus, handed them to Roland, and told him, "Surprise us. And make it good."

"Leave it to me," Roland replied as he wrote something on his pad. He took the menus and left them alone again. They sat there in silence while both took the first sip of wine.

David spoke first. "I need to know and I need you to answer truthfully. Why did you come here tonight? Because of Roland?"

"I came because he asked me. I usually don't turn down dinner invitations from friends."

David shifted in his seat and seemed to study his napkin closely. "That's not what I meant. I need to know if you love me or Roland. He told me about how you kissed him while he was tied to the pole that night. Why did you do that?" David rubbed a clinched fist across the table. "I won't share you with him, so if you prefer him, tell me now. I will bow out without further ado."

"David," Charlea touch his face and turned it toward her. "I'm sorry about my indiscretions with Roland. I don't know what came over me when I found him there. I was scared and I lost control of my senses. Roland is *Adonis*. His appearance is like every woman's dream of manly perfection. But *Adonis* is an image of something that's not real or practical. *Adonis* led me to you." A lump was forming in her throat, threatening to squeeze tears out of her eyes. She fought it and retained her composure. "Roland is a wonderful man, but he's not you. When I'm with you, I feel like I'm where I belong. I feel safe and secure. You, David, are the one that has been in my heart this past year."

"Are you sure? He'll always be around. Can I trust you?"

"You can trust your heart with me. You are my treasure. And where my treasure is, there my heart is."

David's eyes grew moist and he kissed Charlea with love and longing.

For Charlea, it was a kiss sweeter than any offered by *Adonis*. A kiss that took her breath away and gave her comfort to the depths of her soul. In her mind's eye, she saw Mark smile and wave as he walked away from her, leaving her filled with David. He would take care of her now.

Later, Charlea took another sip of wine to get the courage to ask the question that had been plaguing her. "David, that night in the warehouse…did you tell me that you loved me?"

"Yes, Charlea, I said it and I meant it. And I still love you. I have since that first afternoon at the library."

"I love you, David. I've let go of my past and want a future with you in it."

"Those words are music to my ears." David reached inside his jacket and pulled out box wrapped in light pink paper. "I had this made, hoping that someday you would wear it for me."

Charlea gingerly unwrapped the box and opened it. Inside lay a silver necklace with three emeralds set in a silver swirl that formed a heart shape. Her soft gasp signaled that she knew what had happened to part of the gems. David took the necklace and put it around her neck before kissing her passionately again.

The world around them melted away, leaving them surrounded by their love.

About the Author

C.S. grew up in Texas and Colorado. She and her husband moved to South Dakota, Wyoming, and Idaho, following their careers. Upon retirement from her job as a natural resources technical writer, she began to write fiction. In retirement, C.S. enjoys quilting, writing, and traveling with her husband.

Your review of this book on Amazon.com will be greatly appreciated. Please let others know if you enjoyed the book.

Made in the USA
San Bernardino, CA
14 April 2016